A HILL TO DIE ON

ED JAMES

OTHER BOOKS BY ED JAMES

SCOTT CULLEN MYSTERIES SERIES

Eight novels featuring a detective eager to climb the career ladder, covering Edinburgh and its surrounding counties, and further across Scotland.

1. GHOST IN THE MACHINE
2. DEVIL IN THE DETAIL
3. FIRE IN THE BLOOD
4. STAB IN THE DARK
5. COPS & ROBBERS
6. LIARS & THIEVES
7. COWBOYS & INDIANS
8. HEROES & VILLAINS

CULLEN & BAIN SERIES

Six novellas spinning off from the main Cullen series covering the events of the global pandemic in 2020.

1. CITY OF THE DEAD
2. WORLD'S END
3. HELL'S KITCHEN
4. GORE GLEN
5. DEAD IN THE WATER
6. THE LAST DROP

CRAIG HUNTER SERIES

A spin-off series from the Cullen series, with Hunter first featuring in the fifth book, starring an ex-squaddie cop struggling with PTSD, investigating crimes in Scotland and further afield.

1. MISSING
2. HUNTED
3. THE BLACK ISLE

DS VICKY DODDS SERIES

Gritty crime novels set in Dundee and Tayside, featuring a DS juggling being a cop and a single mother.

1. BLOOD & GUTS
2. TOOTH & CLAW
3. FLESH & BLOOD
4. SKIN & BONE

DI SIMON FENCHURCH SERIES

Set in East London, will Fenchurch ever find what happened to his daughter, missing for the last ten years?

1. THE HOPE THAT KILLS
2. WORTH KILLING FOR
3. WHAT DOESN'T KILL YOU
4. IN FOR THE KILL
5. KILL WITH KINDNESS
6. KILL THE MESSENGER
7. DEAD MAN'S SHOES
8. A HILL TO DIE ON
9. THE LAST THING TO DIE (December 2022)

Other Books

Other crime novels, with Senseless set in southern England, and the other three set in Seattle, Washington.

- SENSELESS
- TELL ME LIES
- GONE IN SECONDS

- BEFORE SHE WAKES

DAY 1

Thursday
12th March 2020

PROLOGUE

When PC Chloe Fenchurch yawned, it felt like it'd just keep going and never let go.

Another dark East London street, lit up in sodium yellow unlike the white elsewhere. Late-night off-licenses and kebab shops. The lanes running off were shrouded in darkness.

The tiredness coiled around her again. Like a snake, but it didn't have the venomous bite – it just squeezed and squeezed. Even tighter than her uniform, strapped in by the stab-proof vest and the belt that bit into her thighs. Yeah, maybe she should get that bigger size.

Her first night shift of the week and she'd seen the sun set. Now it rose again, hovering above the low buildings, the heat haze starting to blur everything. Another yawn and she managed to shake herself free of the fatigue.

'Cheer up, kidder.' Adam Burridge gave her that wide grin of his, the one that stretched out the crow's feet around his eyes. He'd started the shift cleanshaven, but now he looked like he'd gone a few days without stepping near a razor. He tucked his thumbs into his stab-proof and looked along the road. 'Not long until this is over.'

Chloe tried nodding, tried smiling. For him, but not for her. Trouble was, she was so dog-tired she couldn't muster anything. 'And then I can spend all day trying and failing to sleep, only to endure this all over again tomorrow night. Great.'

'Nature of the beast. You'll get used to it.' Adam laughed, then started plodding along the street, back in the loose direction of the station. 'After fifteen years, maybe.'

She kept in step with him, her equipment rattling. Cuffs, radio, even her bloody notebook. Fifteen years felt like a hell of a long time. His gear was entirely silent. 'How do you—'

His radio buzzed and crackled, the shards of a voice audible through the noise.

Adam stopped and pressed the button. 'Serial-Alpha receiving, over.'

'Got a report of a robbery at Ibrahim's Store on the Minories, over.'

Chloe looked along the street. There it was, past the boutique hotels sandwiched between two fried chicken places and the Subway franchise. One of those signs of gentrification her old man kept banging on about, how the East End was losing its identity, blah blah blah. Double fronted and painted navy blue with orange lettering, Ibrahim's sat next to a chain shop Chloe didn't recognise the logo of.

'On our way, over.' Adam looked at Chloe, eyebrows raised, jaw clenched. 'You ready for this?'

Truth was, she was loving it. All that training hadn't prepared her for the reality. The months and months at police college were *electric*. But the reality was, she was toiling with the mundanity of her new job. Her old man would capitalise it. The police magazine was called *The Job*. Him and her grandfather talked about the Job in hushed tones, like it was a thing you could touch and feel.

Her fantasy had been seeing police work as a noble enterprise. And, of course, being the third generation of Fenchurch walking the streets of East London as a cop. Doing some good in the world, helping those less fortunate than herself.

And it was so bloody boring. All those forms, all that admin.

Speaking to people.

Doing nothing.

And it was like her prayers had been answered. A robbery, even at this time.

Chloe gave Adam a tight nod. Eyes twitching, teeth almost chattering. 'Let's do it.'

He gripped his baton on his belt, so Chloe did the same, then he walked over to the door. 'Right.' He stopped, took a look at Chloe, then peered inside.

Chloe followed him to the entrance, heart racing, ice climbing her spine.

The shop owner, presumably Ibrahim, stood behind the till, his arms folded across his chest. Stubborn, proud, determined.

A young guy stood on the other side, dressed in the latest trendy clothing. Baggy hoodie, skin-tight jeans tucked into white basketball boots. Face mostly covered by a mask and hidden by a baseball cap. He jabbed a finger towards the owner, his wrist filled with bands of all colours. 'Open the till, man!'

Ibrahim just shook his head.

'Man, just do it.' Wristbands smacked the counter. 'Open up and give me my payday, man!'

'Or what?'

'Or I kill you, man!'

'Here we go.' Adam's whisper faded as he stepped inside the shop, hands raised. 'What seems to be the problem here?'

Chloe followed him in.

Wristbands jerked around and his eyes widened. He reached into his hoodie pocket and pulled out a pistol, side on, training the barrel at Adam.

Chloe took in the situation, trying to assess it like she'd been taught to.

One assailant, armed.

One civilian.

Two cops.

A confined space.

Two exits. Only one definitely led to the street. The other was presumably a storeroom. The backs of the shops were so built up around here that it'd probably been sold off and developed years ago, so wasn't likely to lead to a lane.

It all meant that Wristbands would have to come through them. With his gun. And his anger and desperation, making him more likely to use it.

He thrust the pistol towards Adam, finger on the trigger. 'Get out of my way, man.'

Adam raised his hands higher in the air, fingertips level with his ears. 'How's about you put the gun down and we talk this through, yeah?'

'No, man. I want what's mine!'

'What's that? A prison sentence for armed robbery?'

'Man, this is... This is...' Wristbands walked closer to Adam, pointing the pistol right at his head. 'You want to choose this hill to die on, man?'

'Nobody's dying here, mate. Just put the gun away and it'll all be fine.'

'Man, you do *not* wanna—'

'Shh.' Adam lowered his hands and reached for the gun.

Chloe braced herself, feeling everything clench.

Adam grabbed for the gun and Wristbands punched him, but missed Adam's head, instead catching him on the shoulder.

Adam grabbed him, but Wristbands fell over backwards with Adam on top of him. Not a fair fight, but they were paid to win.

Adam was gripping the gun, twisting as he fell. Wristbands was still trying to keep hold of his weapon and they struggled, but Wristbands stayed on his feet.

The gun pointed towards Chloe.

Chloe's gut plunged.

Wristbands squeezed his finger around the trigger.

Chloe shut her eyes.

Liquid sprayed over her face.

A water pistol.

A bloody water pistol!

She gripped her baton in her damp hands then shot forward,

clubbing Wristbands in the thigh with the metal. He tumbled backwards, falling into a fridge. A long crack ran down the glass. She took another swipe, bashing the metal against his forearm.

Wristbands squealed.

Chloe stood there, panting hard, heart like it was going to burst. But she felt a glow of pride at doing her job. Taking down an armed robber. 'What's your name?'

'Ain't giving you my name!' His fingers were covering his throat. 'Tried to kill me, man!'

Adam grabbed his shoulders and pinned him back against the cracked fridge door. 'Stay. Still.' He looked over at Chloe. 'Well done, kidder. Read him his rights; we'll get the rest out of him later.'

She focused on Wristbands, on Adam holding him down. 'I am arresting you for attempted armed robbery.' She grabbed his wrist, tight, and pulled out her handcuffs, opening one of the rings. 'You do not have to say anything, but it may harm your defence if you do not mention when questioned something which you later rely on in court.' She snapped the cuff on his left wrist. 'Anything you do say may be given in evidence.' Then the right side. 'Do you understand?'

'I understand but I ain't done nothing.'

Adam let go of him and stood up, shaking his head. He held out his hand for Chloe to bump, then turned to Ibrahim. 'Thanks for calling this in, sir.'

Wristbands' arm lashed out, swinging the handcuff out and lashing off Adam's knee.

He collapsed against the counter and went down.

Chloe reached for him and caught the dangling cuff. Wristbands snatched the metal and pulled hard, tugging her forwards. Her head bounced off the fridge and the doors fell off. Bottles of soft drinks rolled out onto the floor.

Wristbands swung out with the cuffs, aiming at Chloe's face.

She caught the movement in time and raised her hands. The metal glanced off her palms and nicked the skin.

Wristbands shot off through the shop, out onto the street.

Chloe set off after him. A 7-Up bottle rolled into her path. She stood on it and went down again.

All she could hear was Wristbands' footsteps pounding along the road outside, fading away as he made for the Tower.

Ibrahim was out from behind his till now, pointing out to the street. 'Get after him!'

Chloe groaned. She wanted to curl up into a ball, go to sleep and wake up whenever the shame had died. And her head was throbbing like she'd headbutted a fridge.

But he was right – she needed to get him.

'Come on, kidder.' Adam reached out his hand and hoisted her up to her feet. 'Let's get him.' He waved at Ibrahim, 'Back in a minute, sir,' then darted off out of the shop.

Chloe gave Ibrahim a tight smile as she left, but she was burning up with shame.

Get over yourself!

She charged on out onto the road, then followed Adam towards the river, their feet thudding off the pavement.

He was about eight stone heavier than her and not built for running, so she caught up by the pub that shared its name with the street. 'Hey, kidder, don't beat yourself up.'

Chloe kept pace with Adam. 'I'm going to beat *him* up.'

'Happens to everyone.' Adam was struggling, his breaths coming in gasps now. 'Rookies either put cuffs on too loosely or with enough force to double as a tourniquet. You did the former. The latter is actually worse.'

Chloe just grunted.

'And in my first month, I ended up...' Adam sucked in a breath as they ran. 'I'll tell you later.' He laughed. 'And you better get used to it. It's not all murders and intrigue. This is real policing. Nonsense and reports.'

'So my dad says.'

Up ahead, Wristbands took the right onto Tower Hill, heading for the tube station. Even this early, the place was crawling with commuters heading to the City, all suited and booted, headphones clamped to their skulls, thumbs hammering their phones as they walked. Wristbands sliced through a group and they went down like skittles at bowling.

Chloe waved ahead of them. 'He's heading for the Tube. We'll lose him in there if he gets inside.'

'Agree.' Adam sucked in a deep breath and reached for his radio. 'Control, we need back up at Tower Hill tube, over.'

Chloe lost the response in amongst the crackles and whistles. Sod it, she needed to take charge here, so she bombed ahead of Adam, her gear rattling hard with each stride.

She was closing on Wristbands.

He made for the path through the gardens up to the tube station, but glanced behind him and made eye contact with her, hurtling towards him. His eyes bulged and he kept on along the street.

The Tower was hidden by railings and the modern buildings springing up around it. Just bars and offices up ahead, but it would be busy enough to lose yourself in. Lots of places to hide and wait it out.

Chloe was five strides behind him now and closing. 'Stop!'

Wristbands shot right, weaving through the Tower Hill Memorial, into the gardens.

Chloe followed him in.

And he'd vanished into thin air. No sign of him. No heaving, no hard breaths.

Just two people sat on separate benches, both looking at their tablets. Nobody running from the police.

She swung around, but there was no sign of him.

How the hell had he got away?

She raced over to the monument building.

There he was. Up on the ledge, trying to jump over some nasty-looking spikes out onto the street.

And off he went, sailing through the sky.

Right as Adam bustled in next to her, lashing sweat from his darkened blond hair. 'You got him?' Breathing hard like he would suffer a heart attack.

'Back!' She swerved around him and raced out to the street again, heavy with commuters.

No sign of Wristbands. He'd lost himself in the throng.

Amazing work....

She'd made a right arse of this.

Chloe wanted to race off in any direction, but she had no idea where he'd gone. Could've gone back the way towards Ibrahim's. Could be down at the Thames. Could be heading into the City. Her dad warned her about how that wasn't their patch, but she didn't really care so long as she caught Wristbands.

She didn't even get his name. Or really see his face. Could've been about three different races. Amazing...

'Help! Police!'

Came from behind her.

Maybe Wristbands had cut around the monument and headed back into the gardens?

Chloe swung around and set off towards the sound.

Over the grass, a woman was clutching a rolled-up umbrella, pointing at the blocks that formed the smaller monument, a long section of wall between two benches which carried the inscription. 'Help me!'

A man lay on top of it, arms folded over his chest. Dressed in trousers and cardigan, but his feet were bare. A rough sleeper, probably.

Chloe scanned around for Adam, but she couldn't see him, so she jogged over the grass. 'Are you okay?'

'I'm fine.' The woman scowled at the man next to her. 'I'm worried about him.'

'Thank you, madam.' Chloe gave a polite smile and stepped towards him. She couldn't tell if he was breathing or not. 'Sir?'

Nothing.

It didn't look like he was breathing. Then again, it was quite cold out, so maybe his heart rate was low. Slowed everything down.

Maybe.

She reached into her belt for a pair of blue nitrile gloves and snapped them on. Then prodded the man.

Again, nothing.

This time, she touched the body and it was cold. Stiff.

A dead body.

Amazing...

She stepped onto the bench at the side, then up onto the wall to get a better look at him.

Eyes wide open, tongue hanging out.

Yep. Dead.

And shit, she recognised him.

1

FENCHURCH

Simon Fenchurch hated to be that guy, but he kept his focus on the clock on the wall. It clicked to seven forty and he felt a little knot of tension disappear. Another minute done, twenty to go.

'Are we boring you, Simon?' Abi was looking at him with narrowed eyes. Hair scraped back in a severe ponytail, revealing her almost-elven ears. No makeup today, just raw and unvarnished Abi.

Abi Fenchurch. His wife. Still, but only just. A three-month separation that was limping towards a divorce.

And only one man in the way of it.

Dr Steven Waugh. Lank hair hanging in curtains around a moon face. Thick beard covering his neck and cheeks. And so Australian it hurt. He smiled, making his cheeks fill up. 'Simon, we need to make sure you're present for these sessions.'

Fenchurch couldn't look at him for long. 'I'm here.'

'I mean, yeah, you are, but it's not just physically present, is it? Mentally too. And from where I'm sitting, you're barely physically present. Literally clock watching.'

Fenchurch shifted his gaze back to stare hard at Waugh, giving him one of his ten most severe glares. Didn't seem to faze Waugh, though.

And Fenchurch kept thinking of him as a surname. First names were for friends and close family. Suspects had surnames. People you didn't trust or couldn't trust. 'What more do you want from me?'

Waugh sat back in his chair. 'Simon, it's polite to engage with us.'

Fenchurch stretched his legs out, linking them at the ankles. 'All I've done is listen to a litany of character flaws.' He glanced over at Abi, but couldn't hold her gaze for long. 'It's like *I'm* the one who had an affair, not her.'

She groaned. 'Simon, the fact you're not listening... It's...' She shook her head, then looked at Waugh. 'Do you see what I'm contending with here?'

Waugh frowned. 'Thing is, Abi, "contending" is a bit of a loaded term, don't you think?'

She shrugged. 'It might be, but I think it's accurate.' She shut her eyes. 'I made a mistake, but *he* won't acknowledge any fault on his part for—'

'Any *fault*?' Fenchurch swung around to stare at her. 'Abi, I didn't sleep with someone else. You did. This is all on you. Not me.'

'And the fact you can't see that—'

'This again.' Fenchurch sucked in a deep breath. Felt like he was drowning here. 'Listen, we've both got busy jobs, I get it. Yours is bad, but I've been a lot more busy than you recently. Maybe that's fair, I don't know, but I try to be there for you. I try to—'

'But you're not. You haven't been for a long time.'

'That's harsh.'

'No, Simon, it's not. Think it through. We both suffered because of... Because of what happened to us fifteen years ago. Losing Chloe. It drove a wedge between us and we separated, but I moved on with my life. I grieved. You didn't. You just stayed in that state where you... where you kept looking for her.' She swallowed hard. 'And you came back to me, Simon. You let yourself grieve and I had my husband back. That's why we remarried.'

'But I found her. Christ, because of me, we found her. We got her back.'

She shut her eyes again and shook her head. 'Simon, I just don't know if you love me anymore.'

Fenchurch sat back. The words stung. 'You were the adulterer, not me. You slept with an old colleague, not me.'

Her eyes were still closed.

Waugh smiled at him. 'Can you see anything in what Abi's trying to say?'

Fenchurch huffed out a deep breath. He tried thinking it all through, but it just ached. 'Okay, maybe she's partly right. I gave up so much of my life for hunting for our daughter, then I found her and...' His throat felt very tight. 'And I had nothing else to hunt for. Took a while, but we reintegrated her back into our lives. We moved on as a family. And we became so close, the three of us. Four of us. Chloe loved her baby brother and... and in a way it... it let us relive her childhood.'

But he still had the trauma of those years without her. Almost eleven years where she'd grown up, into a young woman. And he'd driven a wedge between himself and the rest of the world. Just had that steely focus to find her. And when he wasn't looking or losing himself in his work, he lost himself in a bottle of wine. Most nights. Every night.

Coming back from that was impossible.

And that was her point, wasn't it?

He looked right at her, her eyes open again. 'Abi, I'm sorry for neglecting you. For neglecting us. It's been tough for me.'

'I understand, but you've still been throwing yourself into your job.'

'It's an important one. Just as important as yours.'

'And you martyring yourself while our son grows up without you is worth it, right?'

'Don't be like that.'

'Like what? Telling you the truth?'

'Come on, Ab. This isn't about me.'

'It is, Simon. Of course it is. Alan is three and a half. He spends more time with the nursery staff than he does with you. We were supposed to visit my parents in December for a week, but you had to pull out because of a case. You couldn't delegate to Rod or Kay or anyone else. Just had to be you. Cancelling your family holiday for work.'

Fenchurch nibbled at his thumbnail. 'Fair enough.' He crunched a little sliver off. 'I could've pulled out of that. I could've quit too.'

Abi looked over at him, mouth hanging open.

At this stage in his career, Fenchurch was weighing up his options. Close to getting a pension, maybe time for a second career. The whole bit. Everyone thought about it, more and more as the years turned into decades.

But more often than not, the answer was no. Being a DCI paid more than becoming an ex-cop on the fast track to being an OAP. And that lifestyle was seductive.

All the lonely nights Fenchurch had spent, yeah. He'd been through it all.

'And I should've come down to Cornwall too. I was going to, but...' Fenchurch looked at her. 'Abi, I'm sorry. Sometimes things happen that I can't control. But what I don't understand is how me not being there is somehow the cause for you meeting up with an ex-boyfriend, who you were seeing while we were separated, and having sex with him.'

'Because I felt so lonely, Simon. I was vulnerable. Our son hasn't been a well boy. He's had so many operations considering his age. And I've borne the stress myself.'

She was right. He had to concede that. 'I'm sorry about all of that, Abi. Sorry you feel it, sorry I *made* you feel it, sorry we had to go through that, on top of what happened to Chloe.'

She looked at him, tears glistening in her eyes. 'Do you want to make things work?'

'I'm here, aren't I?'

'I know, but like he said—' She wagged a hand in Waugh's

direction. '—you're not mentally present. Do you want to try and save our marriage?'

Fenchurch didn't know.

He really didn't.

He had that same stirring in his heart whenever he saw Abi. Still wanted to hold her, to kiss her, to walk down any street hand in hand with her.

But she'd had an affair. Slept with someone else. And not just once. He didn't know how many times. She said it was once, but who knew what the truth was? And that time was definitely premeditated.

While he had been Mr Distant, it took Steve bloody Waugh's magical couples therapy for her to open up about it all. To tell the truth.

So he gave her it. 'Abi, the truth is, I'm over it.'

She looked over at him, her forehead twitching. She gasped, short and sharp. 'Well.'

Was he being too harsh? Too brutal? Too... selfish?

'Abi, you hurt me. You slept with someone else. I could maybe understand or forgive once. But after all we've been through, after being separated, after renewing our marriage... I just can't. I just can't understand, can't forgive, can't... Can't do this anymore.'

She reached over for a tissue and honked as she blew into it. 'Well.'

'You keep saying that, Abi.' Waugh steepled his fingers. 'It's like you're hiding something from us. You say "well", when you actually want to say something, but you hold it back from us.'

'From "us"?' She glared at Waugh, but flicked her hand towards Fenchurch. 'This is about him, not you.'

'But you are hiding something.'

'Of course I am. He's hurt me.'

Waugh raised his eyebrows. 'But you had an affair, didn't you?'

'People have affairs for lots of reasons. I've made myself clear on why I was vulnerable to that.'

Waugh leaned forward in his chair, making the mechanism

creak. 'Just so we're all on the same page here, I think it'd be useful for us to go into that in a lot more detail.' He paused. 'Is that okay?'

Abi looked at him, then at Fenchurch. She shrugged. 'Well...'

Waugh looked at Fenchurch. 'What do you think, Simon?'

Fenchurch didn't know how much it'd help. How much could it?

Was it just Waugh being nosy? Peeking into people's lives, getting some sadistic kicks out of it?

Or would it actually lay bare all their flaws, all their history?

Fenchurch gave a similar shrug.

'I'll take those as both yeses, then.' Waugh scribbled something on a notepad. 'Abi, you were involved with this colleague before, am I right?'

She took her time answering, spending it looking at her fingernails. 'When Simon and I were divorced.'

'And you stayed in touch afterwards?'

'Not until... It's a long story, but we bumped into each other at a conference.'

'And you rekindled things romantically?'

'Not initially, no. We were friends. Coffees, that kind of thing.'

'Did Simon know?'

Fenchurch kept his gaze on the spiral carpet. 'No, I didn't.'

'And you didn't think it a bad idea to repeatedly meet an old flame for coffee and similar kinds of things?'

'I'm sorry, Simon.'

Waugh scribbled something down. Took him a while, like he was writing out the Bible from memory. 'I want to ask something that I suspect all of us have been wondering.' He set his pen down on the edge of his chair then snorted, shifting his gaze from Abi to Fenchurch and back. 'Is Alan really Simon's son?'

Fenchurch was on his feet before he knew what hit him. 'What the hell did you say?'

Waugh seemed to shrink into his seat, like he was a cushion. 'Simon, this is a safe space where—'

'You *don't* talk to us like that.' Fenchurch stood over him, hands in pockets. 'Do you hear me?'

'It's a fair question and—'

'Yeah, but you don't ask it. Ever. You hear me?'

'Sure.'

Fenchurch walked over to Abi and looked deep into her eyes. 'I'm sorry he said that to you. It's not fair.'

'It feels like it is fair, though.' She shrugged. 'I mean, the only stupid questions are ones you don't ask. Right?'

'Al's my son, though. He looks a lot like me.'

'And he's a grumpy little sod.'

Fenchurch couldn't help but laugh at that. 'Fair cop.' He collapsed back into his chair. 'Abi, when I said I'm over us, I don't know if I am. What I'm sure of is that I still feel hurt. I feel betrayed by your affair. That you didn't talk to me about how you felt. That... There's just this massive wedge between us and I don't know who put it there.'

She stared right at him. 'I'm sorry, Simon. I should've talked to you about how I felt. That I wasn't happy about all the hours you were working. I work a full-time job too and we've got a toddler and—'

'And you're right, Ab. I should've been open to you. Present in our marriage. I should've been there for you.'

There was a lot of hurt in her eyes. 'Do you want to try to save this?'

He nodded. Out of instinct, maybe, but it happened. 'I do.'

'Do you really?'

'I do. Course I do.'

The clock ticked to eight.

Waugh dared to lean forward in his chair. 'Okay, guys, that's all we've got time for today. It's been a good session, hasn't it?' Fenchurch swore the smug git was looking pleased that his tactic might've worked. 'Same time next week?'

Abi nodded, then gathered up her stuff. She left the tissue on the table, like she did every week.

Fenchurch hadn't spilled a single tear in nine sessions. But he'd just come close to spilling blood. 'Next time, then.' He gathered up his leather jacket. 'But I don't want any more of that kind of nonsense from you.'

Waugh just tilted his head to the side.

Fenchurch didn't know if he agreed, if he was sorry, or what. He headed out into the corridor, stopping for a deep breath.

'You okay?'

Fenchurch looked around at Abi, frowning. He still had that twinge of love in his heart, but it was paired with that sickening churn in his gut. No matter what they'd discussed, that they'd potentially agreed to think about trying to save their marriage... He was still hurt. He still felt that burning on his cheeks. 'This stuff's so close to the bone, Ab. So tough to hear the truth, even harder when it's so raw and so fresh. Just three months since I found out about...'

Since Chloe told him what was going on down in Cornwall.

Since then, it'd been hell. Everything felt wrong.

'How's Chloe getting on as a probationer?'

He looked over at her. 'That's for you to discuss with her.'

'Chloe isn't speaking to me, Simon. And it's eating me up.'

Fenchurch had little sympathy. It wasn't just him who was cut up by this. 'It's not that... it's... Listen, Chloe can make up her own mind about what she says to you. Or doesn't. She's upset about it. Feels let down. After what she's been through, she's got trust issues. Massive trust issues. And adultery isn't helping her.'

'I understand. But she's living with you, Simon. It feels like I've lost her again.'

'I'm not keeping her away from you.'

'I know, but... I just want to know how she's doing. That's all.'

'She's doing us proud. It's a hard month, the first month. She's just about finished it and it'll be plain sailing from there on. I have no doubt she'll become a full officer.'

'I just want to see her.'

'I want you to see her, but it's up to her.'

Abi pressed her lips together. He'd seen that look so many times. 'Do you have time for a coffee just now?'

Right then, Fenchurch's phone blasted out.

'Sorry.' He had to check it. Could be anyone. But it was DI Uzma Ashkani. One of his direct reports. Demanding, but driven. He smiled at Abi. 'Sorry, I'd better take this.'

'Okay, I'll take a rain check on that coffee, then.' But he could see the hurt in her eyes. Being second fiddle to the Job. He hadn't known how much of a strain it was on her, but there it was.

'Rain check.' He sighed *before* answering it. Made that mistake a few times. 'Uzma, what's up?'

'Simon, there's been a body discovered near Tower Hill tube station. Potential murder.'

'Can't you run the—'

'I'm afraid it's a bit more involved than that.' Ashkani sighed. 'Simon, the victim is an ex-cop.'

2

If there was a street name in London more suited to how Fenchurch felt right then, he was buggered if he could name it.

Seething Lane.

Perfect.

Place was rammed full of squad cars, so many it was hard to count, let alone remember all the plates. Dr Pratt's purple Jaguar gleamed like it'd just been polished. Two CSIs were unloading their van, already suited up. Their flats and homes must be immaculate. Not a stray hair anywhere.

Okay, so maybe Bleeding Heart Yard or Savage Gardens would suffice, both not far from here, but Fenchurch *was* seething. He'd agreed to those couples counselling sessions with a view to getting out of his marriage. And now...

Yeah, that bastard called "hope" was back. Prodding him in the guts and stabbing him in the heart, bleeding or not.

Somehow he'd lost his objectivity, his determination and... And he had hope flickering in his guts again. Little butterflies, maybe, but there they were.

Him and Abi, back together again. Them and Chloe and Baby Al. Alan, as they called him now.

Waugh had gloated like he'd been the one to achieve anything.

However many sessions he'd presided over, all Waugh had achieved was make Fenchurch more determined to draw a line under his marriage.

It still got to him. That bitterness in the pit of his stomach. That anger. That rage. That—

Why?

Why did she have to have an affair?

Was it really his fault? His promotion from DI to DCI had meant more time at the office, more stress, more responsibility. Less trudging around, interviewing suspects, and more admin.

Maybe he had been a bear with a sore head, but she hadn't talked to him about it. No, she'd fallen back into the arms of Brendan Holding.

Fenchurch shut his eyes and counted to ten.

He'd get over it. He always did.

He opened the door and stepped out onto Seething Lane. Cold air and the smell of roasting meat from a nearby snack van. Commuters trudging from tube to tube, station to office. Poor bastards.

Yeah, he was still angry, but it was more a vague pissed off than anything else.

He set off down the street towards the memorial on Tower Hill and got that jab in his guts.

No serving cop wanted to investigate the murder of one of their own. Well, not all, but virtually all. It made them think of colleagues, past and present. Of themselves. It asked so many questions.

Fenchurch put on his game face as he neared the crime scene. He didn't recognise the kid manning the outer locus, but then he didn't recognise half of Leman Street these days. Without speaking, he jotted down his name, badge number and time of entry, then handed it back and stepped into the belly of the beast.

The biggest monument was a haunting memorial lining the road that ran around the Tower of London. Greek or Roman columns and empty windows, to serve in place of a grave for merchant seamen and fishermen lost at sea during the First World War. At least, that's what his old man told him when he was a nipper.

The other two were somewhere in the gardens at the back of the space, shrouded by the thirty-or-so officers milling around, none of them achieving much except draining East London of tea.

A few of his team were there, facing away, though, talking to people. Making themselves useful.

A tent was erected over the inscription stone for the Second World War memorial, a massive chunk of wall. It didn't look like a day for rain and there wasn't a lick of wind.

Off to the side, the bulky figure of PC Adam Burridge stood there like a sentry, guarding Chloe.

What the hell was she doing here?

She didn't look upset, but that posture... He'd seen it before, when she was little and more recently. Like she was going to explode.

Fenchurch felt that fist tighten around his stomach as he walked over. He took it slow, giving them space and himself time to read their body language a bit more clearly. 'What's up?'

Despite only being a probationer, Chloe looked every inch the copper. Hair scraped back and tied away in a bun. Immaculate uniform, even at the end of a shift. She was staring into space, though, and that made the fist squeeze that little bit tighter.

Burridge stepped between them. 'Chloe was FAO, sir.'

First Attending Officer.

First person to see the body.

Of someone she knew.

Christ.

Fenchurch had been six months as a full officer before he'd seen his first dead body. And that was a very different London, much rougher and more violent. Some officers had scraped heroin addicts off train tracks on day one.

This was different, though. His own daughter.

And maybe that was it. Abi was right to point out how wrapped up in his own internal machinations he'd been. Here he was, where his daughter needed him, and he was thinking furious thoughts about a counselling session that was supposed to save his marriage, or at least let them move on without wanting to kill each other. What was best for the children.

Yeah. Get over yourself, dickhead.

Chloe saw him and stood ramrod straight, just like her grandfather had told her to. Not that the Fenchurch back was up to much. 'Dad.'

'That's DCI Fenchurch to you.' He smiled at Burridge then at his daughter. 'Chloe, can I have a word?'

Burridge raised a hand. 'Sir, could you give us a minute?'

Fenchurch stepped away and beckoned him to follow. 'She's my daughter. It's up to me to make sure she's okay.'

'With all due respect, sir, she—' He laughed. 'Actually, I take that back and I'm just giving it straight. You can't pull rank on me then try to take her away. It's not on.'

He had a point.

Adam leaned in. 'Listen, she's down in the dumps about two mistakes in a row, okay? Happens to everyone, so I'm giving her the usual advice. She's new, so she's going to screw up, so she needs to make sure she screws up in different ways and not the same ones.' He looked to the side. 'And I know who the little toe rag is, so we'll get the day shift to head around to his flat and pick him up.'

Burridge was clearly a good cop and a better training officer. That was policing. Fix the young, don't eat them. And his experience meant that, even if you don't catch them in a chase, you know where they're going. 'Listen, just give us a minute. Okay? I don't want to tread on your toes, you're clearly one of the best and, if it was any other officer, you as TO would get priority. But after what she's been through?'

Burridge frowned. 'I know what she's been through, sir. If it was an issue, she wouldn't be here.'

'Trust me, I just need a minute.'

'By all means.' Burridge nodded at him, then at Chloe, but the twitching on his forehead maybe betrayed his anger or frustration. 'I'll give you some space, kidder.'

'Sure thing.' Chloe gave him an empty look and her gaze followed his path.

Fenchurch saw the emptiness in her actions and certainly recognised it. Weird how much of a person's behaviour seemed to be genetic or heritable. 'You okay?'

'Depends. Am I talking to Dad or DCI Fenchurch?'

'Either. Both.'

She sighed again. That coping mechanism. Get it out of your system. Be in touch with your body and your feelings. 'I'm fine.'

'Are you sure?'

'What, you think I'll go to pieces over seeing a corpse?' She looked around at him and locked eyes with him. He let go, let her win that round. 'Dad, I'm fine. You don't need to patronise me.'

'It's a big thing seeing a—'

'*Dad.*'

He held up his hands. 'Okay. Just trying to help.'

She smiled now, her lips thin but with some warmth. 'Right. Sorry. Look, I appreciate your concern, but I'm made of tough stuff. Okay?'

'Got it.' Fenchurch gave her the smile back. 'It's the end of your shift now.'

'Right. And?'

'Time to get home.'

She hefted up her stab-proof from the floor. 'Adam's told me to bugger off, but I want to type it all up while it's fresh.'

'I think he's right. Just make sure your notebook's tip top and get home.'

'That an order?'

He laughed. 'You don't report to me.'

'Thank God.' She got out her notebook and opened it at the last page. 'Dad, the thing is, I know the victim.'

Fenchurch frowned at her. 'Who is it?'

'I think it's Grandad's friend. Bert Matthews.'

3

Fenchurch felt that weird claustrophobia from the crime scene suit. The chemical smell, the stale taste. No matter how many times he'd worn one, or how many times he'd told an officer about the importance of preserving crime scenes, the way his breath misted in the goggles...

But it maybe helped a small amount. The transparent plastic distorted and twisted things so they didn't seem so real. Like he wasn't seeing the body of Bert Matthews.

Just lying there on the granite slab, eyes and mouth open. Skin as pale as his ruddy complexion would get. His thick combover dangling down to his neck. Bare feet, but clean and smooth. Otherwise, he could be a homeless man who'd got caught out, but here he was, a friend of his old man's. Pair of them were thick as thieves and just as unreliable at times.

Maybe that was unfair, but Bert and his father went back a long way.

A suited figure turned to look at him. 'Ah, Simon.' Detective Superintendent Julian Loftus, just his baby blue eyes visible through the goggles. 'Thanks for... Well... Thanks for coming.'

'It's my job, boss.' Fenchurch inspected the body again.

Casually dressed and relaxed. Almost looked like a death at home. A heart attack during the night.

But leaving the body here? That pointed to murder.

And Fenchurch had no idea why.

He looked at Loftus. 'Sir, I need to point out the potential conflict of interest here. I'm acquainted with the victim. I understand if—'

'Yes, yes, yes.' Loftus clapped his arm. 'Thing is, everyone who's been on the force longer than five minutes knows Bert Matthews. One of those who'd stick his oar in anywhere it wasn't wanted. A good egg, though. I'd have to go to Manchester or Newcastle to find an investigator worth his, her or their salt who hasn't had their ear bent by one of his many, many stories.' His breath misted his goggles. 'So I need you to get to work. Okay?'

'Understood, sir.'

'Now, I need to bugger off to brief Command, but when it's one of our own, we go the extra mile.' Loftus locked eyes with him. 'Find his killer, Simon.'

'Will do.'

Another pat and Loftus strode off.

Leaving Fenchurch with the corpse.

The morning sunlight had crawled around to catch Bert staring up at the blue sky.

Fenchurch spotted three suited figures just behind the monument. One was comforting another, while the third seemed a bit confused. He made his way over. 'Everything okay?'

'Guv.' The hugger broke free, letting Fenchurch see it was DS Kay Reed. 'It's Lisa, she...'

DS Lisa Bridge was cradling herself in Reed's arms, tears rolling down her cheeks.

'I'll just get back to the victim, then...' The lone figure was Dr Pratt, his bushy eyebrows filling a good chunk of his goggles. He bundled past Fenchurch on his way to Bert's body.

Fenchurch tried to make eye contact with Bridge, but couldn't. 'Are you okay?'

Reed shot him a glare, like she was saying 'does she look okay?'

but didn't have the courage to say it. 'Lisa is Be— the victim's niece.'

'Right.' Fenchurch felt a trickle of sweat running down his back. He'd clean forgotten, assuming he ever knew. 'Kay, can you take her away, please?'

'Of course.' Reed led Bridge back the way he'd come, away from her uncle's body.

Seeing your own flesh and blood dead was one of the hardest things, especially when it was a shock like that... Yeah, that'd break even the strongest of officers. And Bridge was.

Fenchurch set off back to the body.

Dr Pratt was working away at the body, prodding and pressing. 'Om pom tiddly om pom.'

'William, do you mind not doing that for once?'

Pratt looked up with a frown. 'Doing what?'

'The old "Om pom tiddly om pom" stuff.' Fenchurch waved a hand around the area. 'A lot of people worked with or knew the victim.'

'Right, well, of course, but I've no idea what you're talking about.' He reached into his bag for a massive thermometer. 'Om pom pom-pom-pom pom pom.'

Didn't even know he was doing it. Fantastic.

'You got anything for me yet?'

Pratt glanced up at him. 'Well, it's fairly clearly death by drowning.'

'*Drowning?*'

'Indeed. Happened last night too, unless I'm very much mistaken.' Pratt looked around the place. 'But there's no obvious water source here.'

Fenchurch looked over to the river, but it was hidden by the Tower and its surrounding office blocks. The peaks of Tower Bridge climbed above, but looked about half a mile away. Hard to get a body over from there without being spotted and Bert didn't exactly have the tell-tale signs of being in that infernal river.

Back up towards the tube station, there were a few fancy

hotels. They'd probably have hot tubs in each room, rather than a bog-standard bathtub.

'So you're saying he was transported here?'

'Logically, yes.' Pratt pointed back to the larger monument, which had a lot of the CSI attention. 'I believe Tammy and her team have found some water splash patterns, which would indicate his transferral, but said water is long since evaporated.'

'Right, right.'

'And there's obviously no way to identify where the water in his lungs came from.'

'But he was definitely drowned?'

Pratt looked up. 'Definitely. One hundred percent. I don't even need to get him back to Lewisham to know.'

Fenchurch looked around the place. A monument to the maritime war dead. And a drowned victim. It had to be connected.

But why?

He never understood that psychological need to move a dead body to a public place, where it would be discovered. Surely it reduced the chances of avoiding conviction?

Better to leave the body in the bath or body of water you killed the victim in.

Isn't it?

The police would know about it, for starters, and CCTV was everywhere in a city like London, especially these days. Only a matter of time before you're caught.

Of course, if you *wanted* the police to know and you were confident enough to be able to evade detection... Why would anyone want them to know that Bert was dead? And why here?

'Can't detect much through these masks—' Pratt tapped his nose. '—but there's an almighty stench of bleach coming from the body.'

'Someone covering their tracks?'

'Right. I suspect immersion in a volume of bleach, so it's incredibly unlikely any DNA could've survived.'

That little tingle at the back of his neck started up again.

Pointed to someone who knew their onions. 'Okay, William, let me know when the post-mortem will be.'

'Oh, it'll be this afternoon. I've got as clean a slate as I can get these days. Not a lot of deaths at the moment.'

'Excellent, thank you.' Fenchurch took one last look at the body. Dying like that, being dragged here and being left to rest in public. Poor old sod. 'See you there.' He walked back to the inner locus crime scene manager and tugged off his mask and goggles, then started taking off his jacket.

DI Uzma Ashkani stood outside the perimeter, hands on hips. Belly swollen with barely two months to go, just weeks until her maternity leave. 'Sir.'

'Uzma, you're a sight for sore eyes.' Fenchurch kicked off his crime scene suit trousers into the discard pile. 'How was the check up?'

'All good.' She rested a hand on her tummy. 'Doctor wants me to take it easy, but you know me. I just can't.'

Fenchurch hoped she didn't live to regret that. 'Okay, so we've got a puzzle and a half here. Victim appears to have been killed elsewhere, so your highest priority is finding out how he got here. Who transported him? Why?'

'On it.' But she had the narrow-eyed glare of someone who was sick of desk duties. Her eagle eyes swept around the park. 'I guess they brought him here by the Tower Hill tube entrance.'

Fenchurch looked over at the main road. 'Probably, but don't discount it.'

'Fenchurch Street station's up there too. Open till, what, one? Last trains to deepest, darkest Essex. A few hotels too. Will get people going around there.'

The exact same thoughts he'd had. Might not have got off on the right foot, but they were settling into a groove. He was going to miss her when she was off on maternity. But something made him frown. 'You said they brought him here?'

Ashkani frowned. 'What do you mean?'

'Well, either you're using a gender-neutral pronoun or you think more than one person did this?'

'Bert's a big guy. Unless we're hunting a serious weightlifter, I'd assume it's two people. And weightlifters don't necessarily have the cardiovascular stamina to carry him all that way.' She walked her fingers from the entrance to the monument. 'Also, why was he put *here*?' She scanned the place. 'You think he could've been in the navy?'

'Merchant or Royal, yeah. That's my thinking.'

'Which would mean there's something symbolic about this?'

He nodded. 'And if there is, we need to know very quickly. I don't want a serial killer or a bloody terrorist running around London trying to send messages. Or bumping off ex-sailors.'

'Fair enough.' Ashkani looked behind her. 'I understand DS Bridge is related to the victim?'

'Her uncle, yeah.'

'Well, I'll get her to pick up on that. Channel her grief into something useful.'

'Good idea.' Fenchurch chucked the overshoes into the pile and signed out, then walked away. 'My old man was a close friend of Bert's. Colleagues for years. I'll speak to him about Bert, see what's what.'

'Sure thing, sir. I'll head back to the station.' Ashkani winced like her baby was kicking. 'Thank you, sir.'

What for, Fenchurch didn't know, but he watched her walking away.

Lisa Bridge was on the phone to someone. Presumably breaking the news to a family member.

But Chloe and Burridge were still here.

Fenchurch walked over to them, trying to act all casual. 'Chloe, can I give you a lift home?'

Burridge flexed his bulky arms and gave Fenchurch the old up and down. 'Don't worry, sir, I'll look after your little girl and keep her away from any bother.'

Fenchurch felt the blood rush up to his neck.

And he caught himself.

Her own training officer being so patronising about his daughter...

He gave Burridge a stern look. 'Can you give us a second, Constable?'

'Sure thing, sir.' His dormant Geordie accent came out to play, then. Maybe he felt ruffled by Fenchurch. Or protective of Chloe. Either way, he buggered off.

'Dad, that wasn't exactly woke.'

Woke... Christ. 'It's hard to be all sympathetic and understanding when it's about your little girl.'

She shook her head. '*Dad.*'

'Look, Chloe, I get it. Maybe he meant it in a protective way, but you can see how demeaning that is, right? Especially to a new officer, particularly a woman, trying to make it in a man's career.'

'Dad, I am going to finish my shift like a big girl.' Eyebrows raised, so there was a bit of humour in that. 'Okay?'

The stubborn Fenchurch gene was strong in her.

'Okay, I get that. But Burridge should be letting you go home, get some sleep, then tell you to get in early to type it up.'

'Really?'

'That's what happened to me the first time I saw a dead body. And I wasn't a probationer. I was a complete mess. Crying everywhere.'

'Wow.'

'I might be a big, ugly bugger, but I do have a sensitive side.' Fenchurch smiled at her. 'It's just buried really deep inside.'

'Need to start drilling for it.'

'Look, it's the end of your shift and the radio was saying the DLR's shut. And home is kind of on the way to my dad's, so...'

4

It'd been a while since Fenchurch had just pulled up outside his flat without going in. Then again, it'd been only three months he'd been living there after moving out of the family home.

He left the engine running as Chloe unfastened her seatbelt. Dressed in her civvies, her long hair flowing now. 'Dad, you should turn that off when you're waiting.'

'Takes more fuel starting it up again.'

She frowned. 'Does it?'

He laughed. 'I don't know. Sorry.' He hit the button and killed the engine. 'Happy now?'

'Not really.' She slumped back in her seat. 'How was counselling?'

'You know I agreed with your mother not to talk about it.'

'Yeah, but still. It does affect me.'

'Your mother was there. I was there. The dickhead counsellor was there. Only made me want to punch him three times.'

'Never change, Dad.'

'I think we made progress, though.'

'In which direction?'

'I'm not sure. A big part of me wants to forgive your mother, to get back together. To be a happy family unit again.'

'Sure you could ever be happy knowing what she's done?'

'I do feel betrayed, though.'

'And you're happy to begin to think about starting to talk about the slight possibility of change?'

He laughed 'Cheeky cow.'

'I get it, though. It's a big thing to get through.'

'It's a lot of big things to get through, that's the problem.'

'It's tough.' She opened the door. 'Sure getting back together would be a good thing, though? Won't you just always not trust her?'

Fenchurch rolled his shoulder. Trying to act casually. Cool, even. 'That's something we'll have to discuss and work through.' He looked over at her. 'Finding a body is never easy. You can talk to me, you know?'

'This again. Right.' She stepped out. 'Back on at seven, so I'd better get my head down.'

'Should be on at ten, though?'

'Adam said get in early, type up reports.'

'Wise man.' Fenchurch grinned. 'I can have a word and get you time off if you—'

'No.' She rolled her eyes. 'Dad, I've got to be strong about this.'

'Sometimes being strong is all about showing your vulnerabilities.'

'Don't you think I know? I was abducted, they messed with my head. And... And all the other shit. You think I need a hero dad to give me a hug and read me a bedtime story?'

Fenchurch was blushing now. Christ. 'I'm just trying to help.'

'Look, I know you've had the other side of that. Your daughter was kidnapped. You spent eleven years searching for her. And you want to be my guardian and protector forever, but that's not who I am or what I need from you. Dad, you better get used to me fighting my own battles, making my own mistakes and seeing my own dead bodies.'

As hard as it was to hear it, it felt good to know that she'd thought it all through. Knew her limitations, her needs, her fears. And those of her family. 'Okay, I understand.'

'Good.' She ran a hand through her hair, fanning it out. She swallowed. 'Not going to lie, Dad, it was creepy seeing Bert up there. Someone I know, who I played cards with a couple of times with Grandad. But I *will* get through this my own way, right or wrong.'

'Okay, live your life your way.'

'And Dad, I know it's okay to show weakness. And emotion.'

He grinned. 'Typical Fenchurch. Stubborn to the last.'

'Damn straight.'

'Okay, get some sleep and rest.' He turned the engine back on. 'We can talk at dinner.'

5

The old street changed every time Fenchurch visited. The pub was all hipster now, craft beer taps and greasy burgers. Three skips outside tiny houses that were getting the City banker treatment, despite being in the arse end of Limehouse.

Fenchurch stood there, hand hovering over the doorbell.

His old home. The place he grew up in. Assuming that's what he'd actually done and he wasn't still a child. So much happened here, so much grief and trauma, but Dad was still living here.

Yeah, the old Fenchurch stubbornness.

He pressed the bell and the door shot open.

Dad was standing there in his winter coat. Hair streaked back, fancy shirt on. That goatee was back, dyed black. 'Simon?'

'You expecting someone else?'

'Just a parcel.' Dad wasn't looking him in the eye, instead scanning up and down the street. 'Nice to see you, son.'

'And you, Dad.' Fenchurch gestured behind him. 'Need a word inside.'

Dad frowned. 'What's up?'

'Come on.' Fenchurch pushed past into the living room.

Dad had rearranged everything yet again. You'd think fifty

years living in the same place would let you settle on an optimal layout, or at least one you'd settled into, but no.

Still, Fenchurch actually liked it. It made sense for once.

He walked over to the sink and filled the kettle, then set it to boil. He got two mugs out, but the teabags weren't in their usual place. 'Dad, where are the teabags?'

'Left of the sink.'

Fenchurch walked over and found them. Except they were rooibos. 'You got any *tea* tea?'

'Don't drink it anymore, son. That stuff's lovely.' Dad collapsed into his armchair, coat still on. 'What's going on, then?'

Fenchurch gave up on getting a decent cuppa, so perched on the sofa. 'We found a body at the Tower Hill Memorial thing.'

'I heard something on the radio about that.'

'Well, turned out Chloe found it.'

'Chloe? Shit.'

'She...' Fenchurch exhaled. 'Her probation's a bit faster than mine.'

'Not mine, son. I found a dead tramp on my second night.'

'Jesus. I didn't know.'

'Yeah. Absolutely shat myself. And I didn't want people to know.'

'That you'd found a body?'

'No, that I'd shat myself. Literally.' He held his gaze a few seconds, then burst out laughing.

'*Dad*. I'm serious.'

'Sorry, son. Too good an opportunity to pass up.' He wiped at his eyes. 'I did find a tramp though. He wasn't dead, but he'd pissed himself. And not laughing. Clocked me one in the gob. Tooth's still wobbly.'

Fenchurch waited for his laughing to die down. 'Dad, we found Bert's body.'

'Bert who?'

'Matthews.'

Dad stared over to the window. 'Who's Bert Matthews?'

'You worked together?'

'Oh right, yeah. Old Bert. I mean, that's what we called him but he's ten years younger than me.' Dad chuckled. 'Yeah, I did some stuff with him in the archive. Only thing he helped me with was all that Machine stuff we thought would lead to Chloe. And it didn't.'

'Weren't you mates?'

'Just professionally.'

'You sure? Chloe knows him.'

'Right, well. Bert and I played snooker together. Took her along a couple of times, during that period where... Well, she was speaking to me and not you. So she played cards and pool with him, but I wasn't exactly his BFF, know what I mean? And he wasn't mine. Haven't seen nor heard of him since...' He frowned. 'Last October?'

'Any reason for that?'

'Just never that close, son.'

'You got a phone number for him?'

'Sure, let me look.' Dad got up and waddled over to the sideboard, then started chucking stuff around.

Sod it, he was going to be ages looking.

Fenchurch walked over just as the kettle boiled. Slowest kettle in Britain. One of those ancient ones you could fix yourself and repair all the parts. Replace even the element. Not that there was much else to it. Fenchurch put the rooibos teabags in the cups and poured. He didn't fancy his chances of getting a decent drink out of it.

'There you go, son.' Dad passed over a document.

A 1986 desk calendar. All the dates had been scribbled out and A to Z put in every few pages. 'Dad, you know you can get specialised phone books?'

'Yeah, but that's a right faff. My system works.'

Does it...

Tons and tons of names and addresses. Only a few mobile numbers, so Fenchurch wondered how many of them would still be active.

Nothing under M for Matthews.

Nothing under B for Bert.

Must be under A for Albert.

Nope.

'Dad, he's not in here.'

'Give that here.' Dad stomped over like they were both thirty years younger and snatched it off him. 'There you go, you daft bugger, it's under G.'

'G?'

'Gilbert Matthews! Christ, son. Don't you know anything?'

Fenchurch blushed again. Christ, it was becoming a habit. He hadn't known what Bert was short for. Schoolboy error. 'Cheers, Dad.' He copied the phone number down. 'You got a mobile for him?'

'Bert? God no, he's old school like I am.'

Fenchurch handed it back. 'Next question: do you know where he lives?'

DAD STOPPED AND POINTED. 'There you go, son.'

Bert's home was just around the corner from Dad's. A long row of brick two-up two-down houses, built for dockworkers and anyone supporting that.

Nowadays, City boys and girls, or their cousins in Canary Wharf, would kill for a place around here. Tiny little things, but great location. Walking distance to work.

Still, Bert's place was the worst on the street. The window paint was white and cracked rather than that matte olive you saw every-where these days. And a big settlement crack bisected the front door's lintel.

Fenchurch knocked, but didn't expect any response. 'Police. Open up.'

Dad reached for the door, but Fenchurch held him back. 'You're not a copper anymore.'

'Right, sir.' Dad did a mock salute.

Fenchurch put on a glove and tried the door handle. One of

those ancient locks that were about as secure as leaving it wide open with a sign reading 'Please Rob Me'.

Bingo; it opened.

But Fenchurch didn't step inside.

The radio played some shimmering yacht rock that took Fenchurch a few seconds to place – *Guilty* by Barbra Streisand and Barry Gibb. The place smelled of bubble bath. The lavender carpet was soaked, a trail of water leading through from the bathroom.

And the bath.

6

Fenchurch charged along Seething Lane, the cold morning hitting his cheeks, even more seething than before. Not because his space had gone and he had to park up on Pepys Street. No, it was almost City of London territory, so he needed to be careful, otherwise he'd lose a couple of days to mucking about with jurisdictional malarkey.

And he lucked out.

Tammy Saunders was standing by the CSI van, her platinum hair catching the sun. She looked around and saw Fenchurch. Did that thing where people pretend not to see you, then bugger off in the opposite direction.

'Not so fast.' Fenchurch caught her before she'd docked the key in the slot. Didn't even get to slam the door in his face. Fenchurch caught it and held on to it. 'That you finishing up?'

'Right.' She wouldn't make eye contact with him. Wouldn't or couldn't. 'What's up?'

'Well, wondering if you've found anything here?'

Tammy looked back to the monument. 'We won't.'

'Right. Public place?'

'Exactly.' She took a few seconds to meet his gaze. 'Hundreds of DNA traces every square metre, so it's just pointless even looking. And your victim is scrubbed clean. We might get something from the body at the post-mortem, Simon, but I wouldn't hold out much hope for it.'

The usual caveats. The usual reasons they couldn't possibly find a clue that would help track down a murderer. 'So, can you explain how he's been transported here?'

'Not my department. Sorry.'

Fenchurch smiled at her. 'You're getting more and more like your old boss by the day.'

She rolled her eyes. 'Don't.'

'How's Mick doing?'

'Hating West London. Traffic's even worse than over here.'

'Well, that's natural justice.' Fenchurch held the door, but still didn't shut it. 'So, can you explain why it's going to take your lot two days to get around to Bert's flat?'

She shut her eyes. 'Sorry, Simon, but we're run ragged as it is. Three murders within five miles of each other. It's brutal.'

'His flat is as much of a crime scene as here.'

She reopened them and stared hard at him. 'Why?'

'Because there's a big trail of water leading from the bath to the door. Stands to reason that—'

'Fine.' She grabbed her phone from the cradle and started thumbing at the screen. 'I'll get around there now myself and see what's what.'

'Thank you.' Fenchurch stepped aside to let her shut the door. 'I'll see you at the PM.'

'My pleasure.' Tammy slammed the door with a ferocity which pleased Fenchurch.

Nice to be able to get someone doing something when you actually wanted them to.

He stood there, watching the van trundle off down the road, though her left turn was the wrong way if she wanted to get to Limehouse in a hurry. He walked back to the monument, almost tempted to whistle, but the sight of three of his officers standing around put paid to that.

Ashkani was first, her stern look capable of turning cheese

back into milk. 'Sir.' She sighed like he would. 'Getting nowhere, sir. No sightings of anyone transporting a body here.'

'Well.' Fenchurch swung a three-sixty and clocked at least three sets of cameras. 'Get the CCTV and—'

'I know how to do my job.' Ashkani folded her arms over her belly. 'Just waiting on access approval.'

'Why?'

'New protocols in place this week.' She gave him a side eye as she ran a hand over her belly. 'Which you'd know if you'd read the email.'

'Right, well, thank you for that. You do a great job on that side of things. Way better than me.' Or if he'd not been at couple counselling when he was supposed to be briefing. 'So, is there a lot to follow up?'

'Enough.' She flared her nostrils, then set off. 'I'll report back later.'

Leaving Fenchurch on his own. At least he didn't have to contend with her sarcasm any longer, but she was doing his head in. Almost the best officer he had, but with the worst attitude. Everything was a drama, but at least it got done.

DS Lisa Bridge was lurking around near the uniforms guarding entry to the crime scene, still talking on her phone. Her blonde hair was all knotted together. She looked up at Fenchurch and gave him a nod as he approached. 'Thanks, Jon. I'll see you when I get home.' Looked like she was being kept on the line. 'No, I'm fine. And I've got to go. Love you, bye.' She ended the call and looked at Fenchurch. 'Jon says hi.'

'I bet he does.' DI Jon Nelson. Fenchurch's best mate for so long and now... Well, it was a bit cloudier. He joined Bridge leaning against the wall. 'How are you doing?'

'I'm okay, sir. We weren't close, but...' Something caught in her throat. 'It's tough, though. Spoke to my mum and... She was a lot closer to Uncle Bert.'

'Hard to lose someone at the best of times, but when it's a murder?' Fenchurch shook his head. 'Seen so many over the years and I'm lucky to have never had it happen to a family member. If you need time off, then I'm—'

'Thanks, sir, but I'd rather work.'

'I totally understand that.' He looked over his shoulder. 'We think he was attacked at home, then moved here.'

She shut her eyes. 'How?'

'Well, I've only just seen inside his flat, but there's water leading from the bathtub to the door. None outside, but it looks like he was murdered there.'

'And it's definitely drowning?'

'Dr Pratt thinks so, but he'll confirm it at the post-mortem this afternoon.'

'I want to attend, sir.'

Fenchurch fixed her with a hard stare. 'I can't allow that, I'm afraid. There's a huge conflict of interest in you even being here, which I've managed to square off with Loftus.' Which he *would* square off with Loftus if the slimy git ever answered his phone. Which he will square off. And will have to remember to. 'Can you think of any reason someone would drop his body here?'

She blew air up her face. 'I didn't know him that well, sir. Mum was twelve years younger than him, so it's like this weird generational thing? She was just starting school when he joined the navy at sixteen.'

Someone's idea of a joke? Drowning a former Royal Navy sailor, then dumping him at a maritime monument. For the merchant navy.

Fenchurch hoped there wasn't someone hunting down old sailors. Or maybe it was just to mess with the police. 'Know anything about it?'

'Mum wasn't in a good place to say. He didn't last long there, she says. Left at twenty-two and married my Auntie Alice. She died two years ago. I was much closer to her. One of those aunts who spoils their nieces and nephews.' She grimaced. 'Like me.'

Four years wasn't long enough to add much smoke to that particular fire. Bert hadn't served long, hadn't risen the ranks in the navy.

Or the police for that matter. Difficult to build up a particularly nasty rogues' gallery when you're junior.

Still, you'd get some absolute shits who'd want to kill you, but they didn't tend to be sophisticated like this.

'He joined the Met when he got out of the navy. Bought that house he still lives in.'

'Same as my old man. Different times back then. A young lad could buy the house he'd die in.' He held up a hand. 'Sorry, I didn't mean that to sound so rough.'

'No, it's true, though. It's so hard for Jon and me just now. Even him being a DI and me a sergeant...'

And that was Chloe's future. The paltry pay a British cop earned, even in London. Especially in London. Years ago, Fenchurch had worked with a Canadian cop who earned the kind of money you'd get for doing some daft job in a bank. Different over there – a career versus a job, capitalised or not.

'Anyway, Mum said he walked the beat for ten years, then he became a detective.' She shrugged. 'And that's it.'

It wasn't a lot. Guys of that age, of the mindset his old man had, they kept themselves to themselves. Didn't reveal much about what they saw, what they endured.

'He was part of my dad's team, Lisa. Last seven years of his service. Then he retired, but worked with Dad at the archive.'

She looked at him, narrowing her eyes. 'Could it be that?'

Fenchurch had thought about it, but discounted it. All the shit he'd been through in the last few years, Bert had been tangential to helping them find Chloe. Maybe he'd not pissed anyone off as a copper, but the people him and Dad had gone after at the archive, now *they* were sophisticated. Maybe he'd pissed them off sufficiently. Maybe they'd got wind of Bert.

But why now?

And why go for Bert? Surely Dad would be the main target. He was in charge of that shoddy operation, executing the skulduggery required to piece the whole sorry tapestry together.

That was definitely one to ask the old sod about.

Fenchurch looked over at Bridge. 'Your mum mention any friends?'

'Nope.'

'Not even my old man?'

'Nope.'

Interesting. Fenchurch had entirely misunderstood their relationship. 'What about any family?'

'Well, he's got a daughter.'

7

Fenchurch crawled along a street that could be anywhere in London, but was instead an hour away on the Essex coast. Victorian semis on a grid system, cars rammed on both sides just allowing for a thin vein of traffic to pass through. Not that Leigh-on-Sea had much traffic, not at this time. All the commuters would be safely in their offices in London. Some construction work going on, though, enough to keep the local economy thriving.

Bridge pointed up the road. 'Think it's along there.'

Fenchurch pulled in to let a work van past. 'Thought about moving out this way.'

Bridge looked around at him, scowling like he'd gone mad. 'Are you serious?'

Fenchurch shrugged. 'It's a different lifestyle, isn't it? Get into London in an hour.' He smiled. 'Get into Fenchurch Street.'

'That'd be ironic.'

'Nice little stroll over to Leman Street from there.'

'Does Mrs Fenchurch want to?'

'She was more eager than me. Get a good job out here. Better money. And no commuting for her.'

'You didn't think of transferring?'

'I did, but I'd get bored. I'd be running a station or a drugs investigation, probably over in Southend.'

'No murder squad?'

'Up in Colchester, yeah. Not out here. That lot would just come down. Probably send half of our lot over to help out.'

A birch climbed up to block out the sun, then it was gone.

'Thing was, we had a lot on our plates with Chloe and our son and... Well, London house prices being what they are, it can pay to wait.'

Bridge pointed to the side. 'There.'

The parking was less busy down here, so Fenchurch took the bay opposite the house. Not a bad little place, more a villa than the surrounding semis. A garden room extension to one side, a garage on the other. A black Fiat 500 sat outside. The road at the end cut along the back at an angle, so the neighbours overlooked their garden.

Bridge was out first, but she stopped, clenching and unclenching her hands.

Fenchurch joined her. 'You okay?'

She didn't look at him. 'Kath and I are a bit estranged.' She snorted. 'I hate speaking ill of someone who's just lost her father, but... Well. She's a bit up herself.'

'I understand. I've got relatives like that. And it's better to know what I'm dealing with inside.' Fenchurch walked up to the front door and knocked.

It opened with a crack.

Kathryn Bingham stood there, hand resting on her hip. 'Lisa.' She swallowed something down. 'Your mum's just been on the phone. You'd better come in.'

~

THE HOUSE SEEMED different from the inside. Fenchurch looked out across the paved front garden to his car and the houses, with their mock Tudor fronts. A few curtains twitched. One of those areas, then. Maybe not moving out here was a blessing. Then again, he had a high-end camera system looking outside his flat rather than relying on the local spies.

'Now.' Kathryn swung into the room and set a tray down on the coffee table. A plate filled with biscuits surrounded by three tiny espresso cups. 'It was coffee, wasn't it?'

'Thank you.' Fenchurch had asked for tea, but sod it. 'Again, I'm sorry for your loss.'

She took an espresso and sipped at the crema floating on top. 'It is what it is.'

Fenchurch saw exactly what Bridge had meant. He took the armchair at right angles to the sofa and grabbed his cup. Way too small to fit his giant shovels of hands. The biscuits looked tasty and he was starving, but on yet another diet – chocolate and sugar would bugger up his ketosis. 'You off work today?'

'I'm a stay-at-home mum.' She finished her coffee and set it down on the tray, but didn't take a biscuit. 'My husband works in the City. He commutes in.'

Bridge was eating enough biscuits for the three of them. She brushed crumbs away from her mouth. 'Is Darren on his way back?'

'No, I'll see him this evening.' She brushed a hand through her hair. 'I'm sorry, it's just a bit of a shock, really. Not long after we lost my mother and all.'

Fenchurch caught a hint of the Limehouse accent in there. Yeah, Kathryn Bingham wasn't too dissimilar to his own sister. Left behind the East End for a life in a more affluent area. And that accent was a barrier to fitting in, but out it came in times of stress. 'I'm sorry to hear that. Must compound things.'

Kathryn nodded.

This was going to be harder than he expected. 'I gather your father was in the navy?'

'Yeah, but he never talked about his time at sea.'

Lots of men didn't talk about stuff because nothing happened. Some because too much happened. 'Never?'

Kathryn shook her head. 'Not to me, no. Maybe to his mates in the police?'

Fenchurch glanced at Bridge, but it didn't seem like a surprise to her.

'Listen. I know you're here to gather any intelligence you can on Father, but I had a difficult relationship with my dad.'

Everyone had difficult relationships with their parents, but it all came down to precisely how difficult. Maybe a property in Limehouse was enough to murder over. Nice little inheritance. Throw a few curveballs to the police to throw them off the scent. Was that worth it? Hard to say. 'Okay, I understand that. When was the last time you saw him?'

'A few weeks ago.' She frowned and finally took that biscuit. 'Maybe it was Christmas?'

A lot longer than a few weeks, then. 'What about speaking to him?'

'We spoke on the phone every day. So, last night. Well, late afternoon.'

'Did he say what he was doing?'

She frowned. 'He said he was meeting an old friend for snooker.'

'Say who?'

'That's all I know.'

Bridge brushed crumbs from her lap and sat forward to take her coffee. 'Do you know any names?'

'I do, as it happens. In case anything happened to him, he gave me a list of people he played snooker and cards with. All former police officers, some still serving I suspect.' And most will be dead, or in nursing homes wishing they were. 'I can give you his phone number, in case you want to search for anyone he has been speaking to who's not on the list?'

'We've got a landline for him, so if you've got his mobile?'

'Father didn't own a mobile. Didn't trust them. One of those chaps who'd go for walks when he saw people, usually in familiar places. Or he'd show up at their door, asking if they wanted to go for lunch.'

Fenchurch knew a few old timers like that. Said they were protecting themselves or their mates, but usually they just didn't understand technology. Then again, the level of addiction to smartphones in the population, maybe they were the smart ones.

He didn't see much else he could get out of her. A long drive out this way, but it was important for the SIO to show their face at the next of kin's door. He stood and necked the espresso. 'Okay, well, I'll need to get back to the station. Thanks for the coffee and, again, I'm sorry for your loss.'

Kathryn turned away from him to hide her crying.

Bridge raised her eyebrows. 'I'll show you out.'

Fenchurch followed her through and stepped out into the brisk morning. 'Stay here, would you? Comfort her, see if anything comes up.'

Bridge looked into the house, then back at Fenchurch. 'Right, sir. Sure.'

'I know she's a bit prickly, but I can't help but feel she might be hiding something from us. That list could be valuable. Get it, send it to Kay and get units going around those old buggers. See what we can shake down from them that his daughter doesn't know. Hopefully none of them have suffered the same fate.'

'You think that's likely?'

'Not ruling anything out, Lisa.'

'Wise.'

'Okay, well, I'm going to the post-mortem now. See you back at the station.'

'Sir, I don't have a car here.'

'Take the train. Much better than the road. Beautiful journey into London.'

8

CHLOE

The car was moving so fast that Chloe couldn't follow where it was going as it weaved in and out of traffic.

She looked out of the windows but everything was a blur. She saw her dad's face outside, then it was gone, then her mum's, and then she was gone now.

And she was back in the car, with the wolf. He was driving, but his movements... It was like there were three of him, slicking across her vision. She tried to move her hand in front of her face, but it was tied down. Her legs were too.

She was trapped in the car with the wolf.

Just her and him.

It was real this time.

Again.

She tried to speak but no words came out.

What the hell was she going to do? It was happening and—

BUZZ.

Chloe jerked awake and bounced out of bed, fists clenched. Heart pounding, head thumping. The room was a mess, bright light crawling around the curtains. Her eyes stung. Her wound felt like someone had put a live wire to it.

The wolf.

Her hands were shaking.

It'd been a long time since she'd had that dream. Her therapist said it was good to put distance between her, but it being back made her worry. It felt like she was a kid again.

No matter what the people she thought of as her parents as she was growing up did to her brain to remove her memories, some dormant part still persisted. And not just her real parents. Simon and Abi. And her grandfather.

The wolf was still there.

Seeing Bert's body like that, maybe that had shaken stuff loose. Buried memories. Fears. Threats.

The wolf was her child brain's way of rationalising what was happening. They'd kidnapped her, drugged her and would've killed her, but for the actions of one man.

She was safe now. She knew that. But sometimes the inside of her head felt very dangerous. She needed to be very careful now, to make sure the wolf dreams didn't come back on a regular basis.

Maybe that noise was just some innocent noise, something that snapped her out of it.

Maybe.

She sat back on the bed and ran a hand through her hair. Soaking. God.

BUZZ. BUZZ.

No, it was the front door. Right.

She bunched up her hair, tossing it over her shoulder, then padded through to the door. She pressed the button and her mother's face filled the video screen.

Pretty much the last person she'd wanted to see.

She couldn't even make eye contact with a display. 'Mum, I've nothing to say to you.'

'Chloe, please can I come in?' Her voice was thin and shrill. Hard to tell if that was the speakers or not.

'Mum, please.'

'Chloe, I need to speak to you.'

This was the hardest thing she'd ever had to do. Despite all the crap she'd lived through and just about dealt with, her mother's betrayal was the worst. 'It's not going to happen, Mum. You should go or I'll call Dad.'

'Look, Chloe, you don't need to do that. It's important that we—'

'Mum, I've made my peace with you not being in my life. You chose to sleep with that guy behind Dad's back. Hope it was worth it.'

Mum stood there, eyes closed, tears running down her cheek.

Seeing her own mother like that, the woman who'd found her, who'd helped her recover from her ordeal... This was as big a test of Chloe's resolve as seeing a dead body had been.

'Mum, please. I'm on nights just now, so I need to—'

'How's that going? Your work? I'd love to know.'

'It's...' She didn't deserve the truth. 'It's fine.'

'Just a few minutes, that's all. A cup of tea.'

'Mum, I told you. No. Until you respect my position here, we've got nothing to say to you.'

'I want to apologise.'

'Start with saying sorry to Dad.'

'I have.'

'Well, I'll speak to him about it, then, because I don't trust a word that comes out of your mouth.'

'Please, Chloe. Five minutes. That's all.'

'No.'

'Chloe, I'm sorry.'

'After what you did? Sneaking off in the middle of the night when we were on holiday? To have sex with some guy? That's low. Really, really low.'

Mum stared at the screen and it felt like she was staring into Chloe's soul. 'Okay.'

'I've got to go, Mum.' Chloe pressed the button and the screen faded to black. She put the handset back and slumped against the door.

All of her fears surfaced. All the guilt.

Christ, no wonder the wolf was back.

Mum was entirely to blame. What she'd done, or the way she'd done it, her parents' marriage had fallen apart. Shagging that guy.

But Chloe… She knew she could've confronted Mum before telling Dad. Maybe she could've understood her or given her a chance to break the news to Dad. Instead, she went in like a bull in a china shop, smashing it all to shit.

Typical Fenchurch way of doing things.

BUZZ.

Mum's face appeared on the screen again. 'Chloe, *please*. I'm not leaving until you let me in.'

THE DRIVER

He leaned back in the café chair and sipped his latte. The clock showed 15:16. He didn't want to leave it too long there, but this was gold.

The woman on the screen was Fenchurch's wife.

He checked his phone to make sure both cameras were still working. Damn straight, beautiful HD videos of the car park. Where he'd left the car and walked away, letting everything record. Anything record.

She'd been standing at the Entrycom for a few minutes now. Who was she talking to? Fenchurch's car wasn't about, so maybe it was the daughter. What was going on? What were they arguing about?

And was she going to get in?

She seemed to be talking, presumably to the daughter. Fenchurch's daughter, the one who'd been in all the papers. Horrible what happened to her, but now she was a copper and worse things could happen to coppers.

Abi Fenchurch's shoulders slumped. She ran a hand through her hair. Even at this distance, the camera could pick out the detail on her face. Even her eyelashes. It was that good.

And she was walking now, heading away from the car's cameras.

Bollocks.

He sank the rest of his latte, scalding his mouth, and left the café as a big guy shuffled towards him. Had to press himself against the side wall to let him past. Cut down on your cake, dickhead.

And he was outside now, in the cold air, and he jogged towards the car.

Shit.

She walked right past him. Mrs Fenchurch. Soon to be ex-Mrs Fenchurch.

He smiled at her. 'Parking attendant's out!'

She carried on towards her car. Face like thunder. Christ, whatever it'd been about, she wasn't happy.

He got into the driver side and tried to catch his breath. He watched her get into her little Toyota, then drive off out of the car park, heading out into the Isle of Dogs.

Felt wild coming in here. Place was a rabbit warren, but a safe one.

At least, the people who lived here thought it was safe.

He put the car into drive and the electric engine buzzed with the almost-silent motion, just the rub of the tyres on the road.

And he drove off after Abi Fenchurch.

9

FENCHURCH

Fenchurch shut his eyes and listened. The scuffing of shoes against the floor and the slosh of liquid as Dr Pratt worked away at the dead body. The mortuary seemed even colder than usual, chilled air seeping from the vents, but Fenchurch felt as if there was no air in the room.

Only death could make something this cold.

And only the death of someone he'd known in life.

Bert Matthews lay on the slab in the middle, naked and even colder than the room. Staring up at the ceiling now, instead of the sky.

A friend of his father's.

Scratch that. A *colleague* of his father's.

Fenchurch still didn't know where he stood on that one, but they had been close enough. A known associate, as they'd say if they were on the wrong side of the law. Some of the stuff Dad had done over the years had certainly skirted that line.

Could it be connected to what they'd investigated after being serving officers? The help they'd given Fenchurch as he hunted for Chloe and her abductors?

Maybe it was the fact Fenchurch's daughter had discovered Bert's corpse that spooked him. A chance encounter, maybe, but the way she'd described it, that chase from the Minories round to the maritime monument. Could it have been staged?

No, it was an armed robbery with a bloody water pistol.

The thought made him sweat in the ice-cold room.

If that gun had been real, he'd have only one child.

He had to rest against the table and take a deep breath.

'Om pom tiddly om pom pom pom.' Pratt tapped his finger in time with the poms, like he was conducting an orchestra on the last night of the Proms.

Berk.

The door opened and Tammy sauntered in, sipping from a mug of tea. 'Afternoon, gents.'

Fenchurch pointed at her cup. 'Could've got me one.'

'You a fan of rooibos?'

Fenchurch clocked his father lurking about outside. 'Back in a sec.' He left Pratt and Tammy and went out into the hot corridor, like the air conditioning outlet piped all the outflow into that space. 'What are you doing here?'

Dad was standing in the corridor, inspecting the noticeboard. One hand in his pocket, the other clutching a machine coffee. 'Just passing the time, son.'

'Dad, you shouldn't be here.'

He still wouldn't look at Fenchurch. 'My office isn't far from here.'

'No, but you worked with the person on the slab. You can't be here.'

'Fair enough.' Dad looked around at Fenchurch now. 'How's it going?'

'Best not to ask, isn't it?'

Dad laughed, but there was no humour in it. Even less in his eyes. 'How's Chloe bearing up?'

'She's a Fenchurch. It'll take about twenty years for her to feel anything.'

A real laugh now. 'Tell me about it...'

'I'm serious, though. She's not feeling it. I need to coax it out of her. I was in bits when I found my first corpse.'

'And I was the same.' Dad sank his coffee and patted his son's arm. 'I'll see you around, Simon.' He walked off down the corridor with that slight limp.

Fenchurch had inherited it, but on the other side. Too many chases down back streets in this godforsaken city. Too many fights with druggies and idiots. He shook his head and went back into the room.

'Om pom tiddly om pom.' Pratt looked up at Fenchurch. 'There you are.'

'Here I am. I've been here for three hours now, William. You getting anywhere?'

'Well, I have something.' Pratt pointed to an orange bucket. 'The contents of his lungs are bathwater from a domestic tub. A fair amount of bubble bath in there.'

'So he died in his own bath?'

'He died in *a* bath, that's correct. Could be anywhere from Croydon to Walthamstow, though.'

'Why there?'

Pratt frowned. 'Good question. Could be anywhere in the United Kingdom or continental Europe, but you'd have to triangulate that with his movements over—'

'I get it.' Fenchurch looked at Tammy. 'Do you think it was in his own bathroom?'

'I'd stand up in court and say it was highly likely. The water we found on the floor will match what's in his lungs.'

'Will match or does match?'

'Still working on it.'

Fenchurch focused on Pratt now. 'William, talk me through your thinking.'

'My thinking?'

'How did he die?'

'Well, if he was already in the bath, naked, it'd be a trivial matter to hold him down.' Pratt frowned then ran a finger down Bert's bare torso. 'If he was wearing clothes, however, and his assailant overpowered him then tossed him into the full bathtub, then drowned him, then his killer would've had to dry him off and redress him. Which is highly unusual. So it's likely Mr Matthews was in the bath when attacked. Held under the water and drowned. Then moved to where he was found.'

That all checked out. A very simple and basic murder, dressed up with placing the body in a location pertinent to the victim's past.

Fenchurch stared at the corpse. Getting harder to see him as someone he'd drank beer with, even gone to the Hammers with. 'Any defensive wounds? Any blows to the head?'

Pratt shook his head. 'It would appear he didn't see it coming. I'd suggest the likeliest avenue is to lift his legs and hold him under. A man of his age might not have the upper body strength to lift himself up out of the water, for instance.'

That started to make sense.

Bert in the bath, listening to the radio, singing along to whatever was playing, lying back, water up to his ears so he couldn't hear the commotion. Maybe he looked up and saw his attacker, but they were too strong. And then the gut-wrenching act of pinning him down, like they were two wrestlers, but one was deep in his bath, under the line of the water, his lungs filling up with water until he couldn't breathe anymore.

Yep, that made perfect sense.

Fenchurch focused on Tammy now. 'What have you got?'

'Very little, I'm afraid.' She waved a hand at Pratt. 'We were just conferring while you were outside. No signs of sexual assault, struggle, asphyxia or gross wounding, therefore we have nothing on the attacker. No bodily fluids, fingerprints, weapon profiles, yada yada yada.'

'So *you* think it was murder?'

'Simon...' Tammy laughed. 'He was drowned in his own bath and taken to a war memorial. What do you think?'

Fenchurch held up his hands. 'I'm just asking what you'd be comfortable saying in court.'

'You've got a suspect?'

'No, but when we do, I want you singing from my hymn sheet, not your own or someone else's.'

She held his gaze for a few seconds. 'By all means.' She huffed a sigh. 'Given there's no possible DNA from the attacker, we'd—'

'No possible DNA?'

'Well, no. He's been soaked in bleach, by the looks of it.'

'Nothing under his fingernails?'

'No, and they'd been nibbled to the quick, anyway.' She frowned, then shook her head. 'And we'll look at the clothing. We've found three sets of likely clothes resting on an old dining chair in his bedroom, but I wouldn't hold out much hope. Such clothes have all sorts of DNA on them, from the Tube, walking the streets and, well... Listen, I know Bert. He was a clumsy guy, always bumping into people. Could have any number of incidental contacts in ten minutes, let alone in a day. We aren't going to process them all. We can't. And none of them is likely to be his attacker.'

'Why?'

'Well, you and your father discovered the damage to his house.' She narrowed her gaze. 'What's likeliest is someone broke into his home, attacked him and drowned him. Could be anyone. Find them, and we'll do a DNA search of his clothes. As it is, I've got no resources or budget to do a load of busywork.'

'Right, thanks. I'm heading back to the station. Let me know if anything comes up.'

10

Fenchurch parked outside Leman Street and the day was starting to fade. Mid-March, but it felt like the middle of winter. He'd read somewhere about winter actually going from the solstice in December to the equinox in the middle of March. Sure felt like that. Then again, in a month's time, it'd be spring but could feel like summer. Or winter.

Bloody hell. He was dog tired.

Down the street, a van was being inspected by CSIs. He had no idea if they were Tammy's mob or if it was nothing related to his case. Either way, it was a bit close to his patch. But what wasn't on this case?

Fenchurch got out and zipped up his coat. Getting a bit loose with all the weight he'd lost recently. He felt fitter than in years, but the prospect of buying a new wardrobe filled him with dread. He walked towards the van, casually, hands in pockets.

His phone rang.

Chloe calling...

He put it to his ear. 'Hey, are you okay?'

'Not really.' She paused. The washing machine whirred in the background. 'Mum was around.'

Everything clenched. 'And what did she want?'

'Nothing much. We kind of just argued. But...'

'But what?'

'It's the fact she was here, you know? She showed up, despite me telling her I wanted nothing to do with her.'

Fenchurch walked away from the van towards the station's back entrance. 'She's desperate. That's all. Wants to see you. That said, her just turning up like that isn't right. But she's your mother and she wants to make things right between you.'

'Well, she can piss off.'

Yeah, typical Fenchurch. He checked his watch – just after four. 'Listen, I'm still at work. How about we talk about this later? I'll try to get home for about six, get some dinner before your shift.'

'I'm in early, remember?'

'Sure, but we should definitely eat together. It's important.'

'Okay, Dad. I'll see you.' And she was gone.

Fenchurch stopped in the car park and tried to gather his thoughts. Why did his world always have to crumble to shit whenever he had a pain-in-the-arse case to run?

Always, like there was some useless prick somewhere inflicting this bullshit on him.

He tried calling Abi, but she bounced his call to voicemail.

He didn't leave a message, but sent a text:

Call me. ASAP

FENCHURCH SIPPED his tea from an old Glasgow Rangers mug he'd inherited from the office's previous occupant and looked out of his window. The CSIs were still working at that van. A navy Transit, but not a new model. Plates were Y-reg, so in that six-month window from March 2001. Nineteen years old, not far off Chloe's age.

He should've at least asked them what was going on, but then Chloe had called.

He checked his phone, but no new messages or calls. So even Abi was blanking him now. Great, just great. He thought they'd made progress that morning, but maybe he'd just given ground. Too much ground.

All she wanted was to reconnect with her daughter, despite all she'd done to him, to her, to them.

The more he thought about it, the less he wanted to be the big man. The less he wanted to be Mr Nice Guy. He could probably bring himself to forgive her, but it was going to need a hell of a lot from her to make it work again.

Something clunked off the office door and he swung around.

Reed and Ashkani stood in the doorway.

'Have a seat, ladies.' Fenchurch gestured to the pair in front of his desk, then sat behind it. 'How's it going?'

Reed looked at Ashkani, then let her shoulders go. 'Not great.'

'Figures.' Fenchurch winced as his latest bout of hope deflated. 'Just back from the PM, but Pratt and Tammy haven't got much to go on.'

'Great.' Ashkani was rubbing her belly. 'As far as I can tell, Bert was supposed to meet a friend last night, but someone broke into his house, drowned him in his own bath. Dressed him, then dumped him at the maritime monument.'

'We anywhere on how they moved him?'

Reed pulled out some sheets of paper, but kept them to herself. 'We've got CCTV of a van dumping the body at the monument. While there are a few blind spots, we've trailed it from his home over there. Stopped at all the lights, that kind of thing.'

Fenchurch drank some more tea while he chewed it over. The suppositions he'd made Pratt and Tammy sign up to were becoming clearer. Becoming facts. Dots joining up. 'That's good work.'

'And we lucked out, big time.' Reed tossed the first photo over and showed a Y-reg Transit. 'Whoever took him left the van in the lane next to the station. Parked, but the keys were in the engine.'

Fenchurch shot to his feet and walked over to the window. 'That thing out there?'

'Right. Belonging to one Gilbert Finbarr Matthews.'

'Seriously?'

'It's his, guv. Not registered to him, of course, but Bridge confirmed it with her cousin. He'd driven up to Leigh in it a couple of months ago to collect an old cooker from a neighbour of hers.'

Fenchurch finished his tea and rested the mug on the windowsill. 'Any word on the van's forensics?'

'Looking clean, unfortunately.' Ashkani stood up and walked over to join him. 'Whoever splashed Bert with bleach did a number on that too. Any hairs or whatever that Tammy's lot find, we probably won't get anything from it.'

The van was right there. Right outside his window.

Christ, it was like someone was sending Fenchurch a message. A friend of his father, found by his daughter, transported by a van dumped outside his office.

Could be that thing. Confirmation bias? Or just a series of coincidences.

Or it could be real.

Either way, he didn't have any choice but to go with the flow on it.

He looked at Ashkani. 'Didn't any neighbours see anything?'

'Not that we've found.' She was cradling her belly now, soothing the baby inside. 'Got about sixty percent coverage, but nobody saw anything.'

Taking a body out of a house in the middle of the night and nobody saw them. Bloody hell.

'Any CCTV near his house?'

'Nope. Nearest is an ATM at the old bank two streets away. Caught the van but, like all the other cameras, we can't get a good read on the driver. Usual tricks. Hoodie, shades, baseball cap.'

Felt like they were going to struggle to pin this on anyone.

Whoever was behind it all was good. Maybe too good. 'Have either of you got any good news?'

Reed twisted her lips. 'Well, we've got the telephony results back.'

'And I take it there's nothing of note?'

'Right. Only phone number is his landline, unless he's got a secret burner or pay-as-you-go. Nobody we've spoken to ever saw him with a phone.' Reed got out a sheet of paper. 'Only calls he made are to his daughter, Kathryn.'

'Right.' Fenchurch clicked his tongue a few times. That tallied with what she'd told them, how old school her father was. 'What about calls he received?'

'A few of them, yeah. Lot of your scam types. Accident that wasn't your fault. HMRC. All of that.'

'Did Lisa send you a list of his friends and colleagues?'

'She did, yeah. Working on it, guv.' Reed groaned and flicked through her notebook. 'It's going to take time. Tracking these old coppers down is bloody hard work. A lot of them don't want to be found.'

'Okay, just do the grind, Kay. We'll get there.'

'Guv.'

But it was still frustrating the living hell out of Fenchurch. Not a single bloody lead on this whole case.

He was about to let out an almighty sigh, when his mobile rang on his desk.

Abi.

Finally.

He walked over and checked it.

Loftus calling...

'Need to take this. Sorry.' Fenchurch answered it. 'Boss, what's up?'

'Need you to go to the *Post*'s website.' His voice was clipped and straighter than usual. His accent dulled down a notch or two. A voice droned on in the background, but slightly distorted like it was a recording.

Fenchurch unlocked his machine and went to the address. 'What am I looking at, sir?'

Reed was hovering over his left shoulder. Fenchurch hated people doing that.

'The top story.'

Fenchurch saw it. The red box they used for breaking news.

BREAKING: POLICE MARITIME MURDER EXCLUSIVE – LINK TO OLD CASE

Nothing like a hyperbolic headline to get the punters in.

Fenchurch clicked through to the story, but it was just a box of text around an embedded video. He clicked play.

Yvette Farley sat in a small studio, her pink hair all spiky and rough, matching her T-shirt. 'Good evening.' His speakers were up way too loud, so he turned it down a lot. 'I'm here with Rob Lezard, one of the foremost experts on modern policing.'

Across the desk from her was a bearded man, his long hair tied up in a man bun. Sharp navy suit, pale-blue shirt open to the neck. He twisted the St Christopher hanging around his neck. 'Thanks, Yvette, and thank you for this opportunity to get the truth out there.' He had a slow voice, with a dirty East End accent, not a million miles from Fenchurch's own.

'Now, Rob, given your background as a senior officer in the Met, you've been instrumental in some recent exclusives we've published on some police oppression and corruption, but you're here today to talk to us about an ongoing investigation.'

'That's correct.' Lezard looked around at the camera, his silvery eyes shining in the harsh light. His skin made him look mid-forties, but he didn't have the red scar tissue most cops had by that age. Maybe he just wore good makeup for the video. 'Today, the *Post* has been focusing on the discovery of a body at the maritime monument on Tower Hill this morning, which has been a major investigation by the

Met's East London MIT. As a result, the surrounding area was closed for a few hours, disrupting road traffic and entrance to the nearby tube station at Tower Hill. Now, as a former senior officer, and someone used to managing large teams as would be allocated to a case like this, I have offered my services to the officers running the investigation. As of the time of recording, the Met have yet to take me up on that offer.'

'And what is it you're offering?'

'As someone who spent several years of his life serving Her Majesty at various levels in the Metropolitan Police Service, I find it galling that they haven't even taken my calls. But that's by the by.' He ran a hand over his beard, smoothing it down. 'But I'll share it with you, Yvette, and hopefully they'll get the message.'

Lezard looked right into the camera. 'The murder of Bert Matthews directly relates to an investigation he worked back in the day. The case of James Mortimer.'

11

Scotland Yard had that late-afternoon bustle about it, everyone looking busy ahead of their five o'clock briefings. Still had them over here, but out in stations like Leman Street, the cops doing the actual work usually pushed any information downloads to the morning's briefing, in favour of getting on with the bloody job.

At least, that's how Fenchurch saw it.

Though he was being made to feel like he was back at school, waiting outside the headmaster's office. Only this time, his mum wasn't here to smooth things over.

No, Loftus had told him to head over and then didn't answer the bloody door. Cheeky bastard. Thought he was going places, but he was just a useless sod. Ideas above his station.

And Abi still hadn't acknowledged his message, so he sent another. It's not like she was at school. No, she was at home. With their son.

The door opened and Loftus stepped out into the corridor. 'Ready for you now, Simon. Thanks for waiting.'

'Don't mention it.' Though Fenchurch wished he had. Still, he rose to his feet and followed Loftus into the office.

Someone else was in there, standing by the window. A grey

afternoon, but bright enough to conceal his identity until he looked around.

DCI Chris Owen. He hadn't aged a day in the years since Fenchurch had last seen him. Tall, with a tight suit, white shirt and red tie, black leather shoes with a military shine. 'Simon...' He walked over, hand thrust out like a weapon. 'Been a long time.' His Welsh accent had strengthened.

Fenchurch shook it, but kept his distance. 'Back in the big city?'

'Cardiff's a big city, you arsehole.' Owen laughed. 'But yes, I'm back working for the Met again. The Professional Standards and Ethics beat.'

'But overtly, unlike last time.'

'Correct. I'm done with all that covert bollocks.' Owen slumped into the chair next to Fenchurch. 'So, I gather you've made a famous friend?'

'We seem to.' Fenchurch glanced over at Loftus. 'Never heard of this Lezard geezer. Have you?'

'Me neither.' Loftus collapsed into his office chair. 'Says he's ex-Met, and a senior officer to boot, so I dug into it and we don't have any record of him ever serving here.'

'So who the hell is he?' Fenchurch looked between them, but got blank stares. 'And why does Yvette think what he's selling is worth buying?'

'You know how the press works.' Owen rolled his eyes. 'Everything there is rigorously double-sourced, so it's not just Lezard who's talking. There's at least one other person putting their bollocks on the block.'

'But you don't know who and you're going to find out?'

Owen nodded. 'Working on the assumption it's a serving officer. But if it's not, we'll get their pension. Actually, either way, we'll get their pension.'

'That's a bit harsh.'

'They're interfering with an ongoing investigation. Your investigation, Simon. This is going to take up a lot of your time.'

Fenchurch groaned. He hadn't considered that, but of course it would. Fielding calls, reporters following him everywhere. It all just weighed him down. He looked at Loftus. 'Has this Lezard character been in touch with you?'

'My PA fielded a few calls from someone with that name this morning, but I didn't return them.'

'Sir, this could've been averted if—'

'If I'd listened to a potential madman?' Loftus pulled out his keyboard and typed. 'The name didn't mean anything to me, so I didn't bother.'

The door opened again and Fenchurch's dad popped his head in. 'Evening, gents.'

Fenchurch felt his face tighten. 'What are you doing here?'

Dad walked over and took a seat. 'I've no idea, son. Other than these buggers asking me to pitch up.'

Owen was back over by the window, lips pursed. 'Of course you know why you're here.'

Dad laughed. 'Instead of this telepathic bollocks, how about you tell me?'

'Bert Matthews, Ian.' Loftus folded his arms. 'Tell us all you know.'

'What's there to tell? I wasn't a big fan of Bert's, didn't really work with him much. Kind of slippery and lazy.'

Fenchurch got between them. 'Dad, you were friends.'

'No, son. We played pool and so on, but we weren't friends.'

'But you both worked the Mortimer case, right?'

Dad frowned. 'What's this about?'

Loftus stood up and walked over to block the door. 'Ian, you're here because we need to know all you know about that case.'

'Well, I don't remember much about it.'

Loftus threw his hands in the air. 'You were Deputy SIO.'

'Right, right, but I was involved in other cases at the time, so I'll have to go through the archives to refresh my non-existent...'

'Thanks for your valuable contributions, Mr Fenchurch.' Owen pinched his face into a scowl. 'Check the archives... How would we ever get along without you?'

'You cheeky little shit.' Dad sat there, hands shaking as much as his voice. Fenchurch noticed a bit of egg in the corner of his mouth, stuck to his beard. 'You couldn't find your arsehole with both hands.'

Fenchurch wanted to jump in, but his old man was tough as old boots.

'Be that as it may, sir, I have done the reading on that case.' Owen held up a case file. 'You were the Deputy SIO. Someone planted a bomb at the Zeroes concert on tenth of June 2007 at the O2 Arena.'

Dad snorted. 'Right, yeah. Simon was at the concert, so don't you talk to me about—'

Owen was frowning at Fenchurch. 'You're a Zeroes fan?'

Fenchurch shrugged. 'Not my favourite band in the world, but I was there with a mate, who was trying to encourage me to get out more. I left after I got a lead on Chloe, which came to nothing.'

'Sorry to hear that.'

Fenchurch shrugged. 'Got out before the mad stampede, so I was lucky.'

'Right. Security caught a man planting the bomb, didn't they? James Mortimer. And your team investigated. CPS tried him too, but they failed to convict.'

Dad scowled at Owen. 'Nobody's fault, that.'

Owen raised his eyebrows. 'Sure about that?'

Dad snarled at him. 'What do you know, eh?'

'Well, just what's on file, which is why I'm asking you what actually happened.'

'We caught this geezer.' Dad snatched the file out of his hands. 'Red-handed, too. The SIO wasn't so sure. Al Docherty, good geezer. Taught him everything he learnt, God rest his soul. But we pressed on, because it all fit the evidence, didn't it? Ex-squaddie with experience in bomb disposal who had far-right tendencies. Disposal's much harder than building them in the first place. Bingo. He just fit the bill, didn't he?'

'Except he wasn't caught so red-handed, was he?'

Dad scratched at his goatee. 'He was in the boiler room where the bloody bomb was! Of course he'd planted it!'

'But he told you he was going there to defuse it, right?'

Dad shook his head. 'Pack of lies.'

'And an alibi came forward at the last minute, yes?'

'A woman who was seeing Mortimer. Dirty cow was married. Said she was having an affair with him. Hence her not pitching up with her evidence any earlier.'

Fenchurch felt a sting in his gut. Just came out of nowhere and dredged it all up again. Confronting Abi about what she'd done. The denial, then the admission, then the separation. Christ, what a bloody mess.

'And that geezer.' Dad bared his teeth. 'Mortimer, he insisted he was just selling parts for lawnmowers and other appliances on eBay. Absolute bollocks. Of course he was making bombs!'

12

The office was alive with the hum of a thousand fingers pounding on keyboards. Yvette Farley was one of those typing away and didn't look up from her computer. Her desk was a cluttered mess of letters, memos, bills and decisions, like going to press with that video of her and Rob Lezard.

The low sun shone through the window, highlighting Loftus, but casting Fenchurch in shadow.

The air smelled like someone had left a lump of burning wood in the corner, but it seemed to come from Yvette. Still a smoker in the age of vaping, not even the fug of perfume or breath mints could disguise that.

She stopped typing and scanned the screen, her lips twitching as she read, then she hit the return key and sat back, finally looking at them. 'Right, sorry to keep you, gentlemen.'

'It's quite alright.' Loftus wore his full uniform, but it didn't inject that little extra frisson of fear into Yvette. 'So, you obviously know why we're here.'

'Indeed.' She gestured at the computer. 'I imagine it's what I was working on there. Let me confess that the standard of subbing isn't what it was when I started out in this game. Very far from it.'

Loftus smiled. 'Times change and not necessarily for the better.'

'So, why are you here?'

'Your video, Yvette. I wasn't particularly impressed with it.'

'Oh, well, Julian, I'm deeply sorry to have upset you.' She put both hands to her chest. 'Please find it in your heart to forgive me for doing my job.'

'I'm not sure how putting an ongoing murder investigation at risk is doing your job.'

She jabbed a finger at her screen. 'That video went viral. Over a million views and climbing. That's what we're about these days. We'll make about fifty grand in adverts just from that.'

'Well, I hope that pays for your new soul.'

She laughed. 'Come on, Julian, all's fair in love and war.'

'Which is this, though? Feels like war.'

'Touché.' She bunched her hair up and let it fall back. 'Why are you here?'

'We need to speak to Mr Lezard.'

'I'm sure you do, but you had your chance and he won't want to speak to you.' She laughed. 'Listen, Julian. Mate. You know the drill. We have our own database of who's who in the zoo. Unlike you lot, who'd have to go through thirty years of Bert's police history to figure out a motive, we only deal with newsworthy items. Luckily, good old Gilbert Finbarr Matthews came up a few times, and his name was cross-referenced with that case.'

'That's all you've got?'

'Well, of course it's not. Mr Lezard has been instrumental in helping us with a few other stories, so I ran it by him. And yes, Rob worked that case too.'

Loftus looked at Fenchurch, then at her. 'He didn't.'

'Well, you're wrong. He told me. He's got copies of the— Erm, he's got evidence of it.'

'No.' Loftus snorted. 'I've got the whole case file in my office. Robert or Robin Lezard wasn't involved.'

'No, but you need to check his real name, don't you?'

'Okay, so I'll bite. What is it?'

'It's not safe for him to reveal his real name.' She raised an eyebrow. 'And Mr Lezard has other materials, which we will share when the time is right.'

'Yvette, I know how this whole thing works as well as you do. Who is your second source on this?'

'You should know I don't name sources.'

'Okay. But you know if there are any more deaths, they're on your head, right?'

'Sure you'll blame us all the same, Jules.' She tapped her smartwatch. 'Now, I've got a dinner to attend tonight, so please kindly bugger off.'

AND OF COURSE, one of the lifts was broken. The other was stuck down in the basement.

Fenchurch looked over at Loftus. 'You okay with the stairs?'

'Okay?' He laughed. 'I insist on them, but I thought your knees were playing up.' Loftus marched over to the door and pushed through.

Fenchurch caught up with him halfway down the first flight. 'You didn't seem to get what you wanted in there, sir.'

'Never do with her.' His voice echoed around the ornate stairwell. 'I mean, I shouldn't even try sometimes, but you'd think if it's a murder case that she'd cut us some slack?'

'You say that, but the *Post* are going hard on the police brutality angle.'

'I know...' Loftus sighed. 'It's an issue, don't get me wrong, but it's harming our day job. We're the good guys, stopping violent crimes. I despair, Simon, I really do.'

'You getting a lot of aggro from Lezard?'

'Afraid so. He's being a pain in the arse on multiple cases, always ahead of the curve.'

'So why didn't you take his call?'

'Because he's an arsehole.' Loftus powered on faster, making it harder for Fenchurch to follow, especially with his gammy knee.

'When you give people like him oxygen, all you do is make the fire bigger. And he's leaking like a sieve.'

'You've no idea who he really is?'

'Chris Owen is investigating him, which means we will identify him very soon. He's gone through a ton of our cases, but there's no sign of Lezard in any of it. We knew it's likely an alias, but it's nice to have it confirmed. And yes, there is some disguise at work. His footballer haircut. That beard. Those eyes, too, it's like he's wearing contact lenses. So that makes it harder to pin him down.'

'But you must have suspects, right? Each case he leaks on, assuming he worked it, that's a further tightening of the belt.'

'One issue with that.' Loftus stopped on the ground floor but didn't push through to reception. 'The assumption he worked the cases. Nobody fits all of them. About ten officers fit half of them. But he could've worked none of the cases and be reliant on leaks from colleagues. Or ex-colleagues. Or just officers open to a brown envelope.'

'Still, it feels a bit amateur hour that he's getting away with this.'

'Don't you think I know that?' Loftus stepped closer to Fenchurch, making himself bigger, like he was trying to exert authority over him. 'That's why I've got Chris all over this.' He looked away, snorting. 'But I'll be buggered if I know what's going on here.'

'So how do you want to play this, sir?'

'This is where you bloody tell me how I should, isn't it?'

Fenchurch held his gaze, narrowing his eyes. 'Remember our agreement, sir. I catch the crooks, you do the admin. So stop being a prick and let me catch the bloody crooks.'

Loftus wallowed. 'Right, of course.' He looked down at his shoes then back up at Fenchurch with real fear in his eyes. The pen-pusher was struggling with the real street stuff here. 'How the hell do I catch Rob Lezard?'

'It's not him you should be worried about, unless he killed Bert Matthews.'

'Right. Of course.'

'You just let me get on with that, sir. Don't worry.'

'Right. But someone being a pain in the arse is all part of this, isn't it?' Loftus ran a hand over his bald head. 'So, what's your plan?'

'Well, a prick like Lezard doesn't stick his head above the parapet unless he's a hundred percent sure. And an arsehole like Yvette Farley doesn't publish unless she's doubly sure.'

'You think there's something in this Mortimer case?'

'Right. And I need your help, boss. So here's how we're going to progress this. You and DCI Owen should go with my old man to the archive and dig through with Dad's help, should you need it. Get out the dusty old files and start comparing fact and fiction... See if Bert was in any way bent. If my old man squirms, dig deeper. And keep digging.'

'You think your father's bent?'

'No, but he's loyal to a fault. He keeps distancing himself from Bert, but those two were thick as thieves. And we need to dig up the old team. Anyone who worked that case, we need to speak to them. One of them is leaking to Lezard. You don't do that just to cause mayhem.'

'Right. And what about you?'

'Well, I need to catch up with someone who I know was a DC on the case. Maybe he can help me find Mortimer, or at least get in touch with the old team.' Fenchurch blew air up his face. 'But first, I need to take my daughter out for something to eat.'

13

CHLOE

Chloe's mouth was watering already. The place certainly smelled like it made a good burrito. But she'd never seen anyone mixing a burrito like that, but Cantina Broussard didn't seem to do things normally. No bottles of hot sauce on the tables, so it had to be applied at order. The server dug a pair of wooden spoons into a big glass bowl, blending the ingredients all together until it was a mush of rice, beans, salsa, fried onions, peppers, grated cheese and charred steak. She eased it out onto the heated tortilla and sprinkled it with lettuce and glistening guacamole, then folded it much quicker than Chloe'd ever seen before. Maybe the bowls were a good idea, but Chloe didn't fancy the job of cleaning the towering stack sitting by the kitchen.

The cashier had the meal deal all ready to go.

Dad pressed his card against the reader. 'Thanks.' He took both of the baskets containing the silver-foiled tubes. 'Can you grab the drinks?'

'On it.' Chloe took the plastic beakers of cloudy lemonade and charged over to a free table. 'Thanks for this, Dad, but I said I was going to pay.'

He slumped into the booth next to her, his back to the servers but facing the door. 'I said I was going to cook tonight and I haven't.'

'Yeah, but I said I'd buy the next burrito, so...'

'You can pay next time, then. After all, you'll have earned your first payslip by walking the streets.'

'Deal.' She untwirled the top and tore it down, then took a big Fenchurch-sized bite and got a flavour explosion. The chilli heat and the charred meat. Perfection. As she chewed, the fire built up, but her rage simmered down a bit. She hated being patronised, and he'd just been a patronising git.

'But thank you for meeting like this, instead of me cooking.' Dad looked down at his burrito like a wolf finding a stray sheep. 'This case is growing arms and legs.'

'Bert's death?'

Dad stabbed a fork into his burrito salad. 'It's a tough one when it's someone you know.'

'You think you'll catch the killer?'

Dad finished chewing, swallowing it down. 'I'm not sure if we will catch who's done it. I never am, really, but I'm giving it a good shot.'

'Is it because you know him?'

'I give every murder my all, even people who've broken the law themselves. That's part of the problem. But when the victim is a former officer, people tend to go the extra mile when they've lost one of their own.'

She stared into space, resting the burrito on the basket. 'Was he killed where I found him?'

'At home. We think.'

'Jesus. So they broke into his house?'

Her dad had a lump of salsa stuck to his cheek, like her grandfather with his breakfast earlier that morning. 'Looks that way.'

Chloe slurped some lemonade. 'Christ.'

'And I am sorry I didn't cook for you.'

'I'm a grown-up, Dad. I *can* fend for myself.'

'Yeah, but I can't.'

She laughed. 'True. Need to make sure you're looking after yourself.'

'Something home-cooked would be better, right?'

'Not really.' She took another sip through the straw. 'I need carbs, protein and fibre after the gym.' Her hair was still a bit damp, patches fluffing up as they dried. Would need a good brushing when she got to the station.

'But you didn't sleep much.'

'I slept enough. Just... Well. *Mum*.'

Dad winced. 'Well, your mother's not answering my calls.'

'*Typical*.' As she said it, it sounded like she hadn't missed eleven years of parenting, with all the frustrations and habits, as well as the joy and memories. But still, a few years living with someone, you get used to their behaviours. And you see some that you've inherited.

'I'll still try to have a word with her.'

'Thing is, Dad, she seemed a bit upset.' Chloe took a dainty bite of her burrito, but some chilli made her snort.

'Are you okay?'

'It's the chilli.' She shook it off. 'Why wouldn't I be?'

'Well, what's going on with your mother and me has to be stressful.'

'I'm over it, Dad.'

'But you did find a dead body this morning. And it was someone you know.'

Christ, where did he get off? All day, he'd been banging on about this. She was fine. He wasn't, clearly, but she was.

'Dad, I'm fine. I'm a bit tired, but I'm stronger than you give me credit for. After all I've been through, you should cut me some slack.'

Dad rested his fork on the edge of his basket, just under half left. 'I don't want to patronise you, but—'

'You *are* patronising me.'

Dad snorted. 'Look, it's okay to feel fragile. I know you joke about being a chip off the old block, but it's not exactly helped me be a normal or balanced person. Or your grandfather. Take care of how you feel. Okay? Listen to your body.'

'Okay, Dad.' She looked around the place, sipping her lemonade, but gave the slightest shake of her head. This was a mistake. 'Look, I've got to head for my shift early, so I'll see you tomorrow.'

Dad could've gone on about how they were supposed to eat together, but thought he'd come on a bit too strong.

Trouble with running murder inquiries, wasn't it?

And having such a bloody complicated home life.

But no. Instead, he reached over and held her hand. 'Good luck.'

'Don't need it.'

'I know, but I want you to have it all the same.'

She folded up her burrito foil and picked up her drink, then leaned over to peck him on the cheek. 'Thanks, Dad. Have a good evening.' She walked off out of the place, feeling that rage gripping her fists, burning up in her stomach.

Bloody parents.

14

FENCHURCH

Yeah, Fenchurch had being patronising.

Trouble was, she'd been through a lot. A hell of a lot. And while it had arguably made her stronger, it had nearly killed her. And him. And his marriage had been destroyed by it.

Chloe was tough as boots, but she was young. And he was her father. They had so much time to catch up on, so many years he'd not been able to tuck her up in bed, not being able to intimidate her first boyfriend, tell her about the birds and the bees, help Abi with buying her period products. Or do it himself. He was a modern guy, after all.

Maybe, just maybe, having his kid as a serving cop was what terrified him most. Anything could happen on the streets, especially in London. Bomb threats, stabbings, acid attacks, riots. Anything.

Some prick had pointed a gun at her and pulled the trigger. Just blind luck it'd been fake.

Maybe that was what was eating away at her...

No way was she over it, but he wasn't going to press her on it and risk alienating her.

'Guv.' DI Jon Nelson collapsed into the banquette next to

Fenchurch. His girth made the table wobble, shaking Fenchurch's lemonade against the lid. He'd put on a lot of weight since Fenchurch last saw him and the wheezing showed he wasn't getting much exercise. 'Weird seeing Chloe in uniform.'

'Not as weird as it is for me.' Fenchurch rested his burrito back down. 'Been a while, Jon.'

'Hasn't it just.'

'How you doing?'

'Win some, lose some.' Nelson opened up his paper bag and took out a foil tube and a bag of tortillas. Yeah, that was where the mass came from. A burrito was more than enough, but those chips on top of it? Empty calorie central. 'Help yourself.'

'Cheers, Jon, but it'll bugger my ketosis.'

'You're having a salad?'

'Right, but I wish I had the tortilla. Old habits die hard.' Fenchurch looked around the place. They weren't the only serving officers in there. Cantina Broussard was three doors down from the station and gone were the days when off-duty cops self-medicated with booze. At least in public, anyway. Now it was all about comfort eating. Still, the salsa version of The Clash's *I Fought The Law* was loud enough to drown out their conversation. 'Jon, I know there's bad blood between us, so I wanted to clear the air before we get down to business.'

'Not aware of any bad blood.' Nelson dipped a tortilla chip into a pot of salsa. 'I mean, unless you count you kicking me and Lisa out of your flat with barely any notice?'

'I needed it, Jon. Things got bad. Me and Chloe needed—'

'I understand, guv.' Nelson laughed, spraying tortilla over the table. 'I'm just winding you up. We had a place lined up, but I was finding it difficult getting hold of you to break the rental agreement.'

'Oh.'

'I mean, moving was a bit of a pain but isn't it always?' He laughed again. 'And you don't have to talk to me about failed marriages. I wrote the book on them.'

Fenchurch didn't know whether to take him at face value.

Nelson had been a friend over the years, someone who Fenchurch could rely on, someone he could talk to while Chloe was out of his life, someone he *did* talk to.

But he'd more recently been a bit of a nemesis, charting his own course. Him being okay about what happened felt weird, considering he'd blocked Fenchurch's number for a few weeks and didn't reply to any messages.

And Fenchurch didn't know which side of the coin Nelson was on these days. He'd been tangential to a number of cases over the years, instrumental in catching certain people.

Nelson rested his burrito down and took his time chewing. 'So how's Chloe doing?'

'She's doing okay, actually.' Fenchurch tore another strip of foil and a lump of steak fell onto the table. He caught it, but didn't eat it. That myth about the three-second rule, by which time your food was already swarming with bugs. 'I admire her for doing it. Being a cop's a tough gig, especially nowadays and especially in this city.'

'But you still have a healthy fear for her as an officer?'

Fenchurch was chewing and could only nod.

Nelson tore his bag of tortillas open wider. 'It's the same for pretty much everyone when you join up, right? Always worrying about what your parents think when you're out on the street. Doubly hard for you as a son of a cop.'

'Tell me about it.' Fenchurch winced. 'Mum didn't sleep for a year when I started. Thing is, I was always knee-deep in the shit, so it must've driven them crazy. Chloe's different, though. Toeing the line. And she's good at it.' He took another bite, almost down to the sloppy end. No matter how much mixing the server did in the glass bowls, it was always a sludge at the bottom. 'I hope she rises quickly and gets a nice office job somewhere. Or something specialised like Serious Accidents.'

'Got a mate over there who hates it.'

'If he's a mate of yours, Jon, I can understand why. Ex-MIT?'

'Right. Couldn't handle the stress you put yourself under all the time, so he went for something easier. But, despite how well-meaning and important it is, it's boring.'

'Boring would be good. I'd prefer her somewhere leafy like Hertfordshire or western Kent. Surrey, even. Or maybe not even in the police, maybe teaching in a school like her mother.'

Nelson was chewing a big mouthful now, so gave a thumbs up.

'How are you, Jon? Still doing drugs?'

Nelson laughed, then kept nodding until he'd swallowed it down. 'Middle Market Drugs. Street crime, but more strategic.'

'Glad that's paying off for you. Always a gamble when you step sideways.'

'Sideways and up.' Nelson held his gaze for a few seconds. 'Trouble is, Younis's still causing pain.'

Fenchurch slumped back in his seat and tried to unpick the bottom of his burrito without it splashing all over the table or his trousers. But his hands were shaking. 'How can that clown still be running the East End from prison?'

'Search me, guv. Lot of places to hide a phone these days. Amount he makes, though, probably a lot easier to bribe prison officers.'

'Haven't heard from him in a while.'

'Yeah, I know.' Nelson laughed. 'Last time I visited him, it was all I heard. "Where's Fenchy? No visits, no phone calls, no friendly sex talk, just a brick wall. Beginning to think he never really loved me." And that's a quote.'

'Well, it's nice to be out of the picture.' Fenchurch went for it, swallowing the bottom end in one. Some dribbled down his chin, but it was mostly fine. 'So, let's talk about Mortimer.'

'Right.' Nelson dipped another tortilla in salsa and motioned for Fenchurch to take one. He didn't, so Nelson continued. 'Okay, that case was my first gig as a full DC. Working for your old man. With old sods like Bert Matthews and younger sods like Dean Hatton or Tony Wyatt.'

'Never heard of him.'

'Well, you will. He was my partner. Would rather have gone with old Bert, someone who knew the lay of the land, but me and

Dean got on okay. Tony was fine too.' He crunched a handful of tortillas, then wiped his lips with a napkin. 'Anyway. One morning, me and Dean were working a murder case for your old man, and got an action to shake down a CHIS. Nasty bugger, think he got done for underage shenanigans a few years later, but he had his ear to the ground. Ran a shop in Mile End, lot of stuff under the counter. Anyway, he gave us some intel that an ex-army operative had gone rogue.'

'James Mortimer?'

'Right. He'd supposedly built a bomb for some far-right muppets who plotted to blow up that Zeroes concert. Multi-ethnic band, so they were a perfect target for them.'

'I was at that gig.'

'Right, right.' Nelson took a drink of lemonade. 'Anyway. We arrived there, went down into the bowels and we caught Mortimer. I arrested him, we interviewed him, no comment, then we charged him. And he didn't speak.'

'That's what I've learnt so far. What else you got on him?'

'Mortimer was slippery, refused to give any details about his private life. So, we had to dig. Ran a business selling lawnmower parts. Shop in the East End, but the online stuff—Amazon, eBay, his own site—that was very lucrative.'

'How did he get off?'

'Solid alibi came up during the bloody *court case*.'

'Bit late in the day.'

'I know. Got an earful from your old man about it. I mean, it all made perfect sense to us. Mortimer had been in Iraq, dishonourable discharge. Far-right tendencies.' Nelson sighed. 'And who better to blame things on than a guy who actually built bombs while a soldier? Trouble was, we'd put two and two together. The alibi covered the time up to him getting a call and rushing off to the O2. Two days' worth.'

'Shit.'

'Rachel Jones was her name. And she could back it up. Trouble is, you know the CPS. Blackhurst ploughed on with it. Made us all look like muppets. We caught him in the boiler room at the concert venue. Not exactly red-handed, but near enough.'

'Do you think Mortimer wasn't involved in the plot?'

'Hard to say, guv. I certainly thought so at the time. Thing is, if you were some neo-Nazi group, you could get him to handle lawn-mower parts from his website and then incorporate them into a bomb you built and you'd have a very strong scapegoat. Or he actually planted it. Or he could've been involved. But that alibi was enough to get him off. It destroyed our case.'

'Well. You saw the video on the *Post* site?'

'I did. Loftus sent me it.'

Fenchurch didn't know whether his boss going directly to Nelson was a good thing or not. 'Okay, so we need to find Mortimer.' He wrapped his foil and finished his drink, then put them both on the basket. 'Where do we start?'

15

Stepney Square would be the last place Fenchurch would've ever stepped foot, even as a young idiot full of bravado. Now, as an older idiot, he was blown away by the change. No sign of drug dealers or users. Everything was scrubbed clean of the graffiti except for the outline of the giant Banksy on a gable end. Hard to make it out now and Fenchurch couldn't remember what it had been. Whoever owned the building must be furious at Tower Hamlets council for clearing it away.

The wall would've been worth more than the whole square by now.

'This is where he lived.' Nelson pressed the buzzer and took a puff of vape.

'Still doing that?'

He shook the stick in the air. 'It's popcorn lung with this or lung cancer with real cigarettes.'

'Or neither.'

'Nah. Need the nicotine.' Nelson put it away and pressed the buzzer again.

The door opened and a man peered out. 'Can I help you?' Northern Irish accent, lined face.

'Police.' Nelson opened his warrant card. 'Looking for James Mortimer.'

'Aren't we all.' A thick laugh, then he coughed hard, like he'd dislodged a lung. 'I own this place. That prick's not been seen for weeks. And he owes me, big time.'

Nelson looked around at Fenchurch, frowned, then back at the man. 'Mind if we check that for ourselves?'

'You got a warrant?'

'We don't, but it's a formality. Sure a law-abiding man like yourself would love to help the Old Bill out?'

A chuckle this time, but he stepped back against the wall to let them through.

Fenchurch went first, but he stepped into one of those fabled estate agent pictures. A minuscule unit, empty, with all the living space in one room. Even the toilet, hidden behind a curtain at the side. No furniture, no personal possessions.

And definitely no sign of Mortimer.

THREE BLOCKS away and the gentrification machine hadn't caught up, or had got stuck halfway down the street. A block of modern flats climbed higher than the existing buildings. The primary school had recently cleaned bricks. But the second half of the street was a row of knackered old flats, a yard for a security firm and a derelict factory that looked like it was held together by graffiti.

Nelson stepped up to the first flat in the block and rang the buzzer, sucking even more vape, then blowing it out in a cloud of bubble-gum fumes.

This building was in the rough half of the street, but it'd been done up, the brick exterior covered over with Mediterranean or Californian stucco. Three storeys and a basement. Probably a good investment for when the neighbouring flats were upgraded.

'Hello?' A female voice barked out, gruff and harsh.

'Police. Looking for James Mortimer.'

The line crackled. 'What do you want him for?'

'Am I speaking to Rachel Jones?'

'That's me. Can I take your name?'

'DI Jon Nelson.'

A sharp intake of breath. 'And why the bloody hell should I speak to you?'

'It's about James. Mind if we come inside?'

'In you come.' The buzzer's rasp was quieter than her harsh sigh.

Nelson held the door and Fenchurch went inside.

While the exterior looked like it'd been done a couple of years ago, the inside was still a work in progress. Plastic sheeting and work machinery. No sign of any workmen, just a tired-looking woman. Hoodie and paint-spattered leggings, long hair held in a ponytail. 'Sorry about the mess. Doing this place up to sell it now estate agents can come around here without an armed guard.' She barked out a laugh, but her face meant business, focusing on Nelson. 'Well, look who it is.'

Nelson peered around the place like he was a prospective buyer. Maybe he was. 'Doing a great job in here.'

'When my old mum died, I inherited a bit of money, so I'm doing this place up.'

'Looks like it'll make a packet if you choose to sell it.'

'Oh, I'm selling. Hopefully get enough from this place to buy a mansion in Wales.'

'Good luck with it.'

'Cheers.' She shook her head. 'Why do you want Jimbo?'

'I'm afraid that it's an urgent matter, but also a private one that we can't discuss.'

'Well, you've come to the wrong place. Me and Jimbo split up a few years back.'

'Sorry to hear that.'

'Are you? Because you lot took him to hell and back. He might've got off with what you were trying to pin on him, but he... He wasn't the same.'

'What happened?'

'That court case triggered his PTSD from Iraq. Why he left the army, or why he *had* to leave the army. Couldn't cope with what he did over there. And he was fine for years. We were engaged. His business was thriving. But that case broke him.'

Nelson exhaled slowly. 'I'm sorry.'

'It's not me you should apologise to. It's James. And you, Jon Nelson, you tried. You believed me. Listened to me. Wanted to help James. But the rest of them. O'Keefe, Hatton, Fenchurch, Matthews. They all just didn't care.'

Fenchurch was standing by a half-built kitchen island unit. Didn't know where to lean or even if he could. But the fact she knew all the investigators by name, did that mean anything?

'Again, Rachel, I'm deeply sorry. It took a lot for you to come forward like that.'

'James had been protecting me, didn't want me to speak to you lot, not after what I'd been through with the cops.'

Fenchurch frowned. 'And what was that?'

She looked him up and down, a sour look on her face. 'Who the hell are you?'

'DCI Simon Fenchurch.'

Her look got even sourer. 'Any relation?'

'To Ian?' Fenchurch smiled. 'He's my father.'

'No, to that girl who was abducted and—'

'Ah right. Well, that's me. My daughter.'

'My God. You poor thing.'

'Listen, we just need to speak to James. That's all.'

'Well.' She pointed at the front door. 'I can't help.'

'Please, this is a murder case. It's possible James might've murdered someone.'

She shook her head again. 'Not the first time you shower have pointed a finger at him. He ain't done nothing, just like the last time.'

'Still, we'd like to speak to him.'

'Who's died?'

'Bert Matthews.'

She winced. 'Good. He was the worst of a very bad lot.'

And this underlined why they needed to speak to Mortimer.

Nelson took over, getting between Rachel and Fenchurch. 'This doesn't need to go this way. We just need to speak to James, that's all.'

'Heard you say those words before, ain't I?'

'And you were incredibly brave doing that. Standing up in court, backing up what I'd discovered. After what they'd put you through.'

'It was nothing compared to being abused by cops as a child.'

Shit.

Fenchurch felt that sting in his guts.

He recognised the name now. Rachel Jones. A schoolgirl when he started as a cop.

While he'd dealt with bent cops over the years, maybe more than his fair share, they were mostly just arseholes looking for money from local gangsters, the likes of Flick Knife or Younis.

But those craven bastards in Stratford had run a paedophile ring. Twenty of them, with four serving officers covering over scores of victims.

Nobody would listen.

Until the dam broke, and someone looked into it.

Fenchurch gave her an even stare. 'You were Girl A?'

She looked at him with a different gaze, softer somehow. 'That's right.'

Fenchurch felt his nails biting into his palms. 'I'm truly sorry for what you endured at their hands.'

'Well, it happened. It stopped. They ain't doing it to anyone anymore.'

'I can't imagine how difficult it must've been for you to come forward like that.'

'You've got a bloody cheek. Coming here...' She turned away but he could see her snarling. 'You lot lost a conviction, didn't you? My name must be mud in Scotland Yard.'

'The Met isn't like that anymore. Nobody wants an innocent man to go to prison. And James was just trying to protect you from going through an ordeal. Very honourable of him. He'd have gone to prison to spare you. But you stood up in court, you took their questions, let them try to paint you as a guilty party in the abuse you endured.'

She shook her head again and tossed free some strands of hair. 'You've no idea...' Her voice was a gasp.

'I do, Rachel. I really do, and that's the truth.'

But all she had for Nelson was a shrug.

'Listen, we received intelligence that—'

'DI Jon Nelson.' She shook her head again. 'You've done well for yourself, haven't you? Framing people must be held in high regard by the Met for you to have been promoted twice.'

'I haven't framed anyone. Trust me, I tried to get James off but I was new to the job. Nobody would listen to a rookie, least of all a black man.'

She looked at him with an even softer gaze. 'Look, Jon, I'm sorry, but I haven't heard from him in a long time.'

'Is that a concern?'

She checked her nails. 'I don't know where his head's at these days.'

'Where could he be?'

'I don't know. But... Thing is, we split up and it wasn't good.'

'What happened?'

'James was working all hours in that bloody shop of his. Selling stuff to people on eBay and Amazon. Said it was a big success, even took on staff. Thing is, being busy didn't stop him shagging *her* behind my back, did it? After all I'd done for him?'

It always came down to something like that.

Fenchurch knew it took two to tango, that was for sure.

'His bookkeeper. Some *girl* out of college. I mean... Took me way too long to find out what he'd been up to, so I kicked him out on his ear.' She tucked her loose hair back into the ponytail. 'Last I heard, he started working as a Travis driver.'

THE DRIVER

He hated it when he got told to switch targets.

It meant neither got full coverage.

Unless they had someone else covering the mother. Or someone solely watching her home.

But he was now following Chloe Fenchurch. And that meant trailing two cops.

Commercial Road was busy, like it always was, but trying to keep a trail on two cops on foot while you were in a car was tough. Trick was to vary it.

Like now. He was parked ahead of them, could see them in the wing mirror as they talked to a woman at the bus stop. But the bus was approaching, slow and steady, cresting another wave of traffic. They helped the woman onboard, then strolled off up the street, passing his car.

The front camera could trail their movements, keep them on his radar, document everything, but he had to play a few steps ahead. Maybe drive up, do a U-turn and watch them from over the road. No buses due for ten minutes, but then again, one might just be running late. He couldn't lose them.

Chloe and her training officer.

Adam Burridge was a difficult guy. He knew him too, could identify him. So it was a case of not getting spotted by two cops.

He shot ahead of them and pulled that U-turn, then parked with a good view of them as they walked along the road.

Burridge stopped and listened to his radio, looking at Chloe, then back down the street. Burridge set off, running, with her following.

He didn't know where they were going, but it'd make following them a lot easier.

16

CHLOE

Chloe thundered along the street, her feet smacking off the pavement, her equipment rattling. She glanced behind her at Adam, struggling to keep up with her pace, even after she'd spent forty minutes on the treadmill in the gym, and with a burrito slurring around her guts. Lazy bugger.

She weaved around onto the Minories, but slowed as she approached the shop, grabbing her belt to stop everything shaking and making an almighty racket. She stopped by the entrance and peered inside.

They say lightning didn't strike twice, but there it was.

Wristbands was inside the same shop as last night, holding a gun to the shopkeeper. Ibrahim. She even remembered his name without consulting her notebook. Getting better at this.

And this time he'd brought a friend. Another goon with his hood up. Shades on, despite it being night. Didn't hide his pasty complexion, though.

Heroin addicts.

She didn't get why they did the same shop twice in a row, but then the logic of drug abusers was always skewed. They taught them that at Hendon. Expect weird.

And she was thinking like a cop now, despite never having met a drug addict. At least, not knowingly.

Adam slowed to walking pace behind her, sucking in deep breaths. His gear didn't rattle when he ran, unlike hers – she needed to get the secret out of him. He peeked inside the shop, saw what she'd seen, then motioned for her to cross the road, and approach from the other side.

But something didn't feel right here. Procedurally. They should get—what was it called?—an armed squad out? Surely, they should get them.

Chloe made a pistol with her fingers and raised her eyebrows at him.

Adam took another look inside, then made a pistol of his own and squeezed the trigger. He wiped imaginary water from his face, shook his head and pointed inside with walking fingers.

Chloe had to wait for a Travis car to pass before scurrying over the road, then down a few units, and back over so she was on the other side of the shop's entrance.

They had them snared. Wristbands and his mate. And she wasn't going to make the same mistake as this morning.

Still, she didn't know where the inside door went. The fridge was all taped up from this morning's fight.

Adam took out his baton, shook it out without a sound, mouthed, 'On three,' then hit the beat with his pointing finger – one, two, three, which got a much bigger hit, and he barrelled inside the shop.

Chloe was alongside him, clutching her baton in her damp palms, her heart thudding in her ears. The same way her old man said he got.

'Police.' Adam had the baton out like a sword or a lightsabre. 'Put the gun down on the counter! On your knees! Hands on your heads!'

Wristbands took one look at his mate, then laughed. He pointed the gun at Adam. 'Think you're so smart, don't you?'

Chloe could see the menace in his eyes. The hunger, the lack of empathy. He wanted money to feed his addiction and nobody was getting in the way. She stepped forward and lashed out with her baton, cracking metal off the bone of his forearm.

Wristbands yelped and dropped the gun. It landed with a heavy thud. Chloe stepped even closer and interlinked her leg around his knee, then twisted and pushed him down. Grabbed his wrist and bent it around his back.

His mate went down to his knees, hands behind his head, fingers interlinked. 'I was just here for rolling paper, man. Don't know this guy.'

'I don't believe you.' Chloe cuffed Wristbands and pulled him to his feet by the restraints. 'I'm going to arrested you for two counts of attempted armed robbery.'

Sunglasses's head slumped low.

Adam turned away to speak into his radio. 'Need a car to collected us at Ibrahim's on the Minories. Two suspects in custody. Over.'

'Will send them around now, Adam, thanks. Over.'

'Appreciate it. Over.' Adam looked like he relaxed a bit. The rest of the night would be spent away from chases and arrests, just interviewing these two idiots.

His radio crackled again. 'One thing, though. We just got a call from the local school governor. The headmaster of Shadwell Grammar hasn't been seen since Friday night. Need you to report there. Over.'

'Us?' Adam scowled like Chloe's brother when he'd lost a week's TV rights for something he said. 'Why us? Over.'

'Karen Armitage asked for you by name. Over.'

'Right. We'll get around there. Over.' Adam let his radio go and leaned in to whisper to her, 'Best advice I could ever give. Watch who you hand your business card to when you do community outreach work.'

Chloe applied the cuffs to Sunglasses, then saw a meat wagon pull up on the kerb. 'Come on, you two, let's get you outside.'

Adam snapped on a pair of blue nitrile gloves and crouched

down to pick up the water pistol. Then his eyes went wide as he focused on Chloe. 'Shit.'

'What's up?'

'This thing's real. And it's loaded!'

17

FENCHURCH

Nelson stuffed his hand deep into the tortillas, still chewing the last handful. 'God, these are good.'

'Don't know how you can keep eating after that massive burrito.' Fenchurch looked along Mile End Road. Post office and corner shop next to a designer tattoo parlour. Two fried chicken shops sandwiched a boutique whisky shop, three kebab shops ganged up on a gourmet pizza parlour.

Yeah, the hipsters were moving in here, but still hadn't won the battle.

'There he is.' Nelson tossed his bag into the passenger seat of his car.

A Toyota Prius swooshed into the space between their cars, like something from the twenty-fifth century. It wasn't Buck Rogers behind the wheel, though.

A short man crept out of the driver's side, wearing brown. Leather jacket, trousers, T-shirt. Hadn't shaved for a few days and had the grizzled look of an Eastender. He thrust out a hand. 'Will Merton.'

'Jon Nelson.' He shook it. 'Thanks for seeing us.'

Will sniffed, then nodded at Fenchurch. No hand held out. 'You're Fenchurch, right?'

'My reputation must precede me.'

'Hard not to when your face is splashed all over the papers, isn't it? That, and I mentioned your name to my boss just after you called me. He said under no circumstances was I to speak to you. Had to be routed through—'

'Jason Bell. Right.'

Will was frowning. 'Nope. Kieron Sortwell.'

'Oh.'

Will rubbed his hands together. 'Anyway, I thought I'd help you lot out. Must be tough for you these days.'

Nelson frowned. 'Why do you say that?'

'Well, the East End's rough as badgers' arseholes, isn't it? Getting softer by the year, but still. Must pay to have people on the inside.'

'Why do you think this is an East End thing?'

'When you call me up about James Mortimer, it's got to be. I saw that interview with that ponce. Dredging up all that shit about that incident at the O2.' Will snarled. 'Absolute codswallop and no mistaking.'

Fenchurch could see this going any number of weird ways, so he took over. 'Mr Mortimer works for you, right?'

'Right. Good driver. But times are tough at Travis. They sold off Aldgate Tower so they could do everything remotely.' Will grimaced. 'Means I'm managing a team of twenty co-signs from my bloody car!' He held up a hand in apology. 'Co-signs are drivers, because I forget what they're called legally. But yeah, they're our drivers.'

'And Mr Mortimer's one of them?'

'Right. Well, was.'

'What?'

'Jimmy was a solid A driver. Ranged A- to A+ over the course of a year. Hard to keep that kind of rating, but he got very flaky recently and plunged to a C.' He spat out the letter.

'Any idea why?'

'Got a few, yeah.' Will looked up at the dark sky. 'Jimmy hasn't been on in a week, but his last few weeks had been pretty slim pickings. Life's hard when you're a C.'

That didn't feel good. Going missing just before the murder of a member of the squad who framed you for an attempted bombing.

Could be he was involved, sure, but it could be he was another victim.

Fenchurch looked at Nelson and saw his fear reflected like a mirror, then he squared up to Will. 'You mind if we get a list of his recent fares?'

Will looked down from the sky, frowning. 'You're expecting me to say no, aren't you?'

Fenchurch laughed. 'Every time I've dealt with you lot, it's been the same story.'

'Well, it's a different world now. Travis are very co-operative these days. We even volunteer stuff. Two sexual assaults last week. Reported by us to you before the victims even had an inkling.'

'That's a very different operation than I'm used to.'

Will smiled. 'Thanks. It's been a tough road, but we're getting there.' He reached into his car and pulled out a laptop that looked like it weighed less than a phone. 'Went to the liberty of pulling up his fare list when you called.' He rested it on top of the car and stepped back. 'You guys can look at it if you want.'

Fenchurch didn't know whether it was because of his past experience with Travis or anything to do with Will himself, but he smelled a rat. Companies like that never ventured information. Never.

Could be the ultimate form of misdirection. Waste their time.

Still, don't look a gift horse in the mouth.

Nelson sidled up and started looking through it. 'Is this right?'

'I mean, it's every transaction over the last six months.' Will shrugged. 'I doubt this... whatever you're investigating... had anything to do with his employment. Jimmy had lots going on in his private life...'

The affair?

Or something else?

Fenchurch shifted over, trapping Will between him and Nelson. 'What kind of lots of going on?'

'Look, I'm not that close to him, but Jimmy... Brilliant guy, super smart. Like, if you mention anything, he's read it. In detail. Knows all about it. And not just bluffing, but like he really knows and has a deep understanding of all aspects of stuff.'

'But?'

Will looked over at Fenchurch. 'Jimmy's... what's the word... Quirky? Yes, quirky. And he has his demons from back in his service times. And I guess he's overqualified to be a cabbie, but who are we to complain? Same as me, same as lots of us. It's a good job, work your own hours, pay's good. Get a car at cheap rates.'

'But these demons? You mean that plunge in ratings?'

'Right. He didn't say what they were from exactly, or why they came on all of a sudden, but I think it's back in his army days.'

Nelson was looking over at them, eyebrow raised, but he didn't say anything, instead going back to the laptop.

Fenchurch focused on Will. 'We gather he might've suffered PTSD from his time in Iraq.'

Another shrug. 'Yeah.'

'How bad was it?'

'Not sure.'

'You're employing someone with PTSD to drive a car around London? And you're not sure how bad it is?'

'What about if he has a flashback in the Blackwall Tunnel?'

'As long as they're getting treatment for it, we're cool with it. We do a monthly check on all of our drivers. After that case where... Well, I think that was one of yours, wasn't it? The fella who—'

Fenchurch remembered it, but didn't want to. 'Right, so he—'

'Guv?' Nelson was pointing at the screen. 'Got a fare on the twenty-fifth of August. A one-star. Name of Dean Hatton.'

Fenchurch recognised it. 'And who's he?'

Nelson grinned. 'My old partner.'

18

CHLOE

Chloe sat outside the headmaster's office, trying to breathe. Or keep it under control at least. Part of the stress came from the knowledge that Shadwell Grammar was where she could've attended if she hadn't been kidnapped as a small child.

Wasn't it?

Hang on. No.

Her parents lived in Islington, though. Grandad lived near here, in the catchment area. She'd have been to a school up that way, maybe where her mother taught now.

God, her head was a mess.

The gun had been loaded.

They'd assumed it was another water pistol.

But it was a gun.

A real gun.

Loaded with bullets.

Wristbands had pointed it at Adam and was going to kill him if he didn't get the contents of the till.

And Chloe had smashed his arm with her baton.

Taken him down.

Christ.

What if he'd pulled the trigger?

What if the gun had gone off when it dropped?

She looked over at Adam, messing about on his phone on the other side of the headmaster's door. 'We should've called an Armed Response Unit.'

'Come on, kidder, we carried out a risk assessment.' Adam put his phone away. 'We dealt with that idiot this morning. He pulled a water pistol on you, so that felt much more likely.'

'It was *real*, Adam! It was loaded!'

He looked over. 'Okay, so here's the deal. Sometimes you've just got to go with your gut. This isn't New York or LA. It's London. People don't carry guns. And we had prior intel on that guy.'

She shut her eyes and slouched back in the chair. 'Still, it feels like we could've died. You could've died. He was pointing it right at you.'

'My cross to bear, kidder.'

'No!' Chloe jabbed a finger at him. 'If he'd shot you right in front of me, I would've seen it! My training officer getting his head blown off!'

'Safety was on.'

She frowned. 'What?'

'I clocked that. Even if it was live, the dickhead had the safety on, so he couldn't have fired.' He shrugged. 'But I get it. I've lost people in the line of duty. Good men, good women. Some arseholes too. It's why I do this job. Why I train rookies like you. A lot of the time, accidents happen because of accidents, fine. Nothing to be done. But when it's a mistake that comes from inexperience? Well, that can all be fixed by the right training.'

She felt her nostrils sting like she was going to cry. 'I can't believe you—'

'Ah, Adam, thanks for coming in.' A middle-aged bundle of energy powered up to them, tall enough to hug Adam when he was sitting down. Silvery hair cut into a short bob. Thick winter coat that doubled her size. 'Come on in.' She opened the door to the headmaster's office and entered like she owned the place. Still, she didn't sit behind the desk. 'Thank you, Adam, can I get you a cup of tea?'

'No, we're good, Karen. Thanks for—'

'What about you?' She was focusing on Chloe. 'My, you are pretty, aren't you?'

'I'm fine.'

'Don't let men speak for you, young lady. If you want a cup of tea, I can get one fetched for you.'

Chloe smiled, but it was the only defence she had. 'We're fine, thanks. Honestly.'

'Well. I've got one coming.' She pulled off a glove and tossed it onto the desk. 'Well. Anyway, Adam, I tried calling you but you didn't answer. Now why was that, mm?'

'We were responding to a call in the Minories and my phone was on silent.'

'I understand that, of course, and you came as soon as you heard and, well, thanks for coming, it's very much appreciated.' She tossed the other glove on the desk. 'Okay, well, as school governor, it's beholden to me to make a request that you seek out the headmaster.' She looked around the room like his ghost was lurking in the shadows.

'Okay.' Adam took out his notebook and motioned for Chloe to do the same. 'What's his name?'

'It's Brendan Holding. He's been here a good few years. Excellent head, the kind who still takes some classes for the A-level students too, which is very good of him as he's an excellent teacher and it keeps him grounded, you know, and we've had our issues here, of course we have, which school hasn't, but Brendan helped me tackle them all. Drugs, knife crime, even had a student turn up with a gun!'

Chloe looked at Adam with a raised eyebrow.

But he ignored her. 'Okay, Karen, let me take you through the immediate steps of a missing person report. Have you got his home address?'

'This isn't my first rodeo, Adam.' Karen pulled out a document and slid it across the table to him. 'Home address. Parents' address.

Home phone number. Mobile number. Three email addresses. A list of colleagues he's friendly with. A list of ex-colleagues he's still in touch with. Friends, close family.' She smiled like Adam was the teacher and she was the pet. 'Anything else you need? Because I have other items that might be of great use to you and I'd so love it if you found him very soon.'

'This is quite comprehensive, thank you.' And creepy. 'Do you have this for everyone at the school?'

'All part of the vetting process.' Karen tilted her head like she was really proud of herself. 'We don't want just anyone teaching our children, do we?'

'Very true.' Adam took the page and folded it in half. 'Okay, so the main thing we'd look for are any potential troubles he might've—'

'None.'

Adam paused. 'You're sure of that?'

'Absolutely.'

'Because gambling debts or secret affairs, for instance, can often be hidden.'

'I'd know. And why do you raise them, mm?'

'No reason, just standard procedure.' Adam was gritting his teeth. 'I'll get a warrant to obtain his bank details and we can see if there were any unusual withdrawals or deposits.'

'Very well, if that's what you must do,' Karen was frowning, 'but I'm pretty sure you won't find anything because Mr Holding is fairly well off and, as a single man, he hasn't had the same outgoings many of us had over the years.'

'How well off?'

'Oh, nothing extravagant, like minor royalty or a pop star, but Mr Holding has the resources to take a big holiday, which he did a few years ago and was gone for a month, which is nice for him but it was in the summer holidays and I had some pressing school matters to attend to with him.'

'But he didn't take any holidays during term time?'

'Well, that's another matter, isn't it, because there were a couple of years where our summer work ate into his own personal allowance so we let him go on a break during term time.'

Sounded to Chloe like that's exactly what he'd done.

Adam frowned. 'So why call us in?'

'Well, Mr Holding has to book leave, doesn't he, and it has to be approved by the school board, chaired by myself, and it's been days since I've heard from him, when he usually phones me first thing in the morning to reassure me that everything is tickety-boo in here.'

And there it was. Maybe there was more going on between them than she would admit. Or maybe she was just an overbearing type who wanted to control everything.

'Okay.' Adam put his notebook away. 'What myself and PC Fenchurch here will do is go and have a look for Mr Holding. I'm sure he'll be fine.'

'I can only hope.'

19

FENCHURCH

Hatton's address was spitting distance from the Lewisham Police Support Centre, or whatever it was currently branded.

Fenchurch struggled to keep up with all the changes these days, none of which seemed to make any improvements to how fast people worked. Especially Pratt.

The gleaming roof was the only bright object on the dull horizon, catching a thin shard of evening sun. Bert's body was resting in there, the post-mortem now finished, ice cold and waiting for justice that might never come.

Nelson smirked as he pressed the buzzer again. 'Cheer up, you old sod.'

Fenchurch scowled at him. 'What?'

'You look like a wet fortnight in Southend. What's up?'

Fenchurch shrugged. 'Nothing much.'

'So, probably everything?'

'About the size of it, yeah.' Fenchurch yawned into his fist. Christ, he was tired. He needed a cup of tea and some positive news. Neither was likely. Or advisable at quarter to eight at night. 'Anyone in?'

Nelson stepped back and looked up at the brick block of flats.

As old as it got in Lewisham, but probably one of the latest to get gentrified. 'No lights on in the top flat.'

'And this is definitely his address?'

'Right. It was four years ago.'

'Four *years*? Jon, he's probably moved!'

Nelson just took a toot of vape.

'Jon?' A woman was walking down the street, weighed down by two big bags of shopping. Trench coat on, the belt sagging and the lapels flapping in the breeze. Head tilted to the side. 'Jon Nelson?'

'Marianne.' Nelson shot over and held out his hands for the shopping. 'Here, let me.'

'Bugger off, you patronising sod.' She nudged past him then set down her bags with a deep sigh, her breath misting in the air. She had a hard look about her, one that screamed 'cop' to Fenchurch. 'Who's your mate, Jon?'

'Old boss of mine. DCI Simon Fenchurch.'

'Interesting. Heard a lot about you.' Marianne rattled out her keys and stuck them in the door, then focused on Fenchurch. 'And not all of it good.'

Fenchurch could only shrug. 'You Job, then?'

'Nope. I'm a CSI.'

'You work with Tammy Saunders?'

'Not for a while, but I know Tammy.' She twisted the key and nudged the door with her foot. 'What's up?'

Nelson was all smiles. 'Looking for Dean.'

'Just like my solicitors.'

'Oh?'

Marianne's breath plumed in the air, mixing with Nelson's vape mist. 'We're in the middle of a divorce, but it's taking forever. Been going on for two years? Three? Swear he's like the Scarlet Pimpernel. I just want to move on with my life, Jon. That's all. I just want a divorce.'

Nelson nodded. 'You got a last address for him?'

'No, I've got his current one. Just moved in two months ago.' She looked at Fenchurch, seemed to consider something, then back at Nelson. 'Used some contacts to find him, shall we say.

Finally managed to serve notice on him. Should be done and dusted in weeks now.'

'You want to give us this address?'

THE ADDRESS WAS WALKING distance and the cold evening was doing wonders for clearing Fenchurch's head. Almost made him feel alive rather than half dead. 'That sound like Hatton?'

As they walked, Nelson was tucking into some tortillas from the bag in his pocket. 'Dean always was a sneaky sod, guv. Wouldn't put it past him to do that to Marianne.'

'You ever work with her?'

'A bit. She's admin, really. Lab-based.'

'Explains why I've never met her.' But Fenchurch got that grotty feeling in his gut, like a dream where he'd been force-fed something from the bin. 'She didn't work—'

'No, guv. She didn't.'

'You didn't know what I was going to say, Jon.'

'I did. You wondered if Marianne worked the Mortimer case back in the day and if someone's bumping them all off. Is she at risk, blah blah blah. She didn't, so I'd say she's not at risk, even if someone is trying to bump them all off.'

'Right.' Fenchurch laughed, despite himself. 'The thought had crossed my mind.'

'I know how you work, guv.'

Fenchurch stepped aside to let an old geezer past, huffing and wheezing as he staggered down the street, three sheets to the wind. He braced himself against a car, the noxious booze fumes leaking off him, and set off the car alarm.

Fenchurch ploughed on, around the corner. And stopped dead.

The address they were headed for, Krueger House, was a ten-storey tower block, one of many climbing into the night sky around here. A Fire Service van was parked outside and one side of the fifth floor was a blackened mess, gutted by fire.

That rancid taste was back in Fenchurch's mouth again.

Hatton's address was up on that floor.

Had someone got to him?

Fenchurch marched as fast as his clicking knee would let him.

The van's lights switched on and the exhaust spat out a cloud.

Fenchurch stepped onto the street to wave it down.

Unusually for a firefighter, the arrogant prick got out with a smile. 'Can I help you, mate?'

'DCI Simon Fenchurch.' He held out his warrant card and pointed up at the building. 'Looking for the tenant of flat five slash three and I hope that's not why you're here.'

'Forlorn hope, mate.' He got out and seemed to keep coming out. The guy was almost seven foot. And big with it. He'd missed his calling as a basketball player. Probably wouldn't even need to jump at that height. And his voice was an octave too deep. 'Name's Andy Collins. What can I help you with?'

'We're looking for a Dean Hatton.'

'Well, you've found him.' Andy the giant looked up at the building. 'He went up in smoke last night.'

Fenchurch looked around at Nelson, seeing his fear and suspicion. 'He's dead?'

'Body found inside.'

'Who's your Met contact?'

'DI Rod Winter.'

One of Fenchurch's own officers. Great, this was going to make him look like a prize chump. 'He been out?'

'This morning, yeah, but it's open and shut. At least, according to him. Some CSIs were out, talking shit about conducting DNA analysis to help identify him, but DNA and fire don't exactly mix, do they? We could get it from the bone marrow, assuming it's not spoiled.'

'Would have to be an inferno to—'

'It was. Had a few call outs last night, so we didn't get to that one in time.'

Christ. 'Definitely male?'

'Oh yeah.' Andy looked up at the building again. 'We've

finished our initial assessment, so I'll share it with DI Winter when I get back.'

'If you wouldn't mind sharing it now?'

'Oh yeah?'

'Only, we needed to speak to the resident in relation to a murder enquiry.'

'Well, one death just became two.'

'Any chance you could give me a highlights package?'

Andy exhaled slowly. 'It's not exactly protocol.'

'I'm desperate, mate. I'll owe you big time.'

Andy laughed and it was like a truck was rumbling down the street. 'Having a favour from a DCI in my back pocket? That's worth more than a Bitcoin.' He ran a hand across his chin. 'Okay, so I think the daft sod left a charcoal barbecue burning.'

'Inside?'

'Outside, you berk!'

Fenchurch stared up at the building again, mouth hanging open. Sure enough, each flat had a small patio area, though most were stuffed with kids toys or clothes drying racks. 'He had a barbecue up there?'

'That's what I said, didn't I? Only been living here a couple of months, but he was charring his steaks and sausages every night. Neighbours weren't happy and the residents' association kept warning him. Only a matter of time before they kicked him out. Anyway, all kicked off last night. Big fire and we put it out. Went through the embers this morning and we found a body. Passed out drunk, presumably. Had a habit of it, according to the neighbours. Cooking his meat and drinking cider up there every night. What a life.' Andy shook his head. 'Luckily the cladding was replaced last year, otherwise he'd have taken the whole place up with him too.'

Fenchurch didn't want to think about it. One man's stupidity could've led to another Grenfell. Foresight or just plain luck had saved scores of lives and homes. 'Something to be thankful for.'

'Tell me about it.' Andy laughed, but his face was screwed up tight. 'Great way to kill yourself, mind. Get drunk, light the barbecue and never wake up.'

Fenchurch nodded along with it. 'And it's also a great way to murder someone and leave no doubt.'

'Well, that's not my remit. Better take that up with DI Winter. Looks like the fire caught about two in the morning.'

'Seems a bit late to be barbecuing?'

Andy shrugged. 'Don't know about you, but when I've had a skinful, the first thing I want is to eat. Carbs and meat. Stands to reason he'd start cooking when he was absolutely panel beaten.'

20

N elson was behind the wheel, weaving through the arches under the train line, but it felt like they were going round in circles.

A part of East London Fenchurch never visited, despite it being his patch and where he'd spent his early years. He'd zoned out as he checked his messages and hadn't noticed them crossing the river but he swore they were north of it. Stuck down in a valley, so there were no landmarks around he could see.

'What are you thinking, guv?'

Fenchurch watched the boxy houses and the flash cars. Probably had been here, just before they'd been built, when it was fields or old industrial land. 'Couple of possibilities, Jon. Door number one, Dean Hatton was in that flat and died exactly as that berk said. Door two, ditto but someone killed him. Door three, it ain't him in there.'

'I'm thinking it's behind door number one.'

'Care to say why?'

Nelson took the next left, heading down the back of the estate. The wooden fences were all low enough to show the empty gardens, just lawn and bare of trees. 'Well, Dean loved his meat.

Red meat. All he ate, pretty much.' He frowned. 'Actually, is bacon red meat?'

'I think so, yeah.'

'Well, he'd have two bacon sarnies for breakfast from this builders' caff just off the Old Kent Road. Lunch was always a steak sandwich from a place on the Minories. And he was a master barbecuer. Went to a butcher in Crouch End, specialist in certain cuts of meat. No veg, ever. Saw him take slices of cucumber out of a sandwich once. Moaned at the guy behind the till the next day for putting them in.'

'So he was heading for bowel cancer?'

'Probably was, yeah. And he'd barbecue every night. Even on Christmas Day.'

'So you buy it?'

Nelson shrugged. 'I mean, yeah.' He took another turning, heading into an older part of London, but still nowhere Fenchurch recognised. 'But it doesn't mean I'm a hundred percent on it. Just saying it's plausible.'

Fenchurch could press him, but he wouldn't get too far. They needed facts, not conjecture. 'So, where next?'

'Just up here.' Nelson pulled up to a busy roundabout coming out of nowhere. A dual carriageway shot in both directions, but Nelson continued over.

Fenchurch knew where they were now – Dagenham, but he'd no idea how they'd got there. All that redevelopment work down by the river over the last few years had twisted his antenna. Pretty much the last part of London before you got to Essex and the boundaries were now as blurred as between the East End and the City.

Nelson pulled up. 'Here we are.'

They were outside a block of flats that would've been fancy in the Nineties but now looked tired.

'I'll lead here.' Fenchurch got out first and walked over to the Entrycom. Then realised he didn't know why they were here. 'Jon, you know which flat?'

He was smirking. 'Seven.'

Fenchurch hit the button and stepped back. 'Smartarse.'

The buzzer rasped out. 'Hello?' A woman's voice.

And Fenchurch didn't know if she'd heard his insult to Nelson. Schoolboy error. 'Looking for Tony Wyatt.'

'Yeah, me too. He's buggered off to Magaluf on a mate's stag weekend.' She tutted. 'I ask you, is Wednesday to Tuesday a weekend or is it just taking the piss?'

NELSON TURNED INTO A SIDE STREET, then trundled down until the small Sixties homes became bigger Eighties jobs, semi-detached becoming detached and with bigger gardens. 'Here we go.' He parked on a bend in the long straight road, with the views in either direction blocked off by houses, and got out.

Fenchurch followed him into the cold night, but Nelson was on a mission, charging up the front path. Fenchurch had to jog to catch up. Big mistake. His knee cracked like he'd crunched a gearbox, and he yelped.

Nelson stopped, frowning. 'You okay, guv?'

Fenchurch had to stretch out his leg, straightening it, until it popped. 'Christ!'

Nelson didn't seem to know what to do, so just stood there, grimacing. 'What happened?'

'Long story, Jon, but one too many chases down back alleys caught up with me.' Fenchurch got another pop, making him gasp, then he put some weight on it. 'Good to go.'

Nelson shook his head. 'Not so sure about that.' He continued on down the path and knocked on the door.

A big house, two storeys, but set in darkness. Mature garden, but the trees had been pruned to within an inch of their lives. Would take some doing to grow back. Some music played, that odd mix of tinny and bassy that usually meant a radio.

Fenchurch joined Nelson on the top step, a pair of mossy slabs that needed a good pressure washing. He got that rancid taste in his mouth again. 'Let me get this straight, Jon. We've got Bert Matthews and Dean Hatton dead. Now Detective Superintendent Richard O'Keefe, your current boss who was SIO on the original case, isn't answering the door? Tell me that doesn't feel wrong to you?'

'Right, yeah.' Nelson got out his phone and put it to his ear. He looked through the living room window, then stabbed his phone screen again, but pinched his lips together. 'Should be here, guv. He's on annual leave this week.'

'So, he's in the Seychelles or Great Yarmouth. Jon, you had me worried there.'

'No, he said he was staying here all week, working on his vintage cars.'

Fenchurch swallowed. That taste was back again.

The only thing he could focus on was the sound of Steely Dan, twisted by the radio. *Rikki Don't Lose That Number.* One of his old man's favourite tunes. Sounded like it was coming from the garage, so he stepped over to it. Yeah, it got louder. He put his ear to the door, one of those metal ones with a twist handle. Definitely playing in there.

The double garage was wide enough for two cars and deep enough for four. Light shone from below the door.

Nelson walked over and twisted the handle. Something clunked. He slid it up and over.

The music was blaring out now. A strip light hung above two old cars, a navy Mustang and a boxy Volvo that was more wood than metal. An oily smell, mixed with something darker.

Fenchurch stepped into the garage and turned the radio down to a level that wouldn't damage his eardrums. 'Hello?'

Nothing, just his voice and Steely Dan echoing around.

A row of shelves lurked in the darkness at the back. Something wobbled in his vision and he couldn't make it out. He walked between the cars. Another two were parked behind, a Seventies James Bond Aston Martin and a pink Daimler.

A stool lay in a dried pool of motor oil.

Above it, a man hung from the ceiling, slack and dead. A clear bag hung over his head, zip tied at the neck. Something was written in black marker:

I AM A DICKHEAD

O'Keefe had killed himself.

21

CHLOE

B rendan Holding might've worked in Shadwell, one of
London's most deprived areas, but he lived up in leafy
Islington, not far from where Chloe's parents lived.

Had lived.

Where she'd lived with them, briefly.

Where her mother lived alone now.

Somehow, Holding owned a house rather than a flat. Not a big
one, but it had a garden. This is what Karen Armitage meant
about having resources, then.

'On you go, kidder.' Adam stayed back, thumbs tucked into his
belt.

'Okay.' Chloe walked up and pressed the bell. Got a weird
chime for her trouble. And she was so over that word.

Kidder.

It'd gone from being annoying to 'throttle the bastard', but
now right out to 'just meh'.

She hoped it didn't stick as a nickname. As it was, she got more
than enough stick for being the boss's boss's kid. Not that any of
them reported to him, but that didn't stop it. Nepotism was still
rife in the Met, yada yada yada. Heard it all, so many times. And if

Dad had actually been protecting her, she wouldn't get stuck with Adam Burridge, would she?

She tried the bell again, but still no response, so she turned back to Adam. 'Think it's empty.'

'Think isn't good enough.' Adam set off down the street and charged up the next-door neighbour's small front garden, knocking on the door. Barely four metres away, but she had to traipse all the way back to the street and up the path.

This door opened, though. A big man stood there, stubble and shaved head. Maroon T-shirt showing the evolution from ape to man then to drummer. 'Can I help?' Slight Scottish accent.

'Looking for Mr Holding.' Adam thumbed to the side. 'You know him?'

'Sure do, aye.' He coughed, then again. 'Sorry, got something stuck in my throat. Aye, Brendan's a pal of mine.'

'Seen him recently?'

The big guy frowned. 'Not since Thursday or Friday.'

Adam nodded, but Chloe caught a twitch of confusion in there. 'Any chance you've got a key? Or know someone who does?'

'Why, what's happened?'

'Just had a missing person's report, that's all.'

'For Brendo? Shite.' He frowned. 'Just a sec.' He stepped back inside, then came out. His big hairy feet were bare. 'Got a key for watering his plants when he's away.'

Adam kept pace with him, but Chloe had to follow. 'He go away a lot?'

'A fair bit over the summer. Went to Cornwall in December.'

Chloe felt that jolt in her side. When she was there with her mother and infant brother. When her mother slipped off to see the man she was sleeping with. Sneaking off, denying it all.

What had started that whole mess.

Adam stood to the side, peering through a window. 'What's your name, sir?'

'Jamie.' He put the key in the lock and opened it. 'Et voila!' He stepped aside.

'Please wait here, sir.' Adam smiled, then entered the property.

Chloe tried the smile, but Jamie wasn't looking at her. Just standing there, hands in pockets. Charming.

The lights came on automatically, which made Adam jump. 'That's spooky.'

Jamie laughed. 'It's Alexa, not a ghost.'

Adam swung around and grinned. 'Still be saying that when a hand reaches out for you?'

'Yeah, yeah.' Chloe looked into a living room. Two leather sofas and a big TV on the wall. A stereo even bigger than her dad's, two giant speakers and a tall stack of mismatched silver and black boxes. Racks of CDs on the walls like it was the nineties. Some vinyl records stacked against the wall. A PlayStation and an Xbox.

But no sign of Brendan Holding.

A floorboard creaked over her head.

Chloe went out into the hall and peered up.

Adam was looking down over the banister. 'Bedroom, bathroom and an office, all empty. How you doing?'

'God, you're fast.'

'I AM LOOKING for a full-grown man and not a thumb drive.'

'Well, the full-grown man isn't in the lounge.' Chloe entered the kitchen with a lump in her throat, expecting another dead body. Shit, where did *that* come from?

But there wasn't even an alive body in there. Big table, lots of appliances. Blokey ones, like coffee machines, bean grinders, blenders.

Back in the hall and Adam was peering into a downstairs bathroom. 'Bloody TARDIS in there. Could have a party just in the dump station.'

'Can you call it a toilet?' Chloe peered over his shoulder and saw his point. The bathroom seemed bigger than the rest of the house. Toilet, bidet, shower unit and bath. Crazy.

Still, it was empty.

Adam let out a sigh. 'Well, kidder, we've run out of road here.'

'That's it?'

'What did you expect? You and me on an all-expenses-paid trip to his home town to speak to his relatives? Sadly, people go missing all the time, for all sorts of reasons. We need to prove it's suspicious before we have to do anything about it.'

Have to.

That blasé attitude didn't feel right to Chloe. She'd joined the police to help people, not to run away after the first obstacle. A man going missing was suspicious.

Right?

Still, Adam was her training officer. Maybe she should listen to what he had to say. Maybe once she'd seen a few of these cases, she'd appreciate his version of reality.

'We'll punt it over to your dad's detectives to follow up, then we're on to the next call.' Adam walked back outside to speak to Jamie the neighbour.

Chloe took one last look at the place. Must be worth a fortune. She'd never be able to afford it, even with a police mortgage. As it was, she'd need a massive inheritance just to get a bedsit. She joined them outside.

Adam handed over a business card. 'If you see or hear from him, please call me.'

Jamie inspected it. 'Sure.'

Adam walked off down the lane.

Chloe wasn't prepared to end it just yet, staying in Jamie's orbit. 'Did he ever mention anyone who wanted to harm him? Any enemies?'

Jamie looked up at her, then away. Not one for eye contact. 'No, Brendo's sound. Never any of that nonsense.'

'You're close, right?'

'Few beers every so often, aye. Know the type, right? Lover not a fighter.' Jamie laughed.

'Anything in that?'

Jamie frowned. 'Thing is, though, he told me he was seeing a married woman for a bit. She broke it off and came clean to her husband. Ask me, he was struggling with the guilt, maybe. Don't know.' He laughed again. 'Maybe her hubby caught up with him. He was a copper, I think.'

'Maybe.' Chloe gave him a warm smile. 'Okay, thanks for your time, sir.' She left him to lock up and scooted off down the path, losing her smile by the time she got in the car.

'Get anything, kidder?'

'Not sure.' Chloe slammed the door and tugged on her seatbelt.

Adam hared down the street, hitting forty by the junction, which he sailed through.

Chloe had to resist the acceleration. 'What's up?'

'Just got a call about a guy pissing down an alley.'

'So why the hurry?'

'Because he was also finger painting a wall with his own shit.'

'Disgusting.' Chloe was almost sick in the car.

Never mind seeing a dead body, the alive ones did worse things.

She sat back and folded her arms, watching north London slip into east, the houses getting grittier as they skirted around the City.

And she started to wonder.

She got out her phone and checked the display. A text from her mother, looked long and rambling, but she tapped it and started to call her.

'Chloe, thanks for calling me back. I know I shouldn't have—'

'Mummy! Biscuit!'

Chloe's heart melted at the sound of her kid brother. 'Mum, it's...' She took a deep breath. 'Yes or no, the man you had the affair with, was he Brendan Holding?'

'I am not going to dignify that with a response. You don't get to know every aspect of my life. What business is it of yours?'

'I'm working, right? A missing persons case. A headmaster from Shadwell.'

Mum gasped. 'Chloe...'

'This is important. Was it Brendan Holding, just tell me. Yes or no.'

'Fine, yes. Are you happy?'

'No, no I'm not.' Something was gnawing away at Chloe's stomach. 'I'm actually a little scared.'

22

FENCHURCH

'Cheers.' Fenchurch took the cup of tea from Nelson and wrapped his fingers around it. Might be March, but it still felt like the middle of winter. Even had snow in Essex a couple of weeks ago. He sipped it and felt the warmth trickle down into his stomach. 'Ah, that's the ticket.'

They were outside O'Keefe's garage and Fenchurch couldn't even look at it, let alone inside. The body still hanging from the rafters was only part of it. The CSIs' blaring arc lights were the other side, that blue light that cut deep.

A figure walked through the light, like a monster coming from the swamp, but tearing at its mask. 'Om pom tiddly om pom.' Dr Pratt removed it, letting his beard spring free, then dumped his face mask and goggles into the discard pile.

Just by the inner locus entry point that Fenchurch hadn't been through. And wouldn't. He'd seen enough dead bodies for one day.

And that face.

When someone put a bag over their head, tied it tight and drew their final breaths, the bag tended to stick to their face. O'Keefe's last visage was not only horrifying but cartoonish. The worst kind of creepy.

Fenchurch finished his scalding tea but couldn't see where to put the empty, so held on to it. 'William, how goes it?'

Pratt looked around, frowning at his cup. 'Got one for me?'

'I do, as it happens.' Nelson pulled out a paper tray with a cup in it. 'Latte, right?'

'The devil's milkshake.' Pratt was scowling, but he took it anyway.

Before Nelson could take it away, Fenchurch stabbed his tea cup into the holder. 'So, you get anything in there?'

'A suicide note.'

'Anything useful on it?'

'Had a glance. This isn't my first such rodeo, as you should be aware. Suicide notes are a common theme with police officers. Usually cryptic about those they've "wronged" but for the right reasons. His was along the lines of, "I am not a bad guy but it occurs to me that everyone thinks I am so I must have outlived my usefulness. You'll miss me when I am gone blah blah blah." I'm not sure you'll get anything out of it.'

'Still, I'll get someone to look it over.'

Pratt sipped his coffee then made a noise that sounded like 'mnyaw'. 'That's good stuff!' He wiped his beard clean with his sleeve. 'Well, the good news is that lividity matches the position he was found in, so the body wasn't moved after death, but that's about all I can glean at this juncture.'

'Any idea when he died?'

'Sunday afternoon if I was a betting man.' Pratt sucked some more coffee. 'Is there salted caramel in this?'

'A little drop of syrup, yeah.' Nelson sipped from his own cup. 'So, do you think it was suicide?'

'Seen similar cases, myself. I suspect he got himself up there on the stool. Tied it all together, put the bag on, zipped that then, when he was almost passed out, he kicked the stool out from underneath himself... It's a gruesome way to go.' Pratt tore the lid off his coffee and soaked in the aroma. 'And the derogatory remark about himself he'd written on the outside of the bag, well that would be the clincher for me.'

'I am a prick.' Nelson narrowed his eyes. 'It's critical we are *definite* he wasn't killed and that it's suicide, okay?'

'Well, I'll get him on the slab to investigate, which won't be until tomorrow.'

'First thing?'

Pratt groaned. 'As near as I can manage, yes.'

Fenchurch smiled at him. 'Cheers, William.'

Pratt took a big gulp of coffee and coated his moustache in it. 'Richard O'Keefe was a good officer. Worked with him a few times over the years. He'll be missed.'

'Sad loss.' DCI Owen walked over, sniffing hard. 'Where's my latte?'

Nelson turned away and walked off.

'I bloody paid for those!' Owen looked like he was going to tear Nelson apart with his bare hands. 'Come back here, you!'

Fenchurch blocked Owen charging off after him. 'Keep a lid on it, Chris. You're at a crime scene, yeah?'

'That twat's taken my lid!' Owen looked at him with righteous fury, then it softened and his shoulders settled back down. 'Right. Yeah, you're right.' He sucked in a deep breath. 'Managed to speak to DCS Garricks for you.'

Fenchurch avoided his gaze. 'Still won't answer the phone to me.'

'What did you do?'

'Nothing.'

'Come on, he won't do something like that without—'

'I think it was my old man. God knows what he did, but the name Fenchurch shuts doors in certain parts of the Met.'

'Your poor daughter.' Owen ran a hand through his hair. 'Heard she's walking the beat?'

'Against my wishes and better judgment.'

'Hard for a father to let go like that.' Owen clapped his arm. 'Anyway, Garricks told me that O'Keefe was signed off on long-term sick.'

Fenchurch frowned. 'Jon said he was on holiday.'

'That's the cover they agreed. Things got a bit much for him, apparently.'

Fenchurch didn't have much sympathy with that. After all he'd been through, he never missed a shift. Eleven years and not a single one. And murder squad, not an easy beat like Middle Market Drugs. Most of the time they were staring at spreadsheets. More like chartered accountants than police officers.

A car door slammed and footsteps clicked towards them. 'Gentlemen, I heard there was coffee?' Loftus.

'Got to get in fast, haven't you!' Owen rolled his eyes. 'Anyway, I was going to ask Simon here for a *precis* of his case so far.'

Fenchurch shifted his gaze between them, but decided that opening his mouth and letting his belly rumble was the best course of action. 'Well, we've got three members of that old team dead.' He held out his thumb and tilted his head back. 'O'Keefe hung himself.' Forefinger. 'Early hours of this morning, Hatton died in a house fire of his own making.' Middle finger. 'And Bert Matthews was drowned and dumped at the monument.'

'That's not subtle.' Owen stared up at the sky. 'The first two, yeah we'd chalk them up to natural events. Under-pressure super who's off on long-term sick takes his life. A troubled DC either burned himself to death or got so drunk it was an accident. But why not just leave Bert in his home? Would take days to find him, like with O'Keefe here. And an old man like that, stands to reason he could've gone into the bath after a skinful and ended up unable to get out.'

Fenchurch could follow the logic, but only up to a point. 'Trouble is that Bert was moved.'

'Maybe he's getting confident.' Loftus frowned, then looked around like he was going to get into trouble. 'Sorry, I should say "they", shouldn't I?'

'Say what you like, I think it's this Mortimer boy.' Owen rubbed his hands together. 'People do stuff like that to send a message.'

Fenchurch frowned. 'Go on?'

'Well, if Matthews was moved, then it's obvious our killer has some kind of an agenda. If it's Mortimer, then it's a fair shout to suggest that would be getting back at the people who ruined his life. Now, he's got two out of the way in O'Keefe and Hatton, so he gets confident, meaning he's a bit more brazen with Bert. Maybe he needs to get stuff done sooner rather than later... Or maybe he wants us messing about trying to solve a strange murder?'

Loftus was following along, but didn't seem to have much to add to it. 'That's possibly how he sees it, certainly. Sorry, how they see it.' He nodded, definitively. 'And I think it's Mortimer.'

Fenchurch frowned. 'Well, I think we definitely need to speak to him.'

Loftus's nodding got more vigorous. 'Agreed.'

'So, we're all on the same page.' Fenchurch looked around them, all in agreement. He needed to pounce now. 'In that case, I need you to—'

'Guv!' Reed was walking towards them, clutching a laptop. 'We got the CCTV and we've identified there were two men dropping Bert off.'

'Good work, Kay. You get a good look at them?'

'Well, we've got one in shadows, but this one...' She opened the laptop. 'It's Tony Wyatt.'

Fenchurch groaned. The other cop from the team, the one they hadn't tracked down. 'He was in Magaluf?'

'Right. Well, that's the thing. He's clearly not. Or certainly he wasn't this morning at quarter to one.'

'Dig into it. We need to find him. If he's flown there today, I want to know.'

'Guv.'

'Who's the other guy?' Fenchurch tried to zoom the photo in, but he just got a box of distorted pixels in the loose shape of a man. Hood up, shades on. Possibly even masked, unlike Tony Wyatt. He looked at Loftus. 'What I was going to say, well, it's become a lot clearer now. We need a public call for information regarding James Mortimer.'

'Already arranged it, Simon. This is him with Tony Wyatt, isn't it?'

'I don't know, sir, but it's growing more and more likely. I just don't see the connection between them. Wyatt's a cop. Mortimer was a suspect. A defendant who got off.'

Loftus tilted his head to the side, like he spotted the insubordination in amongst the deference. 'The main reason I'm here, Simon, is a uniform super has tapped me on the shoulder, metaphorically, and he needs to speak with you. Immediately.'

23

Not for the first time that day, Fenchurch felt like he was waiting outside the headmaster's office.

It'd been a while since he'd visited this station, let alone the super's office. At least they'd upgraded the coffee machine so he could drink what passed for a real cup of tea. Even tasted like real milk, rather than something grown in a petri dish.

The news played on a TV in the hallway. Another innovation. Felt like he was in a newsroom on a film as the world ended.

Still, the place stank like an open sewer. Some things never changed. Would have to demolish the place and start over again.

Much like Fenchurch's career. Still no idea why he was here. Just Loftus's opaque instruction. Maybe covert activity to pay back some of the colossal debt Loftus owed him.

Or maybe it was his way of getting rid of an officer he didn't trust.

The TV switched to a live press conference from a room Fenchurch knew all too well. Loftus himself, appealing for information on James Mortimer. Fenchurch was glad it was on mute. Last thing he needed was to hear him speaking.

He should be there, leading it. Not his super. Everyone in the force would notice that, or at least the ones who cared about office politics and the runners and riders.

It cut back to the studio, where a newsreader was joined by someone Fenchurch vaguely recognised. The caption filled in the detail – Rob Lezard.

Ex-Met DCI and expert

They'd missed out 'arsehole'.

The mystery man struck again, though. Credit to him – he was an expert at getting himself front and centre of the story.

Footsteps padded towards him down the corridor, soft and careful.

Abi stopped dead, staring at him, mouth hanging open, eyebrows raised. 'Simon?'

'Abi.' Fenchurch hid behind his tea cup, taking a scalding sip. 'The coffee machine is decent.'

'I don't give a shit about coffee machines.' She dumped her bag on the table in front of him. 'I've been called into the police station in the dead of night and had to leave our son with Quentin.'

Fenchurch felt like he'd been punched in the stomach. 'Quentin?'

'He's good with him.'

'I'm not sure he's good for Al, though.'

Abi stared hard at him. 'Why am I here, Simon?'

'Who called you?'

'You know, don't you? This is something you've done.' She tried the door, but got the same response as him. Locked. 'Where is he?'

'Where is who?'

'Evening, Simon.' The long drawn out Brummie vowels of Jason Bell came from behind him.

Fenchurch shut his eyes. What the hell was he doing here?

No.

No, no, no.

They hadn't.

Had they?

Fenchurch wanted to ignore him, but instead he swung around and gave a smile. Hard to keep it up for long.

Bell resembled a puddle now. A puddle of fat someone had sculpted into human shape and covered in skin and some hair, then stuffed into a police uniform with a crown on the epaulets. He was the bloody superintendent. How? Fenchurch didn't understand the senior brass most days, but this?

'Thanks for coming in. Both of you.' Bell grinned at Abi, but his first two chins spread flat. 'And it's been a while, Mrs Fenchurch.'

'I'm going by my maiden name again.'

'Oh.' Bell frowned at Fenchurch. 'Let's do this in my office.' He pulled out a key and opened the door to the superintendent's room. 'Got promoted back in January. Running Islington and most of North London. Tough at the top, eh?' He laughed.

Fenchurch let Abi go first. He finished most of his tea, but left a small amount in the bottom and hid the cup behind the rubber plant standing guard in the doorway. 'So, Jason, what's going on?'

'Have a seat.' Bell gestured at the one next to Abi.

Fenchurch took his time deciding that he had no choice but to play ball, so he sat. And had to swallow his disgust – Bell smelled worse than the corridor. Stale sweat, all acidic and sharp.

'Right.' Bell shifted his gaze between them, taking his time. 'I'm doing this off the books because, well, you're friends.'

If they were Bell's idea of friends, Fenchurch didn't want to go to one of his dinner parties. 'Appreciate it.'

'Okay, so you're here because two of, well, not my officers, but two of our uniformed colleagues from Leman Street responded to a missing persons report from a school governor at Shadwell Grammar. As part of that, they visited an address on my patch. The person in question wasn't at his home, but their investigation led them to connect this individual to you two.'

Fenchurch sat back, stuffing his hands in his pockets. 'What's this got to do with me?'

But Abi was nodding. 'Are you talking about Brendan Holding?'

'That's right.' Bell snorted. 'Now, I gather you've been romantically involved with—'

'Jason, you can't just bring her in here and ask that question.'

Bell wasn't looking at Fenchurch. 'Abi, I'm doing this off the books because I want to make sure this isn't a misunderstanding. Okay? I gather you were romantically involved with Mr Holding?'

'A long time ago.'

'In December?'

Fenchurch wanted to smash his face in. Bang it off the table. Keep banging until it was a bloodied bowl of jelly. But he stuffed his hands deeper into his pockets, gripping his thighs tight.

Abi looked like she wanted to stab him. Instead, she huffed out a sigh. 'Well.' She shook her head, glanced at Fenchurch, then let out another deep breath. 'I'm glad our daughter's doing things by the book.'

'Indeed. I mean, she could've covered it up. Right?'

'Covered what up?'

'Well, the two pertinent facts. First, that Mr Holding is missing. Second, that you had an affair with him in December.'

'Listen to me.' Abi's voice was ice cold. 'I haven't had anything to do with him since the fourteenth of December. I made a huge mistake, but I broke off clean.'

'Okay.' Bell licked his lips. 'But I need a bit more than your word for it.'

'I don't know what you want me to say. It wasn't an *affair*, just one night. I was in Cornwall visiting my parents with both of my children. Chloe was just finishing her time at Hendon Police College, so she deserved a break. Simon was going to join us, but...'

Fenchurch held Bell's gaze. 'I caught a case.'

'Oh, yes, I remember. My actions helped you solve it, right?'

'Wouldn't go that far, but I appreciate what you did for us.' Fenchurch couldn't remember him even being involved.

Bell tilted his head to the side, focusing on Abi. 'Go on?'

'Well, while we were there, I met Brendan for a drink. He happened to be staying at a nearby hotel.'

'Happened to?'

'I didn't ask him to be there.'

'But you'd mentioned it, right?'

Abi shrugged. 'I'd seen him at a conference a few weeks earlier. We exchanged a few texts. That was it.'

'Okay.'

'I feel guilty about it. I got Chloe and my parents to babysit for our son, while... Well, we went on a date. One drink led to sharing a bottle. And... Look, we haven't seen each other since.'

'But you did stay in touch?'

'Like I say, I broke it off, but Brendan wasn't so keen.'

'Very eager, wasn't he?'

Abi nodded. 'I suppose you've got his phone records?'

'He made a few phone calls and some texts.'

'Jason, I love Simon. That's it. We split up over this and it's all my fault. The bottom line is I just want to get back with him.'

Jason Bell was the last person Fenchurch would've chosen as a marriage counsellor, but he'd got deeper into Abi's feelings in five minutes than umpteen sessions with that muppet Waugh had. Maybe having access to someone's phone records did the trick.

'But you were still in touch with him?'

Abi rolled her eyes. 'It's called letting someone down gently. You might've heard of it?'

'I prefer just to be straight with people. Pays off in the long run.' Bell waved around his spacious office. 'Stops you getting brought in to places like this for lying.'

'*Jason.*' Fenchurch waited until he got full eye contact. 'What do you want to know?'

'Texts are one thing, Simon, as you well know.' Bell cradled a tablet in his podgy hands. 'But phone calls, well, we don't get what was said on that call, we only get the metadata. Things like the numbers involved, the duration and when it started. Such as 18.23 on Friday night.'

Abi stared up at the ceiling. 'I can't give you it word for word, but Brendan called me to ask what I was up to later that night.'

Bell glanced at his tablet, grinned, then back at her. 'Go on?'

'Asking if I wanted to meet up with him after he'd seen a friend for a drink.'

'What did you say?'

'That it was over. That it had been over since December. I broke it off with Brendan for a reason. I've been struggling with the extreme guilt, ever since what happened... happened.'

Bell looked at Fenchurch, but his words weren't directed at him. 'Abi, do you know who that friend is?'

'I don't.'

'And do you, Simon?'

Fenchurch shrugged. 'I met Mr Holding at the Prospect of Whitby.'

Abi gasped.

'Lovely little pub, isn't it?' Bell ran his tongue over his lips. 'I'm going to ask you outright, Simon, so I expect the truth. Did you have anything to do with Brendan Holden's disappearance?'

Fenchurch leaned forward, rubbing his hands together. 'You sure you want the truth, Jason?'

'Absolutely sure.'

'Okay. Well. Friday afternoon, I got a call from him.' Fenchurch flicked his hand towards the tablet. 'Suspect you've got that on your gizmo there. He asked if I fancied a drink. Friday was my custody so Chloe looked after Al, our son, while I was out.' He glanced at Abi, but she wasn't looking at him. 'Then I drove there and had a drink. But just one.'

Bell tapped the tablet. 'Your daughter texted her grandfather, to the effect that she was sick of both of you using her as a free babysitter. It was your custody and she was on her off shift. Wanted to see friends.'

That hurt Fenchurch as much as anything. Seeing her anger at them exposed like that. 'I should've seen Holding at another time, but that guy was hard to pin down. Said it was Friday or nothing. And I wanted to be the big man, to hear what had been going on from his mouth. How long, whether he saw a future. All of that.' He folded his arms. 'But he wouldn't say anything. Wasn't denying it, but he wasn't being forthright.'

'So, you bundled him into the back of a van?'

Fenchurch laughed. 'No, Jason, I left him to it. I'd barely touched my drink.'

'And I'm supposed to believe that?'

'Can't say anything other than the truth.' Fenchurch shrugged. 'There's CCTV near that pub. Sure you can get it on your machine there.'

'I'll look into it. But someone like you, Simon, you'll know the CCTV black spots, won't you? Know where to go to avoid detection?'

The walls closed in on Fenchurch.

No way should this be off the record.

The friend routine might work with Abi, but not with Fenchurch.

And both interviews would be recorded, those rooms would each have three different hidden cameras and one not so hidden that they could make a show of unplugging.

Sod it, Fenchurch knew he was being recorded. Knew this was make or break.

Just keep to the truth. The one he wants to hear.

'Jason, I've no idea what's happened to him. Where he went after the pub. I'm sorry. I just went home. I was angry, but I've calmed down now.'

Bell grimaced. 'Thing is, you just got a phone call from him, out of the blue.'

'And?'

'You expect me to believe that?'

Fenchurch shrugged. 'It happened.'

'No messages before? No chance meeting?'

'We had a few texts.'

'WhatsApp?'

'Right.'

Bell grimaced. 'Which is encrypted, so we can't get hold of the messages unless we have his phone or yours.' He held out his hand. 'Sorry, Simon, but I need to take your phone from you.'

24

F enchurch walked along the corridors through Leman Street, phone to his head. Just ringing.

'This is Abi, I'm a bit tied up just now so please leave a message after the beep. Thanks!'

Fenchurch didn't want to think who'd been tying her up.

Beep.

'Hi, Abi, it's Simon. I didn't get a chance to speak when you dashed off after—' He clocked that twat of a uniformed sergeant walking towards him, so he turned away. 'Look, just give me a call. Thanks.' He entered his office.

Chloe was sitting behind his desk, eating the rest of her burrito. She looked up with bulging eyes. 'Dad.'

Fenchurch patted her shoulder. 'Scoot.'

She got up, but spilled a few grains of rice on the floor.

'Just because you're the boss's daughter, doesn't mean it's okay to avoid the big bad cops in the canteen downstairs.'

'Right.' She folded over the top of the foil, but stayed standing. 'Didn't expect to see you, that's all.'

'No, I can imagine.' Fenchurch rested his phone on the desk, face up in case Abi called back. It lit up with another text from Bell, so he flipped it over. 'Look, some people would be pissed off at their daughters for dropping them in the shit. Telling Burridge about... Well, what's gone on between you and your mother.' He smiled at her. 'You did the right thing.'

Her eyebrows pushed up close to her hairline. 'Sure about that?'

'Of course. I mean, if it was anyone else, I'd knock their block off, but seeing as it's you...'

That got a pout. 'Dad, that's not funny.'

'I know, which is why I said it.' Fenchurch looked out of the window at the pitch darkness outside. 'Chloe, I'm not a great man, but I try to do the right thing. Constantly. It's what you agree when you join up to the police. Well, it's what most people do. Some bad eggs out there, but most cops tell the truth. And you're probed for that truth, all the time. You're watched, monitored, assessed. The job is all about you being able to stand up in court and tell the truth as you saw it.' He looked around at her, felt his eyes watering. 'But the truth is... The truth I've found so hard to face is that I'm broken by what your mother did.'

She nodded, but the frown came back for more. 'You mean you're angry at me for telling you about it?'

He shook his head. 'God, no. Chloe, you told me the truth. Your mother lied.'

'Well, you should've been speaking to Mum about that, not him.'

'Right. True. And I shouldn't have asked you to babysit your brother. That was wrong of me.'

She was blushing. 'You were wrong.'

'But I'll always tell you the truth, okay?'

She held his gaze until he had to look away. Not many people could do that. 'So what did happen on Friday?'

'Nothing, really. I met Holding and we had a chat. I got the reassurances I needed. I took that into the couple counselling session I had with your mother this morning.' Fenchurch frowned, feeling like it was a lot longer ago than mere hours. It must be days, right? 'And I left Holding on good terms. No anger. No shouting. No cross words. Just two blokes talking. He only saw Abi once.'

'Which is what Mum said.'

'Right. Exactly. Now, either they've got their stories straight, or they're both telling the truth. I'm going to choose to side with them telling me the truth.'

She finished chewing some more, dainty and covering her mouth just like her mother, not shoving the thing down her throat as quickly as Fenchurch would himself. 'And what are you going to do with that knowledge?'

Hardest question Fenchurch had faced in years. 'I think I want to make things right.'

'You think?'

'Okay, so I'm going to make things right. Al deserves to have both of his parents.'

She stared down at her feet. 'Unlike me.'

'Chloe, you deserved it too.'

'I know, it's just...'

'I would literally give anything to have that time with you. In my head, I've got this big bracketed lump of eleven years where I didn't know what the hell had happened to you. Where the hell you were. Who took you. All I could do was look for you. And... I messed up my relationship with your mother. Drove her away. She was grieving and I wasn't there for her. I hadn't grieved myself; I was still stuck in the anger phase. Stuck in neutral. Coasting down a hill.'

'But you found me.'

'I did, but... But I might not have. So many chance events happened to put me on that path. I'd been looking everywhere and I hadn't found you. We thought you were dead. We found your grave.'

She took another bite and chewed it so slowly. Fenchurch would give anything to be able to know what was going on inside her head, to hear her thoughts. Her reaction. 'Thing is, the fact you kept looking is part of the reason why I chose to live with you rather than Mum.' She swallowed. 'I mean, she shagged someone else, so that's most of it, but you didn't give up on me, Dad.'

He had that fluttering tightness in his chest, spreading down to his stomach. 'You could live on your own, you know?'

'I know. And I could joke about how expensive it is in London, but the truth is, Dad, those eleven years are a big gap for me too. And I can't remember much of what happened before it. They took those memories from me. I've got flickers and flashes, but I can barely remember it. All I get from you and Mum is this warm feeling, like a shadow of a memory, but it's just not there mentally. It's missing. But I want to be close to you. To you both, really. To know my parents.'

Fenchurch got up and walked over to her, wrapping her in a hug. It wasn't like holding a twenty-year-old graduate, but a tearful eight-year-old. And for an instant, it felt like they hadn't gone through all the trauma, that his daughter was safe in his arms.

She nudged him free, but didn't say anything. She sat and ate her burrito. 'Dad, I'll be honest with you. I don't know what to think about you meeting Holding. If you're telling me the truth.'

'Trust has to be earned.' Fenchurch leaned back against his desk, arms folded. 'Listen, this case, I'm not sure you should be investigating it.'

She looked up at him. 'It's a missing persons, Dad, they give that to uniform.'

'I know, but because it involves me and—'

'I'm off it. Soon as I said anything.' She took an angry bite of her burrito, shaking her head as she chewed. 'Thing is, I know I did the right thing, but I'd rather have stayed on the case. I felt like we could've found him. Still feel that.'

'It's good to learn to assess when you're chasing a lost cause.'

'I get that, but it's also like we just give up too early? Looking around someone's house doesn't feel exhaustive, you know?'

'I know, but people go missing all the time. We'd need a force three times the size to do it justice. Sometimes people just don't want to be found.'

'You think Brendan Holding ran off?'

'I've no idea. I'd met the guy once before on a case. Hard to get a read on someone from such a small interaction. But he seems a solid type, not the kind who'd run.'

'So someone's taken him?'

Fenchurch winced. 'I've no idea. Maybe.'

'Well, I feel like I've been side-lined from my first big case because my mother is an adulteress and my father is a cowboy who just maybe took matters into his own hands.'

And there it was. Forget the Fenchurch stubbornness, that kind of bluntness was in the genes.

And she was probably right. She was stuck in the middle of their nonsense, their bullshit. One thing parents should be able to do is insulate their kids from that.

'This better not mess with my career, Dad. I already carry a big enough target as it is.'

'I'm sorry you have to bear that cross, but I had the same from your grandfather and believe me, it was harder back then. But you learn a lot from adversity, makes you tougher and stronger. And you're already tougher and stronger than most, so I've got faith in you.'

'Thanks.' She finished chewing. 'I don't know if I should believe you, though.'

'After all you've been through, that's smart.'

'Is it?'

'Trust but verify is a good motto.'

'Well, right now Adam is running around collecting video from the pub you were in, from outside it and from near Holding's house.' She glared at him. 'Dad, you better be telling me the truth here.'

'I'm not a killer, Chloe.'

She looked him right in the eye. 'Who said anything about you killing him?'

25

Abi was on the sofa, cradling their son, who was so full of impish mischief that he was clearly hours away from sleep. She lifted him up and held him high. 'Come on, tiger, let's get you to bed.' She held him for Fenchurch to kiss.

He leaned over and stroked his son's head, then pecked him. 'Good night, champ.'

'Night night, Daddy.' Eyes drooping, mouth hanging. Yeah, he was actually sleepy.

Abi slipped out into the hallway.

Leaving Fenchurch sitting on the armchair. His chair, the one he'd fallen asleep in a few times. But this already felt like somebody else's home. He'd moved out, back to the bachelor pad he'd bought when they divorced and had almost reverted back to old ways. Taking his hi-fi and CDs. And their daughter. Chloe stopped him sinking bottles of wine every night. Got him on that pain-in-the-arse diet that was actually paying dividends, got him back in the gym, strengthening that knee.

Now he thought about it, the bastard thing throbbed. He tried rubbing it, tried getting it to click, but nothing stopped it. Yeah, he wasn't in the clear on that matter.

A floorboard creaked in the hall. Abi stood in the doorway. She didn't seem to want to join him in the living room. Like he wasn't welcome in their home anymore, like he'd been the one in the wrong. 'You should've handed it over.'

'My phone?'

'Bell asked you for it and you just walked out of there.'

'I don't want Jason Bell going through my private stuff.'

'Why, what are you hiding?'

'Nothing.' But Fenchurch knew there was a warrant coming. Stopping Bell seizing it there and then was one thing, but he couldn't prevent that. Not that there was much to hide, just the thought of it being that slimy prick... 'There's personal stuff on there. Chats with other cops. Chats with you. Chats with Chloe.'

'Sounds like bollocks to me, Simon.'

'Look, you know WhatsApp's end-to-end encrypted, right?'

'Whatever that means.'

'It means whatever you've got on your phone in that app doesn't leave your phone unless someone gets hold of your mobile or the other person's phone. So it's something I can trust, something I can be brutally honest in. I have frank discussions with people on there. Dad, Chloe, Rod, Kay, Uzma. Chloe. Loads of people. It's betraying their trust as much as anything.'

'Sure it's not because it'll prove that you killed Brendan?'

'Abi, I'm telling the truth here.'

'So why not prove it?'

'Because my mobile won't prove anything. There are cops out now rounding up CCTV from near Holding's home and the pub. That'll back up my statements just as well.'

She shook her head. 'Well, I hope they'll get to the bottom of it.'

'Me too. I'm innocent.'

She looked at him long enough, then went over and sat back on the sofa. 'Right.'

'Listen, I'm sorry for being angry earlier. At the counselling. And after. And this evening with that pillock, Bell. I'm trying to rise above it, but it's bloody hard. But the fact you... had an affair, it stings. It really stings.'

'I'm so sorry, Simon. I shouldn't have done it.'

'No, but you did.' He swallowed down thick tears. 'How can we make this right?'

'Can we?' Her forehead twitched as she stared at him. 'Do you really want to?'

He nodded. 'I love you, Ab, that's why it all hurts so badly. I talked to Chloe earlier, just before I knocked off, and I'll tell you the same. I want Al to grow up with two parents. I don't want him to go through what she did, being apart from us.'

'Simon...'

'I know it's... I just want him to be okay. I want us all to be okay. You, me, Al, Chloe. All of us. But you need to learn to respect her boundaries.'

'What?'

'Coming around to our flat like you did today, it's not on.'

'But I want to see my daughter.'

'I'm trying to persuade her to do that, but she's upset. She's got big trust issues.'

'I understand.'

'I'll help you to reconnect, okay? But it won't be easy.'

'Thank you. Let's work on it in counselling, then.'

'I need you to meet me halfway, Ab.'

'I'm trying.'

'And you need to talk to me. Jason bloody Bell was the first person to get you to open up.'

Tears flowed down her cheeks. 'Listen, about Brendan... Why didn't you speak to me? Why go to him?'

'Because I've spoken to you about it. So many times. It's not getting us anywhere. I needed to hear his side of it too. It's how I'm wired. You know that.'

'Be honest with me. Did you threaten him?'

'No. I didn't.' Fenchurch held her gaze. 'I listened to him. Spoke to him, sure. Had some strong words, sure. But I got up and left him alone. Paid the bar tab, then walked out.' He scratched at his neck. 'I looked back in and I saw him twatting about on his phone.' He felt that fluttering in his chest again. 'To be honest, I thought he was messaging you.'

'He wasn't. I've blocked his number.'

'Really?'

'Really. I made a mistake. I can try to defend myself all I want, but I was in the wrong. We drifted apart, you and I, and we can blame each other all we want, but the reality is that I did the wrong thing. I regret it, but I did it. And that's hard to face up to.'

Fenchurch smiled at her. 'I just need to know that you want to fix this.'

'I do.'

'Then I do too.'

Tears streamed down her cheeks. She cleared her throat, dabbing at her eyes. 'Okay, Simon. I've got an early start tomorrow, so...'

'Okay, I'll get out of your hair.' He rose to his feet. 'Goodnight.' He walked past her, and she brushed his arm as he went.

It felt like a kiss. Got him right in the heart.

THE DRIVER

He still didn't know what the hell Fenchurch was doing inside her home.

And nobody was answering his calls. All three of them. Even the special number.

Supposed to just be watching the wife, wasn't he, but no – Fenchurch was there. Him of all people.

And what was he doing inside? Supposed to be divorced or divorcing, weren't they?

The tenement door opened and the big brute charged out, head down. Scanned around the street, like he was looking for something to kick. Or someone.

Made him squeeze down in his seat, under the wheel. The cameras were still rolling, still capturing everything. His phone screen was filled with four videos of Fenchurch glaring at inanimate objects.

Then Fenchurch STARTED WALKING TOWARDS HIM.

Shit!

He could start the engine, shoot off.

Cop like Fenchurch would clock the plates, run them and be around his house before the hour was out.

No. Stay still. If he chapped the window, he'd need to brazen it out.

Fenchurch neared, hands in pockets, shaking his head.

And exactly the *perfect* time for his phone to ring.

He answered it, putting it to his ear. 'Hello?'

Fenchurch walked past, on to his own car, that Mondeo, and got in.

He let himself breathe again. That had been a close-run thing.

'Have you got eyes on her?'

'Got eyes on *him*.'

'What? Seriously?'

'He was visiting her at their old home.'

'Well, that is interesting.'

Fenchurch drove off, far too fast for a residential street.

And everything unclenched. 'He's gone now, driven off.'

'Okay.'

'What do you want me to do?'

'Stay there. Unless you've been made?'

'I don't know. Don't think so.'

'Hard to tell with that one. Okay, let's assume you haven't been. Stay there and I'll let you know what to do next.'

The line went dead and he sat up in his seat, just about able to breathe properly again.

This was way above his pay grade.

26

FENCHURCH

Despite all the high-tech kit the firm had promised to instal, the stairwell light was flickering again. Or was it just that it was still flickering and they hadn't bothered to fix it?

Fenchurch couldn't remember if it'd been like that when he'd stumbled back the previous night, bleary-eyed from yet another brutal shift. But today had been even more brutal and his legs felt like granite as he trudged up the stairs, the light's strobing vibe making him feel like he was in a nightclub.

Perish the thought.

Fenchurch got his keys out and dropped the bloody things on the carpet, slightly askew just like Chloe somehow left it every day. God knows what she did when she left. She usually corrected it when she got back. She wasn't in. Of course she wasn't, she was walking the beat until dawn.

Christ, that was taking some getting used to.

Like everything was.

He unlocked the door and went inside. The place was empty and quiet.

Good.

He sat on the sofa. One thing Fenchurch still liked about

himself was how his memory was sharp as a tack. He scribbled the registration plate down on the back of an envelope.

All the drive back, he'd thrown ideas around in his head. That motor had been there when he arrived at Abi's and was still there when he left. Whoever was behind the wheel must've thought they were being subtle, but you can't really hide on the driver's side.

And Fenchurch had absolutely no idea who he was.

Dark street and parked between streetlights. Just a shape, but one he'd seen a lot of times. Could be anyone. Someone who took a dislike to Fenchurch, which was in four figures probably.

But his first instinct was a cop was following him. Someone working for Owen. When he left Islington nick as a suspect for Holding, refusing to hand over his phone, he'd spotted a car outside, leaving when Abi drove off.

And it had been outside their old flat when he arrived.

He picked up his tablet, the cheap knock-off thing he'd bought off Amazon, but which sort of worked, and logged on to the PNC to run the plates.

Silver Toyota Prius, one of those hybrid things that were everywhere. Taxis and ridesharing drivers loved them. Perfect for city driving, had a decent range and didn't incur the same congestion charge.

Belonged to a Mrs Sarah Ogden.

Meant bugger all to him, so he ran her details. Deceased, six months ago.

Well, that *was* strange.

He ran through everything he knew about the car. Outside the station when he left, but also by Abi's home. Their old home.

He'd gone back to Leman Street to finish up for the night, and that car had followed Abi, not him.

And that really didn't feel good.

So, he could scratch a cop from his list.

He could try and get a favour off someone to run the plates through the ANPR, see where it had been around London or elsewhere. See if it had been following her to school and back home.

Wait a second... She'd been here. Woke Chloe up.

He logged into his home video system and stepped back through the events. A cat dancing across the car park. Commuters returning home in their cars or on foot. That muppet on his scooter. That berk next door on his folding bike.

There, quarter past three.

Abi, getting out of her motor and having a chat with Chloe.

Fenchurch didn't focus on the words, but on the background. The image was pin-sharp, but seemed to focus on Abi in the foreground, with the car park a slight blur behind her, making it hard to spot anything.

A similar if not identical vehicle was parked behind her. Abi walked back to her car and the lens focused on the cars. The low wall blocked the number plate.

Buggeration.

But it only blocked it while it was parked. The car drove off after Abi.

And the plates matched.

Shit, she *was* being followed.

27

The station canteen was in that busy period just before midnight when everyone took their meals over an hour window. Curried fish seemed to be the order of the day and Fenchurch tried to focus on keeping his own dinner down.

And there he was, holding court in the middle of the room. PC Adam Burridge. 'And I told her, doesn't matter who your father is, I'm your—' He spotted Fenchurch and his eyes went wide. 'Sir.' He stood up. 'I wasn't—'

'Need a word, son.' Fenchurch beckoned him back out into the corridor.

Burridge wasn't much younger than him, but it was always useful to patronise someone like him, throw him off guard.

Muted laughter accompanied Burridge's exit from the canteen. Shamed by the boss. Caught talking about his daughter. Poor bastard wouldn't live that down for a few years at least.

Good.

Burridge scratched at his neck. 'Sir, I didn't mean to—'

'Isn't she here with you?'

Burridge shook his head. 'No, I pulled some strings and got her back out on the road with another trainer. Sir, I shouldn't have said what I did just then.'

'It's okay. Just don't do it again so blatantly.'

Burridge frowned. Even seemed a bit hurt. 'I'll try, sir.'

'Listen, I want to say that I changed my mind.'

'Oh?'

'When we spoke earlier, I was over-protective of her.'

'That's natural, sir, especially with what you've been through. With what you've both been through.'

'Right. Well. Chloe shouldn't be held back by me or anyone. She should be encouraged to go as far as she possibly can, because she's going to have to work twice as hard as anyone else to overcome who her father is.'

Burridge smiled at that. 'I agree. Gather you would've been the same?'

'You've met my father?'

'A couple of times, yeah. He's canny, like.'

'Is he.' Fenchurch laughed. 'You're right, though. I've worn the shoes she's wearing, way before I became a detective. She's just going to have to get used to it like I did. All I'll ask of you is, as her training officer, please try and help Chloe get over who her old man is.'

'Will do my best, sir.'

'How's she getting on?'

'She's a good kid. Good instincts so far. Thinks things through, can be calm and rational unlike... well, that is to say, some officers?'

Fenchurch tried to ignore the perceived dig. 'I know what you mean.' He looked at the torn envelope. 'Are you still working the Holding case?'

'I am, sir, but I've been ordered not to speak to you about it.'

'Wise.' Fenchurch pass the note over. 'This might help the case.'

Burridge frowned at it. 'What is it?'

'Spotted a motor when I left Islington nick this evening, then again when I visited my... Chloe's mother.' Fenchurch got out a print-out that'd taken blood, sweat and literal tears to produce back at home. Why did the bloody printer run out of ink every time you needed to use it? He held it up for Burridge. 'This is outside my flat this afternoon, when my wife visited Chloe.'

Burridge looked at it. 'You think this is the same car that followed her?'

Fenchurch shrugged. 'Hard to tell definitively, but the exterior CCTV at the nick might give you a plate. But it was definitely outside her flat. If I was you, I'd look into it.' He narrowed his eyes at Burridge. 'And when you run that plate you'll find it belongs to a dead woman.'

Burridge exhaled slowly. 'Now that is unusual.'

'Tell me about it.'

'Thank you, sir. I'll pass it on to the DC who's working it.' Burridge looked around, up and down the corridor. 'Look, sir, I probably shouldn't be telling you this, but sod it. Chloe talks well about you, I think I can trust you. That DC I mentioned, him and his partner visited the location.'

'What location?'

'The pub down by the river. Pride of Whitby.'

'Prospect, Constable. Prospect of Whitby.'

'Right, right. Well, they found Holding's phone, smashed and broken.'

Fenchurch let out a deep breath. 'Probably some kind of abduction, then.'

Burridge looked away, frowned, then stared down at his feet. 'Listen, if you are behind it, you better get a lawyer in.'

'Excuse me?'

'I'm serious, sir.'

Fenchurch felt the blood thundering in his ears again. 'It's okay; I didn't do it, I am completely innocent.'

'Adam!' A commotion came from the kitchen, centring around a red-faced uniformed sergeant. He spotted Fenchurch and held up his hands. 'Sorry, sir, but we've got a call. Big fight in Tottenham. Possibly a riot.'

Fenchurch clapped Burridge on the arm. 'On you go, Constable. And thanks for the word of warning.'

DAY 2

Friday
13th March, 2020

28

'Coming up next on Friday the thirteenth—' A spooky sound of a crypt opening and bats flying out. '— London's number one breakfast show will be playing a real blast from the past. Can you believe this came out twenty-four years ago? How time flies, eh? This is the mighty Ocean Colour Scene and *The Riverboat Song*.'

Fenchurch pulled into the car park and snapped off the radio.

Way too early for that shit.

Not that it could ever be late enough either.

He opened his door and got out into the glorious morning. A real shift from yesterday. Still air, heat on his neck. Had that summery feel that could lull you into not wearing a jacket. Made him forget most of the shit swirling around in his skull.

The station's back door opened with a thud and a lone figure stomped out. Chloe, face like thunder, heading off towards Tower Gateway and the DLR home.

'Chloe!' Fenchurch set off after her, though his knee didn't allow for anything like the same pace as her young, undamaged ones. 'Chloe!'

She looked around, frowning, and seemed to deflate when she spotted him. 'Dad...'

Fenchurch stopped a couple of metres away, giving her the space she liked. And insisted on, especially near other cops, like the bunch following her out of the door. He stepped aside to let them go past, smiling as they went. 'You okay?'

'I'm fine, Dad. Just finished my shift.' She yawned, screwing her face up tight. 'Mental, Dad. There was almost a riot. Some idiots smashed in a shop up in Tottenham. We got in there, arrested them about midnight, then spent the rest of the shift writing up the charges and processing them. *So* boring.'

'All good experience.'

'Hope so.' Another yawn, one that seemed like it was going to devour her whole. She looked like she was already asleep. Two night shifts after two back shifts, and a mad night like that. It'd knacker anyone. 'Good news is I'm off until Tuesday day shift, so I'm going home to sleep for England. Might even meet up with some friends tonight like a normal person.'

Fenchurch frowned at her. 'You do remember your grandfather's taking you to the football tonight, right?'

She shut her eyes. 'Oh, Christ.'

'You forgot?'

'No, I just thought it was Thursday.'

'No, it's Friday the thirteenth.'

She groaned. 'You'll be there, right?'

'Season ticket next to my old man. Hard for us to get the adjacent seats for you and your brother, but your grandfather has a way with these things.' He rubbed at his neck. 'Listen, I might have to work late tonight, so could you pick up your brother?'

'Sure.' She stood there in silence, then yawned again. She looked like she wanted to say something.

'What's on your mind?'

Chloe pouted. 'When I got back to the station, I spoke to Adam. Adam Burridge.'

'I know him, yeah.'

'Well he says they found Holding's phone near the pub you met him in.'

Fenchurch waited for the accusation.

It didn't come.

Fenchurch smiled at her. 'I hope Brendan's okay. Maybe he got pissed, dropped his phone and he's buggered off somewhere.'

'Doesn't seem likely.' Chloe sniffed. 'Oh. Mum texted me. Said you'd been around there?'

'Another reason I wanted you to collect your brother. Trying to give her space.'

'Does that mean you're going to forgive her for what she did?'

'We'll see how things go, but yeah. It's on the cards.' Fenchurch shrugged. 'Listen, when she came around to ours yesterday, did you see a car hanging around?'

'Dad, there's a car park outside. About fifteen cars.'

'I know, but did you see a silver Prius?'

She shrugged now. 'I don't remember.'

'Chloe...'

'What?'

'Never mind.'

'Don't "never mind" me, Dad. What of it?'

'Nothing.'

'You think someone's following me?'

'No, your mother.'

'And you need me to track them down?'

'No, I've got people doing that. I just wondered if you saw who was driving it.'

'Well, I didn't even see it.'

'Chloe, you need to be more aware than the average punter, okay? You need to be the kind of officer who makes the news rather than reading it.'

She rolled her eyes. 'Okay, Dad.' Then walked off down the street.

Yeah, that was the perfect way to piss her off.

29

Ashkani held his gaze, which was brave of her in front of a room full of bored officers. 'I mean, yes, I could attend the PM for you, sir, but you have already asked me to *personally* dig into the backgrounds of Matthews and O'Keefe to see if we can find any other connections between them, not to mention the rest of the team.'

Right. Back to this.

Fenchurch focused on her. 'But we are still operating on the assumption that all three deaths are connected, yes?'

'That's right, but we don't really know if they're all murders, sir. Bert, sure, but the other two? Possible suicides.'

'Suicides of two members of the same team, right when a third is found dead? Come on, Uzma, we need to be better than that.'

'Which is why we're working on the background data. If we get into the psychology of them, we might be able to identify suicidal indicators, such as O'Keefe's long-term sickness due to stress. Maybe someone has been extorting them? That's the kind of thing that would drive them to take their own lives.'

And she had a point.

'Okay, well, you progress that and I'll attend the post-mortem.' Fenchurch went to the next item in his list. Just two to go, thankfully. 'So you should be aware that, due to the nature of the victims' shared profession—' He raised a finger and smiled at Ashkani. '—*potential* victims' shared profession, that we have full-time support on this case from DCI Chris Owen of Professional Standards and Ethics.' He looked around the room, but settled on Owen. 'Nobody here is under investigation.'

Except for Fenchurch himself...

Someone muttered, 'Investigating cops takes a different kettle of bastard...' A tall officer with a monobrow and spiky hair, looking around for laughs that were stifled at best.

Fenchurch could've hauled him up in front of the whole team, but he didn't, just let him stew under his glare. Truth was, he didn't know the guy's name. One of Ashkani's lot, the older ones, officers he hadn't vetted on their arrival in the team. 'Bottom line, people, is we've got three deaths from the same old squad. Two of them might be innocent. An accident and a suicide. But one is definitely a murder. Our job just now is to figure out the truth and find who killed Bert Matthews. But it's also identifying whether that same someone murdered him, Richard O'Keefe and Dean Hatton. Could be we've got just one murder victim, could be two, but we need to identify the truth amongst all the lies.'

The interrupter twisted his lips together. 'Sir, I've been searching for Tony Wyatt.'

Took Fenchurch a few seconds to remember the name. Nelson's other team member, the one who was missing. A suspect, sure. He looked around the group and spotted Nelson at the back, sucking coffee from the usual posh hipster paper cup. He focused on the spiky-haired interrupter. 'Have you made any progress with that?'

'Kind of.'

'What's that supposed to mean?'

'Well, the trouble is I can't find him going on holiday. No passengers on any flights to Spain or Portugal with that name or any variations.'

Nelson rested his cup down on the table next to him. 'Is it possible he might've killed the others?'

Spiky-hair shrugged. 'No idea, sir.'

'Dig into it, then. Telephony, known associates. Interview Wyatt's wife. All of it. Find him.'

Spike click-winked. 'Sir.'

Ashkani raised a hand. 'I'll take lead on it, Jon. Might need a word after this?'

'Sure thing.' Nelson clearly knew as much as Fenchurch did that she wanted to make sure he didn't undermine one of her officers in a briefing like that.

Still, he was a dickhead.

Fenchurch nodded at Nelson. 'Finally, Jon, how are we on finding James Mortimer?'

Nelson looked around the room, anywhere but at Fenchurch. 'I've shaken a lot of trees, guv, but we can't find him anywhere. Seems to have gone to ground, which is mighty suspicious.'

'Okay, well, keep plugging away at it. And that's us for this morning.' Fenchurch looked as many officers as he could in the eye. 'Let's get out there and find our killer. Okay? Dismissed.'

He set off through the hubbub, making for the door and pretending he didn't hear Owen calling his name.

30

F enchurch took a break from his second post-mortem in twenty-four hours, knowing he'd walked right into a trap. Ashkani should be here, standing around while Pratt worked away, but he'd let her get her way. Again. One too many times.

Still, he could avoid Owen and Loftus. Loftus had been quiet, but Owen was in the briefing, keeping his sights on Fenchurch.

He stood in the area outside the post-mortem rooms, enjoying the blissful silence. Most of it.

While Fenchurch knew Bert Matthews pretty well, these bodies were strangers.

Through one window, the charred remains of Dean Hatton. Could be any age, really. Fenchurch wouldn't be surprised if he'd been dug up from a peat bog, preserved for a few thousand years. He held out little hope of Pratt managing to determine anything other than he'd managed to turn his own body into charcoal briquettes.

Richard O'Keefe lay through the other window.

Fenchurch opened the door and walked back through. It was even quite peaceful listening to Pratt's opera playing over the speakers, if you could filter out the 'om pom tiddly om pom' from Pratt.

Fenchurch was sure he'd met O'Keefe at Hendon, maybe even a couple of times. Despite doing the same job and living in the borough Fenchurch investigated, if your patches weren't geographically adjacent then it was hard to butt heads. And there were so many of them in the Met. London was a country the size of a city, at least twice the population of Scotland, Ireland or Holland, and that was before you took into account all the Home Counties and their commuters.

Still, he'd seemed like a confident man, bordering on arrogant. To call himself a 'dickhead' on his suicide bag?

Pratt looked over at him. 'Am I boring you?'

'Me?' Fenchurch frowned. 'No. Why?'

Pratt raised his arms and spread them around the room, empty save for them and the two bodies. 'Well, my dear Simon, someone in here is yawning and it isn't me.'

Fenchurch covered over another yawn. 'Late night, early morning. Not enough sleep, not enough caffeine.'

'Ah yes, such is the modern experience.'

Fenchurch checked his watch. Only been there half an hour, but it felt like a whole weekend. 'You getting anywhere here?'

'Well, this is going to be a while, as I'm sure you can imagine. Might be an opportune moment to stock up some of that caffeine?'

'Could do.' Fenchurch looked at the body. 'What are the chances of identifying him?'

'Slim.'

'DNA from the bone marrow?'

'Well, yes. Bone marrow extraction from pelvis, femur, teeth... We can extract it here, but it will take some time to process and then we would have to find family to compare it to for a genetic match, unless Hatton's DNA was already on file.'

'It must be, surely?'

'Well, the trouble is, the oil he used as a twisted fire starter—' Pratt chuckled as though a twenty-four-year-old pop culture reference was bleeding-edge comedy. '—became an accelerant, didn't it? Several bottles of the stuff. Which means the fire reached a much higher temperature than the charcoal alone. Normally a barbecue would be roughly five hundred degrees Celsius, enough to cook your steaks or kebabs, even bake a pizza in less than a minute, in the traditional manner. But with the accelerant, it reached over two thousand degrees and for a sustained period, which is enough to effectively cremate the victim. Way in excess of the heat needed to melt and crack teeth as well, so we can't resort to dental records.'

Fenchurch stared at the remains. And they were remains, not a corpse, not a body. 'Poor soul.'

'Indeed. I encountered Mr Hatton once. He attended a post-mortem here when deputising for his DI. Didn't say much, of course, but it's a horrific way to go. And I've pretty much seen them all.'

'Word is he was probably drunk when it happened.'

'Indeed. At least he wouldn't have experienced much or been as aware as if he'd been sober.'

'This tally with what the fire service think?'

'Oh yes, I've spoken to Mr Collins and he's in full agreement.'

Fenchurch got out his phone, thrumming in his pocket. Two missed calls from Owen. He ignored them and put it away. 'What about O'Keefe? Can I get some edited highlights?'

'Not for at least two hours, no.'

Fenchurch's phone rang in his pocket.

Chloe calling...

'Better take this.' He left the room and answered before the door could close. 'You okay?'

'Not sure.' Chloe was outside somewhere, the distant sound of schoolkids in the playground. 'Went round to Mum's to have breakfast with her after my shift. Trying to make up with her, you know?'

'That's good.'

'Dad, she dropped me off outside her school. A Prius followed her all the way here. Mum is definitely being stalked.'

THE DRIVER

He was sure this would get him into trouble.

A single man sitting outside a school, spying on a teacher, but he'd been in the clear so far. And he hoped it continued.

Abi Fenchurch was one of those teachers who liked her children, that was clear. Like, really liked them. Rather than it being a job, something that paid the bills—which must be mostly going on childcare given her full-time job here—this was a calling for her. She was out in the playground, talking to kids, rather than sharing gossip in the canteen with the other teachers.

That kid of theirs, though. The girl. Abi had given her a lift. He hadn't expected that.

And her showing up out of the blue like that...

A cop. Keeping her eyes peeled. Talking to someone as she walked off.

He was told they were estranged, but that was twice in two days.

Most of the time he'd been watching her from a distance over his tablet connection to the cameras mounted on the car, sitting in the relative safety of a café or a bookmaker's, not that he was a gambler. Well, not that much of one.

Chloe couldn't have spotted him.

He was in the clear. It was all okay.

Wait. Whose Mondeo was that?

31

FENCHURCH

Didn't take Fenchurch long to bomb up to Hackney, even at this time of day. He closed in on her school, siren wailing, and tried to keep an eye out for either of them. Chloe or Abi.

His phone rang through the dashboard:

Owen calling...

He bounced the call and slowed to a slow trundle, keeping his eyes on—

There.

Chloe was leaning against a phone box, playing with her phone.

Fenchurch pulled up just past her on the double-yellows, stuck his Official Police Business sign in the windscreen and got out onto the street. 'You okay?'

Chloe looked up at him, yawned, then put her phone away. 'That was quick.'

'I drive like an idiot.' Fenchurch scanned around. The school playground was empty now. The streets were quiet too, just a few parents with younger kids. 'Where's the car?'

She pointed past the school. The kids were all inside now, but the bell rang. Presumably the start of lessons.

And she was right, a silver Prius was parked at the crossroads, facing away from the school. The plates matched the car belonging to Sarah Ogden.

Fenchurch set off towards it. 'You did a good thing calling me.'

'Well, I didn't have much choice after you chastised me for not being aware. I made sure I kept my eyes peeled.' She was keeping up with his furious pace. 'I mean, I was pissed off, so I went to Mum's for some TLC and reassurance, but of course she was busy and running late, so she gave me a lift as she dropped off Al and like, it's halfway home here, so I can walk the rest of the way.'

'And you'd miss swapping from the tube to the DLR at Bank, which is always good.'

'Right.' She laughed. 'And that's when I spotted the car. Matched the plates you texted me. I don't have the juice to do anything with it myself, so I called you.'

'And you're no cowgirl. Right.' Fenchurch stopped by it. Nobody inside, but it had stickers in the window for the holy trinity of ride-sharing apps – Lyft, Uber and Travis. 'But I'm a cowboy.' He crouched down to peer inside.

Forecourt clean, like it'd just been valeted. Made sense if it was a glorified taxi, with passengers rating you on cleanliness as much as speed, safety and chat. The only personalisation was a cradle by the wheel, with a smartphone resting in it. Screen was blank, though.

Fenchurch swung around a full three-sixty, doing an inventory of the location. Pretty quiet, just a couple of women pushing prams. Two bookmakers, both open, both local outfits and small beer. Two craft beer bars, both shut, and an old pub that was open and serving. Corner shop opposite. Deli next door. Three yuppie cafés and two greasy spoons.

Welcome to Hackney.

A bus came along the main drag, stopping a few hundred metres away. A man stepped out of the deli, clutching a brown paper bag. Bearded, hair tied up in a man bun. Sharp suit.

Fenchurch didn't need a caption to recognise him this time.

Rob Lezard.

Ex-Met DCI. Or so he claimed.

Lezard stopped at the crossroads and waited for the green man. He took out a bottle, opened it and drank about half of his smoothie, then ran the back of his hand across his lips.

If Lezard spotted them and scarpered, no way was Fenchurch's knee up to it.

And he wanted to know if Lezard was the arsehole who'd been stalking his wife in a possibly stolen car.

Fenchurch grabbed Chloe's arm. 'Stay back.'

Lezard put the bottle back in the bag as he crossed, heading towards the Prius, oblivious to them.

It *was* him.

Son of a bitch was stalking Fenchurch's wife.

He set off after Lezard, as fast as his knee would allow. 'If he runs for it, you grab him.'

Chloe frowned at him. 'Sure I can do that?'

'Forget that I'm your dad and he's stalking your mum. You're off-duty and following the orders of a senior officer.'

'Okay.'

Lezard stopped just short of the Prius and turned around. His mouth hung open and he dropped his bag. He turned back around and started to run.

'Bastard.' Fenchurch set off after him, but his knee crunched and cracked. All he could do was hop and hobble.

But Chloe was on it, bursting after him. She slowed the gap, then Lezard ran into the middle of the road.

A car thundered towards her, honking its horn.

Fenchurch felt his heart almost explode. 'Chloe! Watch out!'

But she made it over the other side, just as the car blared past.

By the time Fenchurch made it over, she'd locked Lezard's arm behind his back.

Chip off the old block.

32

F enchurch watched from the observation suite, pacing up and down the thin strip of carpet between the two computers in there, close to wearing it down to the creaking floorboards underneath. He stopped to look at the giant TV screen, standing as close to it as his son would sit at home.

Lezard sat on his own, opposite Bridge and Reed. Fenchurch's two best sergeants, one going places and the other who'd refused to even consider it. 'You will let me know when my lawyer turns up, yes?'

'That's correct.' Reed leaned forward, tilting her head to the side. 'As a former officer yourself, you'll appreciate that we're following protocol and ensuring your safety.'

Lezard smiled back, but it was far from genuine.

Fenchurch got out his phone and called Chloe.

She answered straight away with a yawn.

'Hey, sounds like you're heading to bed?'

'Just out of the shower, yeah.' Another yawn. 'How's it going?'

'I'm going to charge him with stalking your mother, then find out what else he's been up to.' Fenchurch stopped himself. The hum of the room seemed to swell up. 'Thing is, Loftus isn't answering his phone.'

'That's a problem?'

'I shouldn't do this off my own bat.'

'Right, right.'

'Good work in taking him down, though. Didn't get a chance to thank you.'

'All part of my training, Dad.'

'Sure. I'll thank Burridge next time I see him.'

'Don't.'

'Okay. Well. I'll let you get to bed, then. See you at the match this evening.'

'Night.'

Fenchurch ended the call and tried Loftus again, but still nothing.

Just what he didn't need. Always the case that when he least wanted him, he'd be on him like a pack of wild dogs, but when he actually needed him? Forget it.

Still, the distance wasn't necessarily a bad thing. God knew what he was up to. Supposed to be working with his old man to find the old team, but Fenchurch and Nelson had done that. Well, what was left of them. Two dead men and a missing one.

Someone knocked on the door.

'Come in.' Fenchurch turned around.

A big lump of a uniform held the door. 'Got someone to see you, sir.' He stepped out of the way. 'In you go.'

A man walked in. Clean-shaven with teeth that gleamed like they'd cost a pretty penny, but were maybe slightly squint. Daft footballer's haircut that looked freshly done. His suit hung off his bony shoulders, wide but with no muscle to them. Trousers up to his shins, one white sock and one pink. Flies undone. 'Are you Simon Fenchurch?' Northern accent, probably Liverpool.

Fenchurch nodded. 'And you are?'

'Angus Percival.'

Fenchurch tried to stop the groan coming out and was only partially successful. He'd never come across the guy before, but he'd heard of him. AKA Percy Pig, the most useless criminal defence lawyer in South London. Based in Croydon, if Fenchurch recalled correctly. Maybe Beckenham. 'Good to meet you.' But he didn't hold out his hand. 'Your reputation precedes you.'

'And it should.' Percival licked his lips and had to close both eyes while he did it. 'Don't call me the Croydon CPS Killer for nothing.'

'Is that right?' Sod it, Fenchurch laughed. 'Who calls you that?'

'The boys in the office. I'm notorious.'

'Sure you are.' Fenchurch gave him a kind look he didn't deserve. 'Thing is, we're not here in court, though. Just dealing with why your client has been stalking my wife.'

'Why, what's she been doing that she shouldn't?'

Five years ago, Fenchurch would've swung for him. 'Nothing. It's what your client's been doing.' He tilted his head towards the door. 'Now why don't you take that big ego of yours across the corridor and we can get on with charging him. Okay?'

'Your cards are marked, Fenchurch.' Percival shot him a glare made of custard and stumbled out of the room. And he left his briefcase in the doorway.

Fenchurch grabbed it. 'Forgot something.' He hurled it at the useless bastard.

It smacked into his arse and he turned to glower. 'That's assault! I'll sue you!'

'Shut up and do your job.'

Percival shook his head and entered the interview room.

Fenchurch stepped back into the obs suite and watched him slide into the room onscreen.

Percival stopped and did up his flies, then sat next to his client. He put his briefcase on the desk and patted it. 'This is where I usually put the hearts of the lawyers who I destroy in court.'

Reed leaned over to the recorder. 'Also present is Angus Percival, representing Mr Lezard.'

Percival grinned at her. 'It's about time you let him go, isn't it?'

Reed laughed. 'We've not even got started.'

'Let him go and I'll not sue you.'

Reed laughed again, then looked at Lezard. 'Let's start with Mrs Sarah Ogden and how you know her?'

Lezard frowned. 'Sarah who?'

Percival leaned in and whispered something.

Lezard scowled. 'But it's bollocks!' He turned back to Reed. 'I've never heard of her.'

Reed slid a page across the table. 'So why have you been driving her car?'

'I haven't.'

'This is her car, right?'

'No idea. Never seen it in my life. Never heard of her either.'

'This car was right next to where you were detained, so that's blatantly untrue.'

'Okay, I'll take your word for it and amend my statement to saying that I've never knowingly seen that car.'

Reed placed more pages on the table. 'Here it is outside the residence of the person who you've been stalking. And here it is outside her daughter's home.'

'Very pleased for you. That's not my car.'

'But that is you driving it, yes?'

'No. It's not my car and I've never knowingly been inside it.'

'Well, it belongs to Sarah Ogden. Legally. But most people would say it *belonged* to her as she died in September.'

'So? It's not me in the car.'

Reed consulted her notebook. 'Mr Lezard, you were spotted outside the school where Mrs Abigail Fenchurch works. That's the woman who you've been stalking.'

Percival's smile glinted. 'As in Simon Fenchurch?'

'Abi is his wife, correct.'

'Well, darling, he shouldn't be involved in this case, should he?'

Reed took a deep breath. 'Well spotted. He's not.'

Percival thumbed behind him. 'But I just spoke to him.'

'He's not interviewing your client, sir. I am. DS Bridge and I directly report to DI Uzma Ashkani. There's no conflict of interest here. But just because she's the wife of a senior officer doesn't make it okay for your client to stalk her.'

Lezard grimaced. 'Hardly been *stalking* her.'

'You're on the record here, Mr Lezard. You were seen in her vicinity. Next to a car that has been seen outside her address and that of her daughter. That all ties together nicely, just need you to turn it into a bow for me.'

Lezard looked at his lawyer. 'What do you think?'

Percival seemed to be sweating. He just crumpled. Couldn't look at anyone, just shrugged. 'Best to tell them the truth, Rob.'

So much for the Croydon CPS Killer.

Lezard ran a hand down his face. 'Okay, if you want the truth, I want him in here.'

'Him, who?'

'Fenchurch.'

Reed frowned, looked at Bridge, then at the camera.

Fenchurch didn't need to think about it. He'd already made up his mind. He left the room, crossed the corridor and stepped inside. 'Let's hear it then.'

Lezard sniffed. 'Just you and me, Fenchurch. And off the record.'

'Okay to you and me. No to "off the record".'

'I'm not—'

'That's the deal.'

'Fine.'

Reed joined Fenchurch by the door. 'You sure about this, guv?'

Fenchurch whispered, 'Sod the conflict of interest, Kay, if this gets that pillock speaking and secures a confession, I'll take the heat.'

'Guv, I don't—'

'Kay, it's my fault.'

'Your grave.' She walked off into the corridor.

Fenchurch blocked Percival. 'You need to stay, Percy.'

Percival raised his arms. Sweat had soaked through his jacket armpits and he stank like a ripe Christmas Stilton you found stuck at the back of the fridge in March. 'No, no, no, you can't do this. I'll have your badge for this.'

'Percy.' Lezard stared at the lawyer. 'Shut up.'

'What?' Percival picked up his briefcase. The bottom fell out of it and paperwork scattered everywhere. But not casework or the hearts of other lawyers. The pages looked like drawings of medieval towns and villages. He gathered up his fantasy life.

Fenchurch grinned at Lezard. 'Did you appoint him on a dare?'

'Something like that. Hard to find the most clueless lawyer in London, but he's managed to waste a lot of your time and get your attention.'

'Well, I don't appreciate it.'

Percival slammed his briefcase down on the table and drummed his fingers off the battered leather.

Fenchurch ignored him and stared right at Lezard. 'Why were you trying to speak to my wife?'

'I wasn't.'

'Okay, but you were outside of her school. Heading back to the car that was stalking her?'

'No, I wasn't.'

'I thought you were going to talk to me?'

'I...' Lezard shook his head. 'Honestly, that wasn't me.'

'Just tell me the truth.'

'Okay. Look, I wasn't following anyone. Her, you, or your daughter. I swear. But there was another geezer there. Saw him getting out of a Prius and head into the bookies next door.'

'Come on. You need to do better than that.'

'Right.' Lezard snorted. 'I saw Jennifer at your place.'

'Jennifer?' Fenchurch snarled. 'Her name is Chloe. It should never have been Jennifer.'

'All grown up now, isn't she? Be nice to interview her about her take on things.'

'So you've been stalking her too?'

'It's intel for a show.'

'A TV show?' Fenchurch felt that stab in his gut. 'A show about *me*? About *us*?'

'Right, about how your girl was taken.' Lezard beamed. 'I'm not all about the harrowing stuff, you know. Serial killers. Bomb threats. No, sometimes I like good news stories.'

'You can't.'

'I mean, I can. Of course I can. And I am. But it is a good news piece. The world's a tough place just now. People are crying out for a tale with a happy ending. And I'm not talking about someone getting justice after years of hunting. No, this story has all the feels. Separation, reunion, then she goes on to become a cop like her old man. That's Hollywood, man!'

'I'm beginning to wish that car had hit you when she took you down.'

'Oh man, I hope my cameraman caught her doing that!'

'Your cameraman?'

Lezard laughed. 'It's an amazing piece of footage, assuming he got it. And such a story. Taken as a small child, now she's all grown up and reconciled with her family. Taking down wrong 'uns like me.' He winced. 'Although I did get wind that the reconciliation with her mother didn't last.'

'That's a personal matter.'

'Come on, Fenchurch. A bit of extracurricular "how's your father", eh? And not on your part either.'

Fenchurch wanted to grab his throat and squeeze. But that was the old Fenchurch. He was smarter now. Wiser. Calmer. And in front of a lawyer, while the cameras and audio recorders captured it all. 'I'm going to charge you with stalking. I don't care if it doesn't stick, I just want you to suffer.'

'Charming.' Lezard sat back and inspected his fingernails. 'Thing is, Fenchurch, you're going to let me go.'

'And why would that be?'

'Because I can help with your case.'

'Which one?'

'All these murders you've found. Matthews. Hatton. O'Keefe. And old Tony Wyatt on the run, eh?'

'What do you know about it?'

'Oh plenty.' Lezard nudged his lawyer. 'And before you start, I've got a solid alibi for time of death. I was on a BBC News programme. They love me over there. Same with the *Post*, which should cover the other times you want.'

Fenchurch hadn't considered him a suspect, but he was always highly suspicious when people offered alibis. 'I'm still going to charge you.'

Lezard sniffed. 'Then I won't pass on the intel I've got about O'Keefe.'

'What intel?'

'I mean, I had some run-ins with O'Keefe over the years; nasty prick.'

'When you were a cop?'

'Right. Heads up Middle Market Drugs these days, right? Well, I did a stint there myself.'

'Funny, because we can't find you as a serving officer, despite all this PR bullshit about you being a former senior officer.'

'Well, that's not my problem, is it? You lot couldn't identify... Ah forget it.'

'No, out with it.'

Lezard shook his head. 'I said forget it.'

'What have you got on O'Keefe?'

Lezard leaned forward. 'Well, for starters, he was entirely to blame for the Mortimer scandal. He persuaded the CPS to plough on, confident he could discredit the alibi. Course, he never did. And Mortimer got off, didn't he? And the Met never caught who the bombers were at that concert.'

'And you know?'

'God, no. I'm just giving you information, Fenchurch. O'Keefe's so bent he's almost straight again. That's where you should be looking.'

'In what way is he bent?'

'Well, Drugs should be the cleanest cops in London, right? But it's funny the things that go on over there. And O'Keefe... Him and a few of his mates were selling secrets to local dealers. Information on other drug investigations. Basically, letting them do what they wanted.'

'Who gave you this intel?'

'James Mortimer.'

The missing bomber.

Fenchurch folded his arms. 'You know I need to find him. I saw you on the news last night talking about it. Why didn't you come forward?'

'Ask your mate, Julian Loftus. He's the one who didn't answer my calls. So I'm paying him back by not answering his.'

'Do you know where he is?'

'No, of course I don't. Jimmy's a very resourceful man. If he wants to disappear, trust me, you ain't finding him.'

'When did you last hear from him?'

'First thing this morning. Woke me up, as it happens. He called me and told me O'Keefe was in the pocket of a certain someone. A good friend of yours. And he's got proof.'

33

At least they'd cleared the visiting room for them.

The place was empty, just Fenchurch and Nelson. A stark room, with walls made of breeze blocks, making it feel like a cross between a warehouse and a high school gym. Low tables lined the sides of the room, all empty. The window let in light as cold as the air, and looked north across the nature reserve and the flat landscape beyond. A pair of ducks came in to land in the middle of a small lake. Maybe a big pond. The wind turbine's rotation was muted by the glass, but it was spinning like Fenchurch's thoughts, churning like his guts.

Whitemoor. Ah, how Fenchurch had missed it.

He sat back down again. 'Been a while, Jon.'

Nelson was flicking through his phone, his eyes lit up by the bright screen. 'Wish I could say the same. Been here every week for the last six months. Hate that drive up, always get stuck in traffic.'

'You worked for O'Keefe. Was he bent?'

Nelson looked up from his phone, his top lip all twisted. 'I'd say I'm sceptical, at best. All the time I worked for him, both stints, O'Keefe *seemed* to be a straight bat. Never any sign of corruption.'

'Isn't that a good indicator? Almost too clean and all that?'

'Could be.' Nelson looked over at Fenchurch, long enough to make eye contact, but then looked away. 'Okay, so I'm going to take the lead when he turns up. Agreed?'

Fenchurch raised his hands. 'I'm just wallpaper.' He looked around the dank room. 'Which would be a massive improvement in here.' He smiled, but Nelson wasn't seeing the funny side. 'I'll just sit here, keeping my distance. You know I'm here if you need me to get him to talk more.'

'Sure.' Nelson went back to his phone. 'But you're assuming I don't get him to talk, guv.'

'When it's just us two, Jon, you don't need to call me "guv".'

'I've called you it for years, guv. Would feel weird to call you Simon.'

Fenchurch laughed. 'Suit yourself.'

The door clanked open and two brick-outhouse guards stepped in, then stood either side of the door like a pair of bookends.

And Dimitri Younis sauntered in. Designer tracksuit, casual enough to not stick out in a Category A prison, but probably cost the best part of five hundred quid. Trainers whiter than the light coming through the window. The row of rings on his eyebrows was all healed up now, but menace and mischief flickered in his gaze. 'Oh. My. Days.' He patted the arm of the guard. 'See who I'm getting double teamed by? Jon Nelson and my old lover, Simon Fenchurch.'

He didn't get a reaction from the guard. 'Just sit, Dimitri.'

'I love it when you use my Sunday name.' Younis swanned over and perched on the seat opposite them. 'Now, what can you two gentlemen do me for?'

Nelson put his phone away. 'Need to ask you a few questions.'

'Oh, I bet you do, but I ain't seen this gorgeous hunk in so bloody long it hurts.'

Nelson smiled, but Fenchurch could see the shame in his eyes. 'On you go, then.'

Younis gave Fenchurch a good visual going over. 'Looking well, Fenchy. Have you lost weight?'

'A bit.' Fenchurch waved a hand around the room. 'How are your new digs?'

Younis snarled but covered it over with another seedy grin. 'Sorry, I keep meaning to drop you a little card with my new number.'

'It's okay, I know precisely where you are at all times.'

'Bet you think of me as you drift off to sleep.'

'And when I wake up screaming in the night.'

Younis bared his teeth. 'I'd love to make you scream in the night.'

'Must be annoying though, being moved from Belmarsh in East London to up here in Cambridgeshire. Far away from your people.'

'Doesn't matter where you are when all you get is an hour outside each day, does it?'

'True enough. Could be in Manchester or Liverpool, Dimitri, so you should be thankful to DI Nelson here that you're only an hour or so up the road from your patch. Still, a Cat A prisoner like you, we can't have you running London's drugs and prostitution from inside.'

'Won't stop me.'

'And it hasn't, has it?'

'*Okay.*' Nelson opened his notebook and splayed it on the table. 'Now, the reason we're here, Dimitri, is to ask you a few questions about Richard O'Keefe.'

'No idea who that is.'

'Detective Superintendent Richard O'Keefe. He died on Sunday.'

'Sad to hear about it. Who's he?'

'Headed up Middle Market Drugs.' Nelson looked around the room. 'The lot who put you in here.'

'Your lot, right?'

'For my sins. See, Mr O'Keefe's death appears to be suicide.'

'Always tragic when someone takes their own life, isn't it? Some people say it's selfish, but that's just them focusing on themselves, the ones who've been left behind and the impact the suicide has on them. Says nothing about some poor sod who's spent the last five years despairing and worrying, then getting to the point where the only solution they can see is to take their own life.'

Nelson raised his eyebrows. 'That's very sensitive for you.'

'I'm a very sensitive man, Inspector.' Younis held out a hand for Fenchurch to shake. 'Congrats on your promotion, by the way.'

'Thanks.' Fenchurch didn't shake it. 'But O'Keefe was on your radar, wasn't he?'

'I've never heard of him. If I was on his, then he never showed up in here or in my old manor down in Belmarsh.' Younis rubbed his hand over the bristles on his head. 'But I can see the sadness in your eyes, Jon. Don't know why you lot bother. You're facing an uphill battle against scumbags like me, people who'd think nothing of selling drugs to kids or exploiting vulnerable people for the sexual kicks of rich men.' He looked over Fenchurch. 'Speaking of which, how's your daughter?'

Fenchurch sat back, arms folded. 'She's good, thanks for asking.'

'Heard word that young Chloe is following in the family business.'

Fenchurch nodded. 'She's a probationer.'

'Well, well. Police Constable Chloe Geraldine Fenchurch.' Younis puckered his lips. 'Has a good ring to it. I'll look forward to ordering some geezers to murder her.'

Fenchurch's blood was pumping, though, starting to thud in his ears. 'Very funny.'

'Oh, I'm deadly serious. Could do it like that.' Younis clicked his fingers. 'Thing is, I've been a bit wistful recently. Starting to feel my age is catching up with me. How I've not bred, unlike you pair. Shame, isn't it? I've got so much to offer a little kid, but chances of getting anyone pregnant in this place aren't great.'

'Didn't think you were that way inclined?'

'Oh, I'll go up any incline, my friend. But I'm thinking I'll find myself a nice wife when I get out of here in a couple weeks.'

Nelson laughed, his bear noise echoing around the room.

'You're not getting out of here except for being moved to another prison.' He tilted his head from side to side, like he was weighing something up. 'Or if someone kills you.'

Younis narrowed his eyes, all trace of banter gone. 'That a threat?'

'No, but I suspect there are a lot of people in here who'd love to take you down. Make a name for themselves.'

'I'm fine, Big Guy, don't you worry about me.' Younis blew him a kiss, then focused on Fenchurch. 'How are things with Mrs F?'

'Peachy.'

'Sure, because I heard you'd moved out of the family home? Leaving the good lady wife and your son? Tut tut. Not a very good example to set, is it?'

'Listen, Dimitri, we're not here to discuss my personal life. Were you or any of his associates responsible?'

'What, O'Keefe?' Younis laughed. 'No. Categorically no.'

'See, we've got intel that he was in the employ of someone in your world.'

'My world, eh?'

'Sorry, I meant you. That you were paying him.'

'So, you drove all the way up here just to ask me that?'

'No, of course not. We've got evidence.' Fenchurch got out the sheet of paper from his pocket and rested it on the table. 'A bank account in Mr O'Keefe's name. Five grand a month paid in over three years. Nice little nest egg. Wonder what he had to do to earn that.'

Younis shrugged. 'Nothing to do with me.'

'Sure about that?'

'Absolutely.'

Fenchurch leaned forward and tapped the page. 'Because it's fairly easy for a man with your connections to set up a fake account, then pay money in. Dirty cash too. That account now has a hundred and eighty grand in it. Looks like a bribe, but we've no actual connection to O'Keefe, other than the name. No proof it's his account, even. But we have got a team of people going through bank security footage looking for the little toe rag who paid that cash in every month.'

'Well, that sounds like a fun task. Pass on my condolences to the poor sods who're doing it. Hope you give them all tea and biscuits.'

'We do get all the fun jobs. Thing is, it's so satisfying when our hard graft lets us connect a crime to one of your lot. Then we can arrest even more of them. Maybe it's Steve Warrington or Josh Connor.'

'Who are they?'

'Two chumps on your visitor log.'

'Oh, them two. Pair of weirdos. Just come in and sit there, don't say anything.'

'Sure. That'll be why you're seeing them on the same day every month?'

'Listen, mate. What's this all about?'

'I think there's two possibilities here. One, you were trying to set up O'Keefe and make him look bent. Seed stories for us to pick up. Two, you were bribing him.'

'Both are very serious accusations.' Younis patted the seat next to him. 'Sure I shouldn't have my gorgeous little lawyer in here to make sure you're not a naughty boy?'

Fenchurch shook his head. 'This is just a friendly visit, so no need for that.'

'Friendly, eh? So, you really think I've got something to do with what happened to O'Keefe?'

'Don't you?'

'Nope. If that sack of shit is responsible for why I'm in here, then I'm glad he died.'

'That's a bit harsh.'

'Nah, good riddance.'

'And you'll die in here, Dimitri. Can only be a matter of time.'

'I'll be out soon enough, don't you worry.' Younis sucked the air like he was tasting a fine wine. 'Saw this story on the telly news while I was between self-love sessions. That berk you work for, Loftus? Asking to speak to one James Mortimer.'

'What of it?'

'Well, you get any response to it?'

Fenchurch got to his feet. 'Well, Jon, this has been a waste of time.'

'Oh come on, Fenchy. You want me to get him to call you?'

34

Fenchurch stopped by the car and took that deep breath he'd been struggling to take while inside the prison. The metallic taste of the place, the stench of cleaning chemicals. The hatred of Dimitri Younis.

'You okay, guv?'

Fenchurch looked over at Nelson. He felt like he was going to be sick. Maybe it'd be a good thing. Maybe it'd get that vermin out of his thoughts. 'I'm fine.'

'You don't look it.'

'Always get this way when I see him.'

'All that flirting, guv, you sure you shouldn't stop him?'

'Playing along with that has led to his downfall in the past, Jon. He gets cocky. Arrogant. Thinks he can run rings around us, but he's the one in here.'

'Yeah, but he's still running things in East London. Even expanding into the North West, by all accounts.' Nelson got out his vape stick and took a deep suck. 'I don't know what you expected to get out of him, but I don't imagine it was that?'

'Jon, I always like to look Younis in the eye. He might be many things, but he ain't a liar. He's not involved in these deaths, I know that much.'

'Hmm. But you think he's up to something.'

'Oh, he's *always* up to something, Jon. Just... what?'

Nelson got in the car without another word.

Fenchurch looked back at the prison walls, hiding the cell blocks. The central tower was the only thing visible, but it was like it was peeking over at Fenchurch.

Christ, Nelson was right – Younis *was* getting at him.

The truth was, the slimy vermin was rotting away in there. He might have eyes and ears on the street, but he was no real threat. What he said about Chloe... Idle. Nothing could come of it.

Fenchurch took out his phone and switched it back on. Two missed calls each from Loftus and Owen. He'd better face the music, listen to their rants as Nelson drove them back to London.

The phone blared out *Does Your Mother Know?*, the only ABBA song Fenchurch could bear.

Ashkani calling...

He answered it. 'Uzma, what's up?'

'I'm at the post-mortem, sir.' Her voice was all frosty, like the very idea of her having to attend something that was part of her job description was beneath her. 'Dr Pratt thinks it's definitely suicide, but it's a murder.'

'Wait, what? That doesn't make any sense. How can it be a murder *and* a suicide?'

Ashkani sighed. 'He's been complaining ever since I got here, sir, saying about how this is what happens when you rush things.'

Nelson popped his head out of the car. 'Guv?'

Fenchurch looked away from him. 'Can you take me through it, please?'

'Okay, I'll try. Bottom line is, a suicide would usually have a few tell-tale signs. Trouble is, Pratt thinks they're not really apparent here. What are present, however, are burn marks on his palms.'

'Isn't that him regretting it?'

'No. When someone regrets their actions, they'd try to pull up the rope, but he thinks these are like he's resisted for a long time, like he'd been fighting against someone.'

Fenchurch looked back at the prison. Maybe Younis had been lying when he'd looked him in the eye. 'So he thinks someone's hung him up there and made it look like suicide?'

'Correct. Trouble is proving it.'

'Always the way.'

'Pratt's ordering an inquest.'

Fenchurch exhaled slowly. 'That'll take months.'

'Exactly. Look, I've got people all over this, sir. I know we're already operating under the assumption that he was murdered, but we will check everything out.'

'Wise move. And thanks.'

'No problem, sir. How do you want to play it?'

'Let's treat it as a murder, first and foremost. We've been careful so far, but let's treat that garage as a crime scene, not where someone took their own life. I need Tammy's lot to comb that place.'

'Sure thing. I'll speak to her after this.'

'Excellent. Is there anything on that bank account?'

'I've got DS Bridge on it. Still nothing to pin it to Mr O'Keefe, sir, but we'll get the CCTV by lunchtime, then it's a case of throwing bodies at it. But we've got transaction times, so it should be quicker than just looking for someone, right?'

'Good.' It stopped Fenchurch demanding the impossible. Maybe she was getting better at managing up the way, by getting stuff done rather than avoiding it. 'Okay, we're going to be a couple of hours getting back, so can we catch up in my office?'

'Sure. Did you get anything?'

'Just a bit of cramp from the drive up. Thanks, Uzma, and thanks for attending for me.'

'Don't mention it, sir. Personal stuff always comes up.' And she was gone.

But her words stayed with Fenchurch. The judgement. The thinly veiled accusation.

Personal stuff.

'What's up, guv?' Nelson was out of the car now.

'That was Uzma.'

Nelson laughed. 'Still got issues with her?'

'Not as many as we used to have. Pratt sees reasonable doubt for O'Keefe not being a suicide. An inquest.'

'Well, that makes it interesting. You think it was Younis?'

'Could be, but I'm not so sure. His lot would usually be less subtle. And framing O'Keefe with that bank account? Does that seem like him?'

'Assuming he was framed. That's a lot of cash, guv. Hush money.'

'But it's not a *lot* of cash, is it? O'Keefe would lose his pension. He's a super, so we're talking a decent wedge.'

Fenchurch's phone rang again.

Unknown caller...

He put it to his ear. 'Hello?'

'Is that Fenchurch?' Northern Irish accent, but soft.

'Speaking.'

'It's James Mortimer. I've just had a call from a mutual friend. I think we need to meet up. Alone.'

35

T he clock on the church next door hit two o'clock and Fenchurch looked around the place. The building site reeked of that mixture of fresh concrete and damp earth, a decomposing corpse.

And it was like a film set at night, lit by a single overhead lamp, despite being mid-afternoon. A man in a dirty trench coat stood in the middle of the circle of men and sucked on a vape stick while the other men messed about on their phones. All wore hard hats, but no work was going on.

A dragon's nest of freshly scooped earth, boulders, and building material. Tons of it. Enough to build a castle, but it was just yet more yuppie flats in the arse end of Stratford, spitting distance from spitting distance from the Olympic Park.

No trees, no flowers, no wildlife. A shipping container stood in the middle of a clearing. The smell of burning plastic and grease. The stack of bricks was rough and unweathered. A crane towered over them, an orange glow shining down.

And no sign of James Mortimer.

Fenchurch checked his phone. Nothing, just another text from Owen.

He got that feeling deep in his guts, that he was making a

mistake. He didn't want to look around at where Nelson stood, in case he was made. Someone like Mortimer, with his training and experience, when they told you to come alone, you made sure you came alone.

Report it up the way—or across to Owen—and he'd have a supposedly covert protection unit, who someone like Mortimer would spot in seconds and from half a mile away.

So you came alone.

Or your companion was so well hidden, even they didn't know they were there.

The nearest workman was maybe two hundred metres away, so if Mortimer wanted to kill Fenchurch, he could. Easily. With minimal protection or witnesses.

'Inspector.' Mortimer stepped out of the shadows. Shaved head, thick beard. Combat trousers. Camo jacket. Rucksack. Desperate eyes searching around. 'You come alone, I trust?'

Fenchurch nodded. 'And it's Chief Inspector.'

'Right.' Mortimer walked over to him and dropped his bag at his feet. He looked Fenchurch up and down, then twirled his fingers around in a circle. 'Spin.'

Fenchurch folded his arms. 'I've had enough of being ordered around by people today. Why are we meeting here?'

Mortimer was now looking everywhere but at Fenchurch. Scanning the site, the people, the machinery, the equipment. 'We're meeting here because I know it's secure. Can trust it's secure.'

'You worked here?'

'Right.' Mortimer sniffed. His inspection seemed to be over now. 'I'm here. You wanted to speak? Speak.'

'I should arrest you.'

'But you won't. Will you?'

'Not yet, anyway.' Fenchurch let his arms hang by his sides. 'Listen, the reason I want to speak to you is because you're chief suspect in a murder. Possibly another two. Probably another one.'

'So why aren't you arresting me?'

'Because I want to hear you out and you're a slippery bugger.'

That got a laugh. 'Why me?'

'It's the old case, James. Back to you trying to blow up a concert venue.'

'Wasn't me.'

'Sure about that? You were caught red-handed.'

'I'm not here to re-litigate a case I was exonerated of. Your lot didn't even try again. You knew I wasn't the bomber. I wasn't involved.'

'That's a bit of a stretch. You *were* involved, James. Like I say, caught red-handed. Now, it might be that you were trying to stop it.' Fenchurch shrugged. 'I get that. Could be. But your prints were everywhere.'

'Rob advised me not to speak to you.' He made to leave.

Fenchurch stopped him. 'Rob Lezard?'

Mortimer frowned. 'He's our mutual friend.'

Fenchurch groaned. 'Lezard is?'

'Who did you think I was talking about?'

'Dimitri Younis.'

'I've no idea who that is.'

'I'd just visited him in prison, he said he'd call you.'

'Well, I've never heard of him. Our mutual friend is Rob Lezard. And time is running out, so focus on me. I'm here. Why do you want to speak to me?'

'Three men are dead. All members of the team that worked that case. Bert Matthews. Dean Hatton. Richard O'Keefe. The men who arrested you. Another is missing, possibly dead, possibly not.'

'I'm innocent, like I told you. You think I'd kill people who tried to frame me?'

'Stands to reason.'

'Look, there might be something in it, but not for the reason you think.' Mortimer looked off towards the crane, then narrowed his eyes at something. 'Standing in your shoes, I'd be thinking of things in a different way. That case went to court, but I got off because I was innocent. You lot didn't find out who had planted the bomb.'

'Correction, we couldn't prove you'd planted the bomb.'

'I swear I'm innocent. Swear on my kids' lives.'

'Assuming you have them.'

'Two boys. Kris and Kieron. And I'm a hero. I was there trying to defuse that bomb. Shit, I *did* defuse it. Probably didn't hear that, did you?'

Fenchurch shook his head.

'Nelson and Hatton were going to arrest me, but that thing was on a timer, so I persuaded them to let me defuse it. Didn't do much, did it? They did me for a crime I didn't commit.'

Fenchurch saw the fury in his eyes, the anger at having to leave his home, become a stray man because the police were looking for him. 'I know you had an alibi for when the bomb was planted. Fair enough. Are you saying you know who did it?'

'Right. I do.'

'Who?'

'Not so fast. First, you want to know who fitted me up for it, don't you?'

Fenchurch shrugged. 'Go on.'

Mortimer ran his hand down his beard. 'I got a call from these arseholes. They sounded official, but they wouldn't say who they were. There'd been a series of credible bomb threats at the time. Al-Qaeda. Islamic State. Real IRA were back. You name it. They said they needed me to consult with them on these bomb threats. Trouble is, they were stitching me up to take the blame for the bombing.'

'How did they do that?'

'I'd been out of the game a few years. Bought my brother's spare parts business. Had a shop in Croydon, started selling stuff on eBay. And lots of it. Bosch and Flymo and whatever was selling. Enabling people to fix their own gear, kind of like what I'd done as an engineer in the army.'

'That's very noble of you.'

'Right to repair is a big thing now. People throw their stuff away all the time and we wonder why the planet's burning up?' He snarled. 'Thing is, when you sell volume of anything over the internet, you stop knowing who you're selling to. And I did it all myself. Most of it. If you bought ten things from me, over a few different orders and different days, chances are you'd get five or six things with my prints on them. A lot of that stuff wasn't just for your cordless mower. No, it could be jury-rigged as part of a bomb. And... And I got wind of the bomb threat at that concert through some mates.'

'Some mates, yeah? You seem to know a hell of a lot about this threat for someone not involved.'

'I'm ex-army, mate. Royal Engineers. I know people in MI6.'

'So you just turned up to defuse it?'

'Right. I pieced it together with what these guys told me.'

'And you acted the superhero? Just happened to know precisely where it'd be?'

'That particular bomb, the destructive force was enough to level that place. Same as any modern events building, there's only one place to put it and that's down in the boiler room. Always in the basement. Take that out, place sinks.' Mortimer stared at him with wild eyes. 'Listen to me. The guys who I consulted for? They tried to frame me. I didn't know them at the time, but I recognised them recently. They were cops in the original investigation. Tony Wyatt and another man I didn't recognise.'

Fenchurch felt like he'd been punched. The wind escaped his lips.

If this was true, if Lezard had the proof, then it'd be public knowledge soon enough.

'Can you back that up?'

'I gave evidence to Rob Lezard. A ton of it. As far as I'm aware, he's not done anything with it yet.'

Fenchurch grabbed his wrist. 'We should do this down at the station.'

'No.'

'You're not in charge here, James.' Fenchurch tightened his grip. 'Come on.'

Mortimer was staring at the crane again. 'You lying bastard. I told you to come alone.'

Nelson was walking towards them, still wearing his trench coat and hardhat.

Mortimer dug his elbow into Fenchurch's gut, then into his throat. He deflated like a balloon and sank to his knees, feeling like he was coughing up his lungs.

Mortimer shot away from Nelson.

Fenchurch tried to stand, but he didn't have any breath. And couldn't take any in. Like his windpipe had been smashed. He tried to move, tried to put one foot in front of the other.

Nelson ran past, feet splashing through the puddles.

Mortimer was at the perimeter, heading for the tunnel Fenchurch had entered by. But he stopped shy of it, crouching down to shift something.

Nelson was closing, his huge frame powering towards him.

Mortimer noticed too late. Nelson speared him, shoulder smashing into his waist, and he went over, rolling back into the mud. Nelson knelt on him, but slipped over. Then Mortimer was on top.

Fenchurch tried to run, but couldn't. He had to skip, like he was six years old, but his breathing and his knee were conspiring against him. In the end, all he could manage was a quick hobble.

Nelson lay in a heap and Mortimer got up. He clocked Fenchurch, then darted away. He rolled a manhole cover and disappeared down into it.

Fenchurch closed in on it, his knee throbbing. He could check Nelson was okay, or go after Mortimer.

No real choice.

He put his weight on the first step, then looked down.

Mortimer was swinging down the ladder like a monkey in the zoo.

Fenchurch had one move here. He placed his feet on the sides of the ladder, then let go of his grip. Those years helping the fire brigade paid off and he slid down the ladder, but just missed his target. His feet slammed into the brickwork and pain screamed up his legs.

Mortimer was running along a corridor, hot pipes on either side.

Fenchurch tried to race after him, but his knee was making bad sounds again. He lost Mortimer at a corner, then weaved around and saw him, racing across a train track.

Christ, Fenchurch had no idea what line that was. Must be overground.

Air blew him back and a train whistled past. Three carriages. Four. Five. Six. Then it was gone.

And there was no sign of Mortimer. He couldn't have grabbed the train at that speed, but he'd couldn't have disappeared into thin air.

Fenchurch stepped out onto the side of the track, onto the loose stones slippery with years of diesel.

Mortimer was nowhere.

36

F enchurch trudged back out into the building site. He got out his phone and had a few texts from Loftus, a couple of missed calls.

Simon, please call me

Is your phone off? Call me

CALL ME ASAP

He tried calling.

Loftus finally picked up. 'Simon. Where the devil are you?'

'Stratford.'

'What the hell are you doing there?'

'Long story, sir, but we've made contact with James Mortimer.'

'And? Is he in custody?'

'He escaped.'

'Lord save us.' Loftus laughed, but it sounded cold and empty. 'What did he say.'

'Well, he swears he's innocent, sir. Insists he didn't plant the bomb back in the day.'

'Did he give you any evidence?'

'Said it was Wyatt and a colleague who set him up. Didn't recognise the other.'

Loftus hissed down the line. 'Wyatt.'

'Are you sure, sir?'

'Well, he is still a suspect.'

'An accomplice, sure, but the main guy?'

'It fits. Perfectly. He's gone missing, thinking he had an alibi. Can you come back here?'

'On my way, sir.' Fenchurch got that tickling at the back of his neck. 'Though I was going to pay someone a visit first.'

'Oh?'

'Rob Lezard. Mortimer said he gave him evidence.'

'Very well.'

'Thanks, sir. I'll see you back at the station.'

Fenchurch swivelled around and saw Nelson at the bottom of the crane, so he made his way over.

Finding Lezard could lead to Mortimer, couldn't it? That was the smart move here. That evidence would lead to Wyatt's accomplice.

Loftus was focusing on Wyatt as chief suspect, but was that right? The only other people surviving from that team were Fenchurch's father and Nelson.

Shit.

Mortimer had shat a brick when he saw Nelson.

That was what happened, wasn't it?

He kept trying to replay it all, but it came down to that, Mortimer running off when he saw Nelson approaching.

Could just be because he saw someone, but it was possible it was because of who it was.

Mortimer would've come in with him to divulge everything, but he saw Nelson and ran off. Then just disappeared in a puff of smoke.

Trouble with someone arranging where to meet, they'd know all the exits. The timing of the train was one thing, but maybe he had another few tricks up his sleeve in that rabbit warren. Have at least three exits well prepped in advance in case things went south.

And seeing one of the men you thought had framed you back in the day... That was definitely things heading south.

It all came down to whether Nelson was bent and Fenchurch just didn't know anymore.

They'd worked together for eight years, more on than off. Fenchurch had trusted him during those lonely nights when he'd been divorced and hunting for Chloe. He'd even helped. But maybe that was because Fenchurch was vulnerable. Take your time, insinuate your way into someone's life.

Yeah... That worked too.

And three of Nelson's ex-colleagues were dead. Matthews, Hatton, O'Keefe. With Wyatt missing.

And what's worse, O'Keefe was a current colleague. His boss, investigating the criminal empire Younis was still running from prison.

Christ.

Nelson stopped a few feet away. 'You okay, guv?'

He shrugged. 'You found him?'

'Crane operator's got a telescope up there for a bit of cheeky astronomy. Trained it on the streets around here, no sign of Mortimer.'

'Right, let's try and find Lezard, then.' Fenchurch set off towards the car, wondering if this was the smartest move of his career.

Or the biggest mistake.

37

Fenchurch stretched out in the passenger seat. His knee was throbbing and he stank of Deep Heat spray, but the cold stuff. Deep Cold? Anyway, it still stank and didn't seem to help any.

Nelson drove through East London, skirting around the City. All places Fenchurch knew well, like he thought he knew Nelson.

'Jon, you ever work with Tony Wyatt?'

'Knew him.' He grimaced. 'Dirty cop.' Takes one to know one. 'Left the force a couple of years ago.'

'Any idea why?'

'No, heard he was hushed up. But that was just a rumour.'

'You think he's been killing people?'

'He's an idiot, guv.'

'But is he a killer?'

'Only if someone told him to. Guy's thick as pig shit.' Nelson laughed. 'Here we are, guv.' He got out of his car.

Fenchurch joined him in the cool air.

Lezard's address was an old art deco building on Fairclough Street. Curved bricks and the kind of paint job that showed the place wasn't like it'd been twenty years ago. The Mercs, Golfs and Teslas parked outside doubled down on that. Look left and you saw the rotting towers of the East End, right and you got the gleaming new ones being thrown up in the City.

Lezard was the only lead they had.

If what Mortimer had said was true, then Fenchurch needed to keep an eye on Nelson as much as find Wyatt. But he needed proof and he needed it soon.

Fenchurch walked along the ground floor until he got to the third door. Quiet inside and dark too, despite it being early afternoon. The sun was around the other side of the building, but the day was gloomy. He knocked on the door and listened. His knee was all numb now. Could barely feel anything.

A ground floor was a stupid address for someone like Lezard who wanted privacy, but a cracking flat for someone wanting a quick escape. The law might be on to him, but he'd be out either window in seconds. Probably a back entrance leading to an old laundry room.

Still, he couldn't hear any tell-tale signs of someone scarpering. If Lezard was in, he wasn't running away.

Fenchurch looked at Nelson, twatting about on his phone. Not the actions of a bent cop. Yeah, he needed to just play along and see what Nelson brought to the table.

Still, no getting away from it. Lazard wasn't home. And Fenchurch needed to see the evidence Mortimer had given to Lezard. Maybe it was here, but there was only one way of finding out.

Fenchurch checked the door for weak points. Five panes of glass in a loose X shape. That'd do it.

Hang on.

The bottom-right pane, closest to the door handle...

He pressed it with his gloved finger and it popped in a touch. 'Would you look at that...' He eased it out of the frame and rested it on the ground at the side, then reached in and unlocked the door.

'Guv, I'm not sure we should—'

'Just intel, Jon. Door was open. Right?'

Nelson pocketed his vape stick. 'Right.'

Fenchurch opened the door and stepped into the flat. Tastefully decorated with a long corridor leading deep into the bowels of the building.

An open door to the right, a bachelor's living room – TV, sound bar, games consoles, beer fridge.

Opposite was a kitchen. The kettle and toaster were ice cold, the fridge silent like it hadn't been opened in hours.

Fenchurch walked to the last two doors. Left was a bedroom, the bed made with military precision, fresh like a hotel room. Cupboards and wardrobes, all too small for anyone to hide in, let alone Rob Lezard. Alarm clock on the bedside table, alongside two hardback novels – *Marked for Death* by Tony Kent and *Dead Man's Grave* by Neil Lancaster, which had a bookmark in about halfway.

Nelson was standing at the other door, but wasn't going in.

Fenchurch barged past, opening it and stopping dead.

A home office, big IKEA desk filled with computers and gadgets. Filing cabinets lining the walls, but the drawers were all hanging open. Paper files strewn everywhere. A whiteboard hung on the wall, but it was wiped clean.

The room had been tossed, and by a professional in Fenchurch's estimation.

The only question was if it was Lezard himself or someone else.

38

Chapman and Wright's office felt more like an estate agents or upmarket barber's than a gritty criminal defence lawyer. Probably because it was. And fancy properties too, all those white and chrome modern things. Tiny places, and they charged the same as you could buy a mansion in Cornwall for.

Maybe Fenchurch should see if they wanted to sell his flat.

Christ, he still needed that flat. He couldn't imagine what it'd be like if he'd sold it. Staying in a bloody hotel. Christ.

Nelson was over at the desk, flashing his warrant card.

The receptionist picked up her phone and spoke into it.

Fenchurch didn't know what to make of him still. It was going to gnaw away at him until he could prove it either way. And that was assuming he ever could.

The receptionist put her phone down and said something to Nelson, but Fenchurch was too far away to hear.

'Guv?' Nelson tiled an eyebrow, then followed her through to the back office area.

Angus Percival was perched on a stool, hunched over a laptop, mobile phone to his ear. He looked around and groaned at their approach.

Fenchurch stood over him. 'Would've thought a brutal lawyer like yourself would have an office to himself?'

Percival put the phone away and shifted his gaze between them, but it was like it lingered all over Nelson. 'Who's your friend here.'

'DI Jon Nelson.' He thrust out a hand. 'Pleasure.'

'No, it's all mine.' Percival was fluttering eyelashes at Nelson.

Which let Fenchurch get a look at his laptop screen.

Pretty far from some aggressive defence work – a Tower Hamlets council form for Shane Macclesfield, a publican, to get rates relief on the Happy Factory. Fenchurch knew the pub, knew to avoid it unless you wanted to speak to members of a weird cult. Harmless, though they didn't seem to think so. Seemed like he was applying for some religious exemption.

Fenchurch laughed. 'Not quite the work of a criminal defence lawyer this, is it?'

Percival still only had eyes for Nelson. 'I'm expanding my repertoire. Can show you a few things.' He'd added a slight lisp to his voice now.

'I bet you can.' Nelson grinned. 'But we're looking for your client. Mr Lezard. We can't get hold of him.'

'Okay.' Percival picked up his phone and put it to his ear. He pursed his lips. 'Sorry, it's just ringing.'

Nelson stood up tall, towering over him. 'We've just been to his flat.' He glanced at Fenchurch. 'Someone's broken in. We're concerned for his safety.'

'Okay, sure. Uh.' Percival took a deep breath, then started working at his laptop. 'Okay, let me just drag up the original client form.' He frowned. 'Oh yes, Rob Lezard is a pseudonym to protect his loved ones.'

Nelson narrowed his eyes. 'You got his real name?'

39

F enchurch was absolutely starving. Nothing since a slice of homemade sourdough at breakfast and his stomach was rumbling like a chainsaw. The archive rooms were the other side of the Lewisham canteen, so Fenchurch charged through the smell of sweet cakes and dirty chips, which made it even worse. And the buggers had shut early, just leaving the ghostly scents to torment him.

Not hard to find them, though, as Dad was in one of his tirades and his voice echoed around the corridor. 'Julian, I've asked and I've asked but they just won't give me the staff. Just one civilian, that's all I ask. Of course, with Bert gone...' He scratched at his neck. 'I mean...'

Loftus and Owen were sitting at the desk, which was covered in paper files, but they were clearly being polite and enduring the rant in the misapprehension that they'd get something useful out of him. Something that would solve the case.

Loftus smiled at Dad. 'I'm sure I can review the application and see if I can expedite matters. I may have some budget free.'

'Not that it's going to help you find— Simon?' Dad was frowning at his son.

'Afternoon, gents.' Fenchurch nodded at him, then Loftus, then Owen. 'You lot getting anywhere?'

Owen rose to his feet, eyebrows raised. 'Well, look who's here, eh?'

Fenchurch walked over to him. 'You should get your phone checked, Chris. Doesn't seem to be ringing.'

Owen frowned at him, then got out an old Nokia that just screamed burner phone. 'Bugger. There's no reception in here.' He looked over at Dad. 'How can you work in here without phone reception?'

'That's *why* I can work, you dizzy sod. Nobody interrupting me all the time, lets me get on with the important stuff.'

'Right.' Owen looked back at Fenchurch. 'Well, it's good to see you, my friend, because we need to have a serious word.'

Fenchurch ignored him. 'Have you come across a Steven Vickers in your search?'

Loftus sat back and folded his arms. 'Steven who?'

'Vickers. It's the real name of Rob Lezard.'

Loftus shot over to the computer and his fingers danced across the keyboard. 'My god.' He scooted over to a filing cabinet and pulled a file out. Fenchurch had never seen anyone move so fast, let alone him, usually so sloth-like. He shook his head, then showed a photo to Fenchurch.

A skinhead, clean-shaven, but with the same dark eyes as Rob Lezard, just missing the man bun, beard and glasses.

Fenchurch handed it back. 'Definitely the same man. But who the hell is he?'

'Well, well, well.' Dad was sitting at a steam-powered desktop computer that made more unwanted noise than Fenchurch's knees. 'Looks like he comes from a slight amount of money. Family owned a fashion empire, of all things. Private education at the kind of school that would get you in the government cabinet these days. Then they lost it all in '92. Over-extended everything. Parents divorced and our man lived with Mum. Attended the local comp, Shadwell Grammar. Bit of a step down, isn't it? After that toughened him up, he joined the cops.'

Loftus worked away at his own machine. 'Five years walking the beat in Croydon and Sutton, then seems to have been a junior DC in South MIT, where he lasted three months. Usual donkey-work for that grade. Ferrying people around, taking statements, fetching coffees.'

Fenchurch found it strange seeing Loftus doing something he excelled at for once, rather than seeming massively out of his depth. That ability to collate and present disparate information sources was pretty bloody impressive. 'So he's not a big hitter like he claims.' He almost smiled at the gall of Lezard. Vickers. Whatever his name was.

The cheek of some people. He lived this bullshit, putting himself on the line every day, having a ruined marriage and a knackered knee to show for his troubles. Some arseholes just wanted to live a fantasy, make-believe that they were important.

Fenchurch frowned at Loftus. 'Why did he leave?'

'Not through choice.' Loftus grimaced. 'Kicked off the force for lying under oath.'

'That'd explain his grudge against the Met, then.' Fenchurch joined Loftus at the machine and saw that face again, staring out with dead eyes. 'Being such a blatant liar about it? That takes balls, doesn't it?'

Loftus frowned. 'And it doesn't explain why he's all over this case in particular.'

'Or why he's been digging into my history.'

Loftus looked around at him. 'He's what?'

'Long story, but he's making a documentary film about me. About Chloe.'

Loftus nodded, but didn't seem impressed. 'He appears to be an opportunist, we know that much, so he's striking where he sees opportunity.' He flicked over, but didn't seem to get any more insight. 'He's got to be connected to this case somehow, but I can't pin it down.'

Owen joined them at the computer, taking over from Loftus. 'You were South MIT for a while, weren't you, Julian?'

Loftus folded his arms. 'Not for very long, though, and our paths didn't cross. Three years apart.'

Fenchurch tried to piece it together. 'Maybe you pissed off someone you both worked with?'

Loftus shook his head. 'I'll have a think, rustle up a few names and see if there's anyone in it, but I can't see it. I was a murder squad detective there, though. He was a beat cop. I was extremely careful not to unsettle the natives.'

Owen punched the desk. 'I've found it.' He looked around the three faces. 'He trained with Wyatt.'

Fenchurch frowned. 'Tony Wyatt?'

'Right. Same class at Hendon. Same training cohort in South London, based in Sutton.'

Fenchurch took Loftus's empty seat, still warm. He couldn't fathom it out. 'Did he kill Hatton?'

Loftus looked at Owen and got a shrug. 'Why would you think that?'

'Well, we're operating on the assumption Hatton's death was murder dressed up as an accident. O'Keefe was a suicide. Matthews was different, murdered in his bath then transported to the maritime monument at Tower Hill.'

'And you think *Lezard's* behind it?'

'Could be.' Fenchurch shrugged, but he felt an itch at the back of his skull. 'But there's another possibility.' He paused, couldn't believe he was even thinking it, but he had no choice. 'Jon Nelson.'

Loftus scowled at him. 'What?'

Dad was shaking his head.

Owen was tilting his. 'Go on?'

'When I met Mortimer, he—'

'Jesus Christ.' Loftus shut his eyes. 'You *met* him?' He groaned, then reopened his eyes. 'What the hell have you been playing at? Why haven't you told me?'

'I did try, sir, but you obviously weren't paying attention.'

Owen raised a hand. 'Let's not kill the messenger here, Julian.' He walked over to Fenchurch, but kept a distance from him. 'What did Mortimer say?'

'That he was framed by two cops. One was Tony Wyatt. The other he didn't know, but he was a colleague.'

'You think it was Nelson?'

'I don't know. When we met, he saw Jon and scarpered. Could be an innocent explanation for that, or it could be that Jon is the one who framed him.'

'Do you believe Mortimer?'

'Hard to say. What he said was plausible, but he's had years to come up with a watertight story, or just a convincing one.' Fenchurch tilted his head from side to side. 'Still, nobody was convicted of that crime. Once Mortimer got let off, the heat died down. But he said he was fitted up by Wyatt and someone else.'

Owen snorted. 'Okay, so he's got a good reason to go after them. Bert Matthews was a junior member of the team, despite his age. But maybe he was sworn to secrecy or maybe they just didn't like a loose end.'

Loftus was staring up at the ductwork on the ceiling. 'O'Keefe was Nelson's old DI back then, but he's his current boss.'

'Christ.' Owen pinched his nose. 'Middle Market Drugs is an area we've got a focus on, for obvious reasons. We need the best cops in there, the most honest, the most trustworthy. Too easy to turn a blind eye to things.'

Fenchurch put his hands in his pockets. 'We unearthed an account in O'Keefe's name. A hundred and eighty grand's worth of dirty money.'

'Jesus Christ.'

'Never accessed by him, though. We're trying to identify who's been paying the five grand in every month, but it's taking its time. DI Ashkani reckons a week.'

Owen breathed out slowly. 'Okay, so let's recap here. Of that team, Hatton, Bert and O'Keefe have all died in the last week. Possibly murdered. Probably murdered. The other three members, Wyatt, Nelson and Ian here are—'

'I ain't going into protective custody.' Dad was working away at his machine. 'You'll have to arrest me to make me break my Hammers streak of not missing a match since 1989.'

'Nobody's suggesting that.' Owen rolled his eyes. 'Of those three, Mortimer suggests that Wyatt was framing him. And he was working with another team member. Given he knows the Fenchurch family from this documentary, he'd have known if it was Ian.'

'Thank you.'

'So Nelson was working with Wyatt to frame him, but Mortimer got off with it.' Owen squinted at Fenchurch. 'What I want to know is why Mortimer never grassed them up for framing him.'

'Thought had crossed my mind.' Fenchurch felt that chill settle on his spine. 'He was acting like a superhero, like he'd saved everyone at the concert. But he seemed reluctant to use a very valid alibi to get himself off. And the prosecution ploughed on, thinking they could discredit it.'

Owen looked at Loftus, then they both let out similar-magnitude sighs.

'Wait a sec.' Dad looked up from a paper file he was poring over. 'Listen, I thought I was right, but I just had to check. The old grey matter isn't as good as it once was. Something was telling me that Jon Nelson and Tony Wyatt were in every single interview with Mortimer and I was right. Turns out I watched them all, tried coaching them two buggers in how to prosecute them.'

Fenchurch had seen this play out so many times – a long and winding anecdote from him that would lead nowhere. 'What are you saying, Dad?'

'That maybe Mortimer had no opportunity to grass. If one of my team was bent, then... Christ, this is all my bloody fault.' Dad tugged at his goatee. 'If one of them was dirty, it's on me.'

Fenchurch walked over and rested a hand on his arm. 'It's okay, Dad. Don't worry.'

'Right, son.' Dad nestled into him like Fenchurch's son would. Strange how things got inverted like that. 'You're saying that he couldn't speak up because Wyatt was in all of the interviews. If he did, Wyatt would speak to the people who had leverage over him and—' Dad did a cutthroat gesture. '—bang.'

Fenchurch tried to play it all through and could see the shape of it. 'Mortimer hadn't spoken up because he couldn't. Right. If he said anything about Wyatt, then either of our suspects would get him. Nelson was in the room with him. Wyatt would be aware of anything.'

Loftus was pacing around, looking like he wanted to punch something. 'Who was his lawyer?'

Dad winced. 'Defended himself.'

One of those arrogant idiots who thought that moral outrage would stand up in court against a thousand years of law.

Fenchurch sat back in his chair and tried to piece it all together. Nelson was a friend, a very good one. How could he think he was bent?

Christ.

Loftus was frowning at Fenchurch. 'What's up?'

'Could Jon Nelson really have killed all those people? Former colleagues. A current boss.' Fenchurch didn't like the sour taste in his mouth. 'Why? To cover over some ancient crime? I just don't see it.'

'Just finding it hard to—'

His phone rang.

'Seems like I'm the only one with mobile reception down here.' Fenchurch checked the display.

Chloe calling...

'Back in a sec.' He left the room and went back into the canteen, making his stomach rumble all over again, then answered it. 'Are you okay?'

'Are you near a computer?'

'Can be, why?'

'Suggest you go to Rob Lezard's YouTube channel.'

Fenchurch felt a stab in his guts. He raced back to Dad's office as quickly as he could. 'What's going on?'

'Better if you watch it, Dad.'

Fenchurch sat down in front of the computer and googled 'rob lezard YouTube'.

His sombre face stared out of the screen, all earnest and pious despite being a lying charlatan. A video was posted twenty-three minutes ago:

Friday Night's Alright For Abduction

Fenchurch clicked it, his heart thumping hard.

'Hey guys.' Lezard's voice crackled out of the speakers, followed by a rasping sigh. 'Rob here, fighting the good fight as ever. Okay. For once, I'll do the housekeeping at the end. Time for something new, something *explosive*.' He sucked in a deep breath. 'Okay. Imagine the scene. You're a cop. Upstairs in your flat, washing the dishes, when your daughter's playing outside. Can keep an eye on her. Then you have a discussion with your wife about a garage bill, you look outside and she's gone.'

Fenchurch shut his eyes and bit down on his teeth.

'Every parent's worst nightmare. But it shouldn't happen to a cop. Especially not DI Simon Fenchurch of the Met. A rising star at the time. Now, I've been building up a profile of him over the last few years, about the tragic tale.'

Fenchurch felt his dad's hand slide over his and didn't resist it.

'Fenchurch found his daughter, Chloe, almost four years ago, living under the name Jennifer Simon. Her parents, the people who raised her, are both serving life sentences. But that's all old news. I want to cover something new. Something very, very juicy.'

Fenchurch opened his eyes and saw a photo of him and Brendan Holding in the pub.

'Now, this is DI Fenchurch. Sorry, I should say DCI Fenchurch. My old rank, as you all know. Fenchurch was meeting Brendan Holding here in the Prospect of Whitby, down on the banks of the Thames. Why were they meeting? Well, only these two men can attest to that. Problem is, one has been missing since that night. The other is DCI Fenchurch, who was recently made aware of Mr

Holding having an affair with his wife. Could even be the father of his son. Who knows.'

The image was replaced by Lezard's face again. 'But what have we here?' His mouth opened and his eyes went wide.

Another photo filled the screen.

Holding standing by an open car boot, like he was pleading with someone.

Then he was inside the boot, staring out with a split lip.

Then the boot was shut.

Lezard appeared back on the screen. 'What happened to Brendan Holding on Friday night? Only DCI Fenchurch can answer that question.'

40

Fenchurch ate the blandest sandwich he'd ever tasted. 'I really could do with some Tabasco sauce on this.'

Sergeant Colin Scott scowled at him. A big fuzzy bear of a cop, his suit crumpled and frayed, half of the pinstripes invisible against the faded navy. And the stain on the lapel, could be tears, could be something much worse. Still, as Police Federation Reps went, he was one of the best, a whole community in one body. Just, why did he have such terrible taste in sandwiches? 'Chilli will rot your guts.'

'And cheese and tomato won't?' Fenchurch took another bite, but it was hitting a spot, if not *the* spot.

This was his favourite interview room, but sitting on this side of the table, with the mic on its stand aimed right at *his* mouth, with the camera pointing more towards him than the interviewers...

Christ almighty.

Fenchurch swallowed, but his throat felt tight. 'Anyway, thanks for it. And thanks for being on this side of the table.'

'Any cop who tries to do the right thing is bound to end up on the wrong side of the table at least once, Si.' Scott shrugged. 'And I'm glad to help. Very glad.'

Fenchurch was as glad of his help. 'So, how do I play this?'

'Well, the thing is, it all comes down to what you've got on Loftus and Owen. This isn't an official investigation, not yet anyway. If you have something on them, you can get them to bugger off. But if they're as squeaky clean as I fear, then...' Scott exhaled, deep and slow. 'Good luck. Might need a lawyer in here instead of me.'

'Thanks for the vote of confidence.' Fenchurch rolled his eyes, dramatically, but there was a big chunk of truth in it. 'There's a murderer at large. That's what I should be focusing on, not this bollocks. And Lezard... He's a liar and a cheat and... Bloody hell.'

'Seriously, Si. No point in denying anything or playing games. Just lay it on the line. Tell the truth. If you've done nothing, then don't hide anything. And I mean, anything.'

'Fair enough.'

'You ready?'

Fenchurch took a deep breath, crushed up his sandwich wrapper. No time like the present. 'Let's do it.'

'Okay.' Scott walked over to the door, knocked and stepped back to his chair.

Owen entered, slouching and avoiding eye contact. His companion, a female plainclothes officer Fenchurch didn't recognise, sat next to him and got out a yellow legal pad. She leaned forward, introduced them, then started scribbling on her pad.

This was real. This was formal.

Owen stared at Fenchurch, his gaze scanning across his face, like he could see the truth instead of pockmarks and stubble. 'DCI Fenchurch, do you know why you're here?'

'I do.' Fenchurch took a deep breath. 'I want to help you find Mr Holding.'

Owen clenched his jaw. 'Okay, so that's how you're going to play it?'

'I'm going to be entirely honest with you. My side of what happened. But I want to be clear here, I didn't do anything to Mr Holding and I want to help you find him.'

Owen gave a flash of his eyebrows. 'Okay, so let's go back to Friday night, then.'

Fenchurch locked eyes with him, staring hard for a few seconds, then leaned forward so his lips were level with the microphone. No messing about, no misheard words. Just the truth. 'This weekend, I had custody of my son. I asked my daughter, Chloe, to babysit him while I met with Mr Holding for a pint of beer. Though I took maybe two sips of it.'

'Thank you. And why did you meet?'

'Because I wanted to hear his side of the story.'

'What story would that be?'

'Mr Holding had been involved with my wife, Abi. A few years ago, when we were divorced. They were colleagues, but it developed into something else.'

'You remarried?'

'Right. February 2016.'

'Just over four years ago. And your son was born not long after?'

'That's correct. And that's a matter I don't wish to discuss.'

'Because you're not the father?'

'I am his father, Chris. That's not in question. Never been in doubt.'

'Okay, I'm sorry. Years of experience of dealing with people who lie to me. But I need to know why don't you wish to discuss it?'

'Because it's not material to whatever you're looking into here.' Fenchurch held his gaze until he looked away. 'Mr Holding had seen Abi a few times when we were divorced. More than a few. They were briefly an item. Then... they rekindled it last year. Met once, then agreed not to do it again. That's what my wife told me.'

'And that's what you wanted to discuss with Mr Holding?'

'Correct. He said the exact same thing to me on Friday.'

'And what did that make you think?'

'A lot of conflicted emotions. I mean, I've got to accept my part in what happened, that a lot of it is my fault. I'd been working late after my recent promotion, meaning I was distant at home, while our daughter was reintegrated into our lives and... Abi was stressed by it all. Who wouldn't be? A career, a toddler, a daughter who we'd lost for eleven years and... And I didn't help her. The final straw was in December. I caught a case, just before I was supposed to head down to Cornwall, where Abi was staying with her parents and our children. One night, she went out to meet a friend.'

'Mr Holding?'

'Correct, but she told Chloe it was someone from school, someone who'd moved down there like Abi's parents had. But that was it, one night in Cornwall. Chloe babysat for Abi.'

'Just like you on Friday. And you're saying she broke it off?'

'I do. The way she's explained it, Abi regrets it. She wants to recommit to our marriage.'

'And you?'

'I just don't know. It's a betrayal. But...'

Owen left him a pause, but no way was Fenchurch going to fill it. He'd slipped there, giving away a bit too much emotion. And Owen knew it, judging by his wolfish grin. 'Simon, did you kill Brendan Holding?'

'No.'

'Did you harm him?'

'No.'

'Did you arrange for anyone to take him or harm him?'

'No. I drove home. Didn't even finish my pint, like I said. I stopped for a bottle of wine on the way home and drank that with my daughter. You can check with her.'

'And you've no idea what happened to Mr Holding?'

'Look, I'm not angry with him. He's just someone who...' Fenchurch tasted the bile in his throat. 'Really, if it wasn't Brendan Holding it would've been someone else who wasn't me. I blame myself, not him. And I don't blame Abi either. It's all on me.'

Owen sat back and stared up at the ceiling. His lips twitched, but he didn't say anything. He looked back down at Fenchurch, then leaned forward. 'Interview terminated at seventeen thirteen.' He glanced at the camera and waited until the red light went off.

The door opened and Loftus entered, hands in pockets, eyes narrowed. 'Thank you, Jess.'

'Right, sir. Okay.' She got up and left the room.

Loftus nodded at Scott. 'You too, Colin.'

He folded his arms across his chest. 'Sure about that?'

Loftus smiled. 'Positive.'

Scott nudged Fenchurch in the arm. 'Simon?'

'Let's see what they've got to say. I'll catch you later.'

'Be good to get out of this suit and back into my uniform.' Scott patted Fenchurch on the arm, then hauled himself up with cracking knees. 'I'll be outside, okay? Any shenanigans, let me know.'

'Sure.' Fenchurch watched Scott leave the room.

Loftus walked over to the table, sat, then unplugged the microphone and camera. 'Okay, this is entirely off the record.' He stared hard at Fenchurch, his pupils wobbling. 'I want the unvarnished truth, Simon. Did you do anything to Holding?'

'You want the unvarnished truth?' Fenchurch shook his head. 'You just had it. On that video. I had nothing to do with whatever's happened to him.'

'Swear to God?'

'I'm not religious, Julian, but I'll swear on the lives of my kids.'

'Wow. That's... Well.' Loftus raised his eyebrows. 'So what happened to him, then?'

'I've no idea. Like I keep telling people, I left him in the pub. Drove home. Never saw him again. Now, whatever Lezard thinks he's got on me, it's not on me. If that makes sense. It's on someone else. Looks like someone chucked him in a car boot.'

Owen reached into a wallet and got out a sheet of A4, but he didn't show it to Fenchurch. 'We've pulled the CCTV from outside the pub from when you left. We've got you driving off.' He passed the page over, but Fenchurch didn't look at it. 'We also found two guys frog marching Mr Holding off into the darkness, out of range of the cameras.'

Fenchurch looked at it now. The two figures were blurry,

masked and hooded. One of them held a knife against Holding's back. 'Christ, so someone's taken him.'

Owen narrowed his eyes at him. 'Was it you, Fenchurch?'

'Of course it's not. You just said I drove off!'

'Did you drive back?'

'No!' Fenchurch tapped the page, right above the timecode. 'I was in Sainsbury's buying a bottle of wine. I gave you my receipt.'

'Could belong to anyone.'

'Paid with my phone, Chris. I was there. You should pull *that* CCTV.'

Owen smirked. 'Okay, Simon, I want to believe you. You're a good cop and a good guy. But we need to be careful here. Very careful.'

'Why? Has Lezard given you something?'

Owen laughed now. 'Is there something he could give?'

'No. I just wonder how good he is at photoshopping.'

'Listen, Rob Lezard is an untrustworthy individual. We know that. Thanks to you, we've got an identity for him. A real name, someone we can pin things to. For some reason, he's trying to destabilise things. Now, we know he's been stalking your wife, Simon. That's not good behaviour. But we need to investigate these allegations.'

'I understand that.' Fenchurch switched his gaze between Owen and Loftus. Neither of them were giving anything away. 'So, what's going to happen? Suspension?'

Owen looked at Loftus, then leaned over the table. 'We're not suspending you, Simon, but I am going to spend the next two shifts working with you. You won't get out of my sight, okay?'

Fenchurch could shout and scream for Colin Scott to come back in, but what would that achieve? Make them suspect him more? He gave a shrug. 'Fair enough.'

Owen held out his hand. 'Phone.'

'What?'

'Superintendent Bell asked you for it last night and you disobeyed a direct order.'

Fenchurch rubbed his temples. 'No, I went to the toilet and couldn't find him afterwards.'

'A likely tale.' Owen gestured with his hand again. 'Phone.'

Fenchurch had no choice here. 'Thing is, Chris, if I was guilty, all those end-to-end encrypted messages would be erased. And the phone would be at the bottom of the Thames in a thousand fish-sized pieces.'

'Still, I want it.'

Fenchurch reached into his pocket and passed it over. 'Passcode is 2868.'

'Very funny.' Owen popped it into an evidence bag. 'Thanks for complying.'

'What'll I do—'

'Here.' Owen passed him a replacement. 'You'll need to give this number to your contacts.'

Fenchurch took it. Nothing like as expensive. 'There's probably no spyware or tracking devices on this, right?'

Owen laughed. 'Hardly any.'

'And I'll never find them.'

'Hard to find things that aren't there. I'll warn you – all of your messages will be read, all of your calls listened to. And I reserve the right to demand immediate access at any time.'

Fenchurch tried to act calm, but his heart was thumping. 'When do I get my old one back?'

'When you're cleared.' Owen smiled. 'Or when you get out of prison.'

THE DRIVER

Abi Fenchurch was standing in the window of the flat upstairs, looking out, holding her infant son in her arms and talking to him, whispering sweet nothings.

The air was cold, but he was sweating. Fear, stress. His heart rate was all over the place. Maybe his watch was double counting, but maybe not.

He'd got a job to do and he was doing it.

Now.

He opened the door, but an old car rattled up alongside his.

Fenchurch's dad was behind the wheel.

41

CHLOE

Grandad pulled in outside Mum's flat, but it didn't look like he was going to get out. Meaning it was time for another of those lectures. 'You never think about learning to drive, love?'

Well. That wasn't the one Chloe expected to receive. She peered up to the flat and saw her mother in the window, holding her brother up to the glass. He was getting too old for that, but after all the stuff he'd been through in his short life, maybe he needed a little bit more affection than other kids. Or Mum needed to give him it.

Yeah, that's what it meant to be a Fenchurch. Suffering. Lots of it.

She looked over at Grandad. 'I took a few lessons before... All this. And living in London, it's so much easier to get the tube or the bus or whatever than a car.'

'Different times, eh? Remember when your old man was a nipper, all he wanted was his motor. Gave him freedom, he said. Last thing his mother wanted. Lock him up in his room and keep him safe, that's what she said. Then he became a cop and, well, all the stress she got from me being on the Job, well it was double when it was her little boy, wasn't it?'

And there it was. Took a few extra moves, but the lecture had arrived. 'This your way of asking how I'm getting on as a cop?'

He glanced over. 'How is it going?'

'Tough.' She shuddered as she yawned. It crawled right down her body, down into her stomach and her legs. 'They don't tell you how bad working a shift pattern is in the leaflets, do they?'

'Brutal, love.' Grandad laughed. 'Overnight, then morning, then back, when you just don't know where you are. Half the reason most become detectives is you're mostly nine-ish to five-ish. Course, it never works out that way. Seven to bloody midnight.'

'Seems to be the way with Dad.'

'Your old man's a bit of a masochist, it has to be said.'

Chloe raised her eyebrows. 'Oh?'

'He's got a hero complex, hasn't he? Thinks he can save the world. Number of times he's got himself in a scrape with some muppet... Probably all down to—'

'Yeah, I get it.'

Something battered off the window.

Mum was peering in, scowling at them, Al in her arms, motioning for Grandad to wind down the windows. Christ, Chloe hadn't seen her.

'Hold your horses, love.' Grandad got both back windows to open, then Chloe's. 'Bloody hell!' Finally his own wound down. 'You alright, Ab?'

'Had better, Ian. Do you want to put him in his car seat?'

'I'll help.' Chloe got out and raced around the car.

Her brother was dressed in the latest West Ham home kit, the claret torso and pale-blue arms, his sleeves covering his tiny hands. Socks went up past his knees. Even had boots on. Super cute. He spun around and thumbed at the back. 'Daddy got me this, Ko-wee.'

Fenchurch

9

As cute as a button, and that speech impediment made him even cuter.

'It's super cute, Al. Super cute.'

'Ah-wee, pwease. Super Ah-wee Fenchurch. I gonna score, Ko-wee.'

She laughed, then opened the back door as the window wound up. She tugged at the car seat and it felt like it would support her father's bulk, let alone her baby brother.

'Abi, look, I just think you should listen to what he's got to say.'

'I appreciate you're trying to mend things between Simon and I, but I need you to butt out, okay?'

Grandad scowled at her. 'Charming.'

'Oh, Ian, don't be like that. Please.'

'Love, I'm just trying to save my son's marriage. For the second time.'

'Maybe you need to leave it to us?'

'Right. Maybe.'

Chloe clicked the last belt in and gave the whole thing a shake. Rock solid. 'You okay, little man?'

'Yes, Ko-wee. Wanna see Tonio.'

'See who?'

'Michail Antonio.' Grandad rubbed Al's head. 'He's West Ham's best striker.' He winked. 'Ko-wee.'

'I wike Tonio.'

'I don't know if he's playing, Al.' She smiled. 'Ally. Well, Super Ally Fenchurch, that's you locked in. Next stop, the Olympic Stadium.'

'Wondon Stadium.'

'Okay.' She kissed his forehead and eased the door shut, save for any stray fingers.

Grandad was behind the wheel, the engine rattling.

Mum was standing on Chloe's side, like she was going to pounce on her. 'Can I have a word?'

'Maybe tomorrow, Mum.' She pecked her on the cheek, then darted past her before she was grabbed and got in. 'Let's go.'

Grandad put the car in gear and drove off. 'You okay there, sunshine?'

'I'm *fantastic*, Grampa.'

Grandad laughed, stopped at the corner waiting for the traffic to clear. 'Good boy, son.'

Her brother started singing, 'Ah-w, Ah-w, super Ah-w! Ah-w, Ah-w, super Ah-w! Ah-w, Ah-w, super Ah-w! Super Ah-wee Fenchurch!'

Grandad laughed. 'That's the one, son!'

Chloe took another look at that car. Was it the same one as outside her mother's school? She got out her phone and scanned through the texts to her dad. There.

Her blood ran cold.

Same car.

Grandad pulled off along the street, going way faster than an old man should. 'You okay, love?'

'It might be nothing.'

'What might?'

'There was a car outside Mum's school this morning.'

'Heard about that. Your old man arrested that stalking pri—' Kid in the car. '—ince, didn't he?'

'They let him go, though.' She frowned. 'And he's back, watching Mum's flat again.'

'Didn't your old man arrest him?'

'Yeah, but he let him go. Rob Lezard.'

'Him?' Grandad stopped. 'Sure it's him?'

'Well, no. Why?'

'Because we're searching for him.' Grandad pulled a U-turn in front of a white four-by-four.

'Super Ah-w! Super Ah-wee Fenchurch!'

Grandad drove back towards the street Mum's flat was on, slowing as he passed, then speeding up after it. 'God, my eyes ain't what they used to be. Is that Lezard behind the wheel?'

'If it's not him, who is it?'

'I've no idea.' Grandad slowed again at the lights. 'Lezard got your old man into a bit of hot water, as it happens. Call him.'

Chloe hit dial, but it didn't ring. Just hit voicemail. She tried again, same result. 'His phone's off.'

Grandad thumped the steering wheel. 'Buggering thing was seized!'

'Why buggy thing sneezed, Grampa?'

'Sorry, little man.' Grandad turned up the radio, the announcer reading out the teams, then smiled at Chloe. 'Antonio's starting.'

'Yay!'

Grandad looked over at her. 'They took your old man's phone after... what happened.'

Chloe went through her contacts and found another number, then hit dial.

42

FENCHURCH

Fenchurch stood on the street, one he'd walked down hundreds of times and which he knew inside out. Knew a few people in the flats overlooking it. But there was danger here.

Well, maybe.

He glanced at Owen. 'Only shadow I've usually got is my son. Now I've got to deal with you.'

Owen smirked. 'Maybe you shouldn't have murdered the man your wife had an affair with?'

'That's a bit close to the bone.'

Owen shrugged like it was nothing. 'How old's your lad?'

'Three years, four months.'

'Not quite at that point where you stop counting the months, then?'

'Not with him. *Never* with him. After everything we've been through, every day is precious. I spoil the little rascal something rotten. Bought him a full West Ham kit on a whim.'

'Bless him. I got a Swansea one for my lad. Cost a pretty penny, I tell you. The price of *socks...*' Owen looked Fenchurch up and down. 'You okay, Simon?'

'Not really. Lezard... He's been stalking my wife, staking out her home. I warned him and he... He bloody ignored me. Went straight back to it. *Here.*'

'All the same, you're here at my discretion. This goes south, you're out of here.'

Fenchurch could argue, but what was the point? He needed to be here, so he needed to be on his best behaviour.

His radio crackled. 'Control, Delta-Seven-Three.'

'Delta-Seven-Three, Control.'

'Advise Alpha-One-Four the location is secure. Over.'

'Alpha-One-Four, Control. DCI Fenchurch copies.'

'Control, Clear... Sir.'

Fenchurch smiled. 'Cheers, Adam. Appreciate it.' He beckoned for Owen to follow, then set off towards the street.

'You know this Burridge well?'

'He's my daughter's TO.' Fenchurch frowned. 'Well, he was. I'm not sure if he still is or not. Chloe trusts him enough to call him to call me, so in my book that means he's good people.'

'Good people.' Owen laughed. 'You sound American.'

'Spent a while over there. Therapy for what happened with Chloe, but it didn't work out like that.' Fenchurch stopped where he could get a good look at the street. 'Anyway.'

The street was blocked off by a squad car. Adam Burridge stood there, arms folded. Dressed down for his days off, but he seemed to be the kind of officer who'd work whenever he was asked.

Fenchurch spotted the car, Lezard's car, and his stomach lurched. 'It's bloody empty.'

Burridge frowned. 'What?'

'Well, when you spoke to my daughter, she said someone was in it. Possibly Lezard.' Fenchurch set off back towards his own car, trying to call Chloe, but it didn't ring.

Of course – they'd be at the bloody London Stadium now. The signal was always overloaded there, despite all the promises from the board for decent wi-fi and what have you.

Someone was walking towards them, clutching a coffee cup.

Hood up, his face lost to the dark evening. He clocked Fenchurch and stopped dead. Then dropped his coffee and sprinted off.

Fenchurch took it slower than he wanted to, just about managing a jog, though Owen could shift and soon outstripped him. Fenchurch got as far as the car before his knee cracked. He bit through the pain and got in, twisting the key and slamming it in gear, then shooting off after Lezard.

Had to be him, thinking the hoodie would disguise him.

Owen wasn't too far behind Lezard now, each step narrowing the gap.

Fenchurch jerked the wheel to the side and slammed on the brakes, cutting across the pavement and almost crashing into the wall.

Lezard jumped over the bonnet without breaking his stride.

Shit.

Owen had to stop and run around the car, his eyes full of rage and fury, his ire doubling when he saw who was behind the wheel.

Lezard had turned around and headed back towards Abi's flat.

And Burridge.

Fenchurch put the car into reverse then whizzed back, shooting off along the street and keeping pace with Owen.

Lezard was getting into a Prius, parked over the road from Abi's side street. The stolen Prius, belonging to someone Ogden.

Burridge had secured the street, but hadn't secured Lezard's car. Probably had a good view of the flat from there.

Lezard's car shot off towards Upper Street.

Fenchurch knew these roads well, though. Better than anyone. He reached over and let Owen into the car. 'Get in.'

Fenchurch powered along, then slowed as he cut onto the main road and followed Lezard north, past all the restaurants and pubs he knew so well. He pulled up behind the queue of traffic at the lights.

Lezard's car shot straight through the red.

A car cut in from the side and smashed into it.

Both cars spun, but Lezard's vehicle slammed into a bus stop, mercifully empty, but the sickening thud was loud through the windscreen.

'Call an ambulance!' Fenchurch got out and ran across the road to Lezard's car, crumpled and broken.

Lezard was slumped against the wheel.

Fenchurch reached over, eased down the hood and recognised him.

It wasn't Lezard.

It was Will Merton, James Mortimer's boss from Travis.

43

The whole street was chaos. Stopped cars honking horns. Pedestrians on their phones or just gawping at the destruction.

Fenchurch had no idea what to do. Everything flashed around in his head. All the possibilities. All the threats.

Fenchurch thought he had Lezard, but it'd been Will Merton. Will thought he'd got away from them, but he must've clocked them, gambled at the junction and the gamble didn't pay off. He got hit. Fenchurch hoped no innocent people were going to spend time in hospital because of Will's choice.

Will had been the one tailing Abi, not Lezard. Staking out her house. Watching her.

Shit.

Fenchurch wondered if he should go back to see if Abi was okay. No, he needed to focus on this. Here and now.

He reached over and felt Will's neck for a pulse. 'He's still alive.' He looked over at Owen. 'Call it in!'

'Right.' He dashed off back to the car.

Hard to survive a collision like that, but Will Merton had. Fenchurch inspected his wounds. He'd seen a lot worse. Seemed mostly superficial.

Owen was holding his radio to his ear. 'I need an ambulance to...' He stopped, frowning. 'Where is this?'

'Upper Street, junction with Canonbury Lane.'

Fenchurch had other priorities right then. 'Stay with him.' He shot across to the other car, mangled and crushed like it'd been through machines at the scrapyard.

Two men in the car.

Shit.

The man behind the wheel was bloodied and cut. He stared at Fenchurch with concussed eyes, rolling around in his head, struggling to decide which Fenchurch to focus on.

The passenger wasn't much better, just sitting there swearing.

'Chris!' Fenchurch swung around. 'Need three ambulances!' He stopped trying to take control of the here and now.

He took out his phone and called Abi.

'Hello?'

'Abi, it's Simon. Are you okay?'

'Your number didn't show up.'

'Long story. Are you okay?'

'I'm fine. Just going to meet up with Kay for a drink.'

'Right.' Weird situation where her best mate worked for Fenchurch. 'Listen, we've caught your stalker. He's—'

'Rob Lezard?'

'No. Someone else.'

A squad car pulled up and Burridge got out.

'Listen, I've got to go, but I just wanted to see if you were okay.'

'I'm fine, Simon. Thank you for checking in.'

'Don't mention it.' Fenchurch killed the call and walked over as fast as his clicking knee would let him. 'Adam, can you take charge of this?'

He was nodding, cool as you like. 'Sure thing, sir.'

'Good man.' Fenchurch charged over to the smashed Prius.

Owen was leaning against the car door, holding his radio out like a kid on the bus listening to their tunes on their phone. 'Ambulances all on the way. ETA five minutes for the first.'

'We can triage them, right?'

'Merton seems the least bad. Agreed?'

'Well, not sure. One is certainly a lot worse, but the other seems okay. I don't want to take any risks, though.' Fenchurch stared at Will.

He needed to find out what the hell Will Merton was up to. But he needed to make sure he was okay.

Will was awake, but his pupils were like manhole covers. Blood ran down to his eyes from a cut on his forehead.

Christ. What a mess.

By the time Fenchurch got to the car, Nelson was there, sitting in the passenger side.

He looked over at Fenchurch. 'The ambulance is on the way.'

Will coughed. 'Thank you.'

Fenchurch stared at him across Nelson. 'You've been snooping on my wife?'

'I haven't.'

'No, you have. This car was seen at her school. At my flat. Now, it's here. I chased you from outside her flat. Why?'

'Can't tell you.'

'Can't? Or won't?'

'You'll just waste time trying to find out.'

'Right, sod this.' Nelson grabbed Will's hand, all smeared with blood, and applied pressure to the back, right where the bone was. 'You came after his family. His wife. His son. His daughter. Why?'

'That's sore.' Will stared at his hand. 'What do you think you're doing?'

'This is nothing.' Nelson leaned in, his voice shrill and sinister, and grabbed Will by the throat, squeezing tight and cutting off his air. 'When I give you back your air you better use it wisely or those words will be your last.'

Fenchurch grabbed him by the arm and tried to pull him away. 'Stop!'

Nelson wouldn't be deterred. 'If you don't talk to me, I'm going to hurt you. I know about seven ways I can break a finger, all of which will look like an injury you sustained in your crash.'

'I'm recording this.'

Nelson let go of the hand. 'What?'

'There are cameras everywhere.' Will pointed at the radio and, sure enough, there was a lens in there. Same with the air vents.

Shit.

Nelson was screwed. Threatening a suspect on camera. And while it was illegal surveillance, it would end his career.

Intel.

'How do I access the footage?'

Will coughed and blood dribbled down his cheek. 'On my phone, but you're screwed. It's all backed up to the cloud. My bosses can access it.'

Shit. Whoever Will worked for, they'd already have this. Possibly be watching right now.

'Why are you stalking my family?'

'No idea.' Another cough. 'I do what I'm told to.'

'By Travis?'

'Hardly. By someone who wants to know.'

Could be undercover, could be underworld. Either way, Nelson was screwed.

Fenchurch grabbed Nelson and pulled him out of the car. 'Jon, you need to get out of here. Okay?'

'Guv.' But he looked lost. He just stood there, staring into space.

Fenchurch took his seat. 'You should talk to me.'

Will rubbed at his cheek with his free hand. 'You thought I was Rob Lezard, didn't you?'

'Why do you think that?'

'Because I was there when you caught him. Getting a coffee from a deli. I'm not stupid. I park this car nearby then leave it. It records for me. Many more cameras on the outside than the ones you're aware of. Keep my distance. Keep myself safe.' Another cough, sounded like he tore his lung open. 'And you got Lezard, thought he was driving this car. But he's not exactly innocent. He's been snooping around at your wife's too. Asking her questions she didn't want to answer.'

'Show me.'

Will hit a button on the dashboard and the screen came to life. Rather than choosing radio stations, it showed a file structure, like Fenchurch had seen on the CCTV system in the station.

Dates, times, places.

Fourth bottom was Abi's address earlier this afternoon. Would be after she'd finished school and collected Al from childcare. Before Dad had picked him up to take him to the match.

Will pressed the screen and the video started playing, a four shot of images in vibrant colour.

Will's car was on the main road near the flat, with two of the four cameras pointing towards Abi's flat. One along the street, one up at it.

A car swerved in to the street and double-parked opposite. One of those SUV Teslas that weren't quite everywhere, but certainly becoming popular. Lezard got out of the driver's side, stuffed his hands into his pockets and laughed.

Someone else must've been in the car.

Lezard just walked over to the door and pressed the buzzer. Nobody answered, but Lezard was giving the street a good going over.

That old chestnut – check who was in before you broke in.

Then Abi's car pulled up.

Lezard walked over to the Tesla, giving a blink-and-you'll-miss-it cutthroat gesture, then got in behind the wheel and drove off.

Fenchurch didn't get a good look at the passenger, but there was one.

Still, he got a great view of the number plate.

44

Fenchurch was driving slowly, through one of those bits of Hackney the hipsters hadn't even heard of, let alone turned into craft breweries and bike cafés. One side of the road was lock-ups, the other was an old primary school and two factories, one making clothes, the other furniture. 'God, remember when this city used to make things?'

'When this *country* used to.' Owen exhaled slowly. 'Well, I don't see anyone here.'

'No, but let's keep looking. Those lock-ups are mighty tempting. We should have a look inside.'

Owen laughed. 'Simon, there's no way we can get a warrant based on illegally obtained recordings.'

He was right, of course.

Fenchurch had to get Lezard. Had to. *How* was the bastard problem he couldn't solve.

'So far, we've managed to narrow the car's location to this area because he triggered one ANPR camera—' Owen waved behind them. '—but didn't come out somewhere over there. You're the expert here. This is your patch. So when you tell me there's no other way out, I have to believe you but—'

'Chris, we're sandwiched between train lines and the marshes here.'

'Right, but that's a lot of ground to cover, which means we've got to get lucky.'

'Or what? You'll kick me off the force?'

'I could give you a cute answer, Simon, but the jury's still out on that one.'

Fenchurch pulled up and tried to think it all through.

What did he know?

Lezard wasn't on his own, but was with someone.

Mortimer?

Made sense.

But why was he stalking Abi? Lezard had said he was doing a documentary about their hunt for Chloe.

So why visit the house?

Did they want to abduct her?

Or speak to her about him? Confront her about what happened between Fenchurch and Brendan Holding on Friday night.

That felt more like it – instead of going after his family, they'd go after the next best thing.

His career.

And Owen was right. He'd need amazing luck if he was to find Lezard.

Wait a second.

Lezard was really Steven Vickers.

Dad had said he'd come from a well-off family. Privately educated, then it all fell apart. Lost their business, shuttered in the recession in 1992.

He looked back at the factories, but it was hard to make out the names.

SCC Clothing Enterprises Ltd.

Veejay's World of Leather.

Bingo. It wasn't furniture; they made leather jackets. Used to, a very long time ago.

'Back in a second.' Fenchurch got out and his knee crunched

like his old man chewing pork scratchings. He walked along the lane to the factory.

Two big corrugated iron gates, lashed with layers of graffiti. One was padlocked, so Fenchurch grabbed the other one and tried it. Heavy, but he managed to open it wide enough to peer inside.

A huge storage room, but not quite dark.

In the middle, a man sat on a chair beneath a single light bulb. Beaten and bloody.

He looked over at Fenchurch.

James Mortimer.

Fenchurch hauled the gate up, letting it ride up to the ceiling as he raced inside the room. He stood over Mortimer and, just like back with Will Merton, he reached for a pulse.

Alive, just.

Then something pressed into Fenchurch's neck. Something cold, hard and made of metal. 'Give me your car keys.' Male voice, London too.

Fenchurch raised his hands. 'They're still in the car.'

'Great. Stay there, then.' He stepped towards the car, heading away from Fenchurch.

And he saw his face.

Rob Lezard.

Lezard took a deep breath, pointed the gun at Mortimer, and shot him.

45

The report from the gun rattled around the factory space.
Mortimer slumped back in his chair. Dead.

Christ. Fenchurch had thought Lezard was an idiot. A mischief maker. They'd badly underestimated him.

Owen was in the doorway, hands in the air, mouth slack and wide. 'Shit.'

Lezard shifted the gun to aim at Owen.

A car horn honked, one long blast.

Lezard looked over. A car pulled along the lane, slowly.

Fenchurch had to screw his eyes to see who was behind the wheel.

Tony Wyatt.

Lezard slammed the pistol into Owen's skull and he went down.

Fenchurch set off towards him.

Lezard pointed the gun at him, right way up. 'Oh no, you don't.' He backed away along the lane, slowly, aiming at Fenchurch.

No back-up in the vicinity, just a getaway car in an empty street.

Lezard got into Wyatt's car and it sped off, the passenger door slamming as it passed.

A bullet whizzed past Fenchurch, just as he dived on the ground.

The car slid around the corner, but Fenchurch clocked the plates.

Fenchurch raced back to Owen. 'You okay?'

'Barely touched me.' Owen patted at his temple. 'Went down like a sack of spuds, though, to make him think—'

'So you let him get away?!'

Owen got up, scowling. 'One, he had a gun on us. And two, your car's being tracked.'

'Tracked?' Fenchurch felt the realisation hit like a hammer to the skull. Owen's team were monitoring him. For how long, he didn't know. 'Right, well.'

'Means we can track Lezard.'

'No. He's in Tony Wyatt's motor, so we need to get after him.' Fenchurch walked back inside, as calm as he could muster as he got out the replacement phone. 'Call it in.'

Mortimer's body slumped on the chair. Shot in the chest, the blood already dyeing his white vest crimson. His eyes opened. 'You?'

Alive, but barely.

Fenchurch called over to Owen. 'Get one of those ambulances here, Chris.' He turned back to Mortimer and tore his vest down the middle.

The bullet looked like it had missed his heart, but the shot still cut through flesh and bone, with blood pouring out. Probably missed any veins or arteries, but Fenchurch was no expert.

Mortimer spat blood onto the floor. 'Vickers. Lezard. I don't know who he is now. I don't know if he does. He framed me for that bomb at the concert.'

Fenchurch couldn't see it, couldn't follow it to its conclusion. 'But you got off with it?'

'Right. Rachel stood up and backed me. O'Keefe kept it under his hat, tried to push through my conviction. I got off and they hated that. A free man.'

'Why didn't you come forward?'

'I can't trust the police after what they did. Lezard's going to do it again. He has another bomb.'

'Where?'

'It's an old one, broken. Someone was supposed to fix it, but they pulled out, so he got someone else to do it, but it blew up on him. Needed my help to fix it. I tried to refuse again, but you see what they did to me. I had no choice.'

'Guy like you, James. Ex-army. Faced death every time you defused a bomb. Come on, takes a lot more than a gun to frighten you.'

'When someone points a gun at you, you tend to let them lead.'

'You put your own life ahead of other's?'

'I'm weak. What can I say?' Mortimer swallowed. 'You need to stop him. Lezard's planted a bomb somewhere. He's going to blow it up tonight.'

'Where?'

'I don't know.'

Fenchurch put his phone to his ear. 'Kay, it's Simon. I need a location on Sierra Zulu 65 Sierra Kilo Alpha.'

'Hold on, guv.'

Fenchurch felt every single nerve twitching in his body. Felt like hours.

'Okay, you're in luck. It's just pulled up outside the London Stadium.'

46

CHLOE

Chloe *finally* got her phone to connect to the London Stadium's wi-fi, but it wasn't exactly like at home. The BBC website took ages to bring up the first page. All those stories her ex, Robert, had told her about how slow the internet used to be... This is what she imagined it was like. How did people cope?

No calls from her dad. Maybe she'd been wrong. Maybe it wasn't the right car. Christ, he'd be down on her like a ton of bricks if she'd made a mess of it.

Or maybe Adam had been all hero and done it all himself.

Maybe.

'Put the phone away.' Grandad was slurping tea from the big beaker. 'Your whole generation, you'll only be happy when you've got chips inside your heads.'

She looked at him and maybe he was right. She was here with her grandfather and her kid brother. She should be present. In the moment. 'I just wanted to see if Dad caught the guy.'

'Given he's not here, he'll be in an interview with him right now.' Grandad checked his watch again.

Chloe looked around and got goosebumps from being inside the stadium.

Seven Nation Army by the White Stripes blasted out, but the fans sang a rude song about Millwall along to the riff.

The players were down on the hyperreal green pitch, stretching and kicking balls around under bright lights that seemed bluer than daylight. The ex-players from Sky TV stood at the end, by the goal far away from them, talking to the camera.

Chloe felt as excited as Al. Super Ally Fenchurch. Well, maybe.

His little legs were swinging on the seat. He looked around at her, his mouth smeared with ketchup. 'Yellow, Ko-wee!'

'What?'

'Yellow strip, Ko-wee!'

'Who are?'

'Newcasteh-w.'

'That's good.' She rubbed his head, then the song faded abruptly.

The voice boomed out, 'You lot ready for the teams tonight?'

The crowd roared in response.

'Well, in goal we've got number one, Lukasz—'

'FABIANSKI!'

Al was shouting along with them. 'Woooo!'

'At right back, number three, Aaron—'

'CRESSWELL!'

Al stood up on his seat and punched the air, then did a little dance.

Chloe leaned over to Grandad. 'Can I get you another tea?'

'Sure thing, love.'

She brushed past and made her way along the crowd towards the stairs, having to connect her phone to the wi-fi all over again.

Impossible!

47

FENCHURCH

F enchurch got out of the squad car and almost dropped his phone, catching it on the way down. He tried calling again, but it just went to voicemail.

'This is Chloe. Leave a message and I'll call you back.' Still professional sounding from all those interviews she'd booked before becoming a cop.

He killed it, figuring the three he'd left already were enough, then texted her again:

Are you at the match? Need you to keep calm, but there's a bomb there.
CALL ME

Burridge was speaking to the stewards, flashing his credentials and arguing the toss.

Fenchurch's police radio chimed. 'Control, Alpha-Eight-Six, can you raise Alpha-One-Four.'

'Alpha-One-Four DCI Fenchurch, Control.'

'Christ!' Fenchurch clutched the radio tight. 'Receiving. Owen, what the hell is going on?'

'Operations are running this now, okay? You need to stand down.'

'What does that mean?'

'Well, you've got over fifty thousand people in there; this is their job. But we need credible intelligence that there's actually a bomb and it's not just Mortimer playing silly buggers with us.'

'Right. How is he?'

'Mortimer? Touch and go.'

'Okay. He give you any more about this bomb?'

'Just that it's a manual detonation. Timer charge. Ten minute countdown. Remote is unreliable, especially in a place like a football stadium during a match.'

So Fenchurch had ten minutes once it started.

Great.

'Okay, if you can stay with him. I might need his help.'

'What part of "stand down" didn't you understand?'

When a building was on fire, Fenchurch was the man who ran inside. 'I'll keep you updated. Fenchurch out.' He checked his phone—nothing—then followed Burridge's path towards the car.

A graphite Volkswagen SUV.

Nobody inside.

A male uniformed officer had blue gloves on and tried the door. It opened. He walked around the back of the car and opened the boot.

A woman jumped out, wild-eyed and furious. Hoodie and paint-spattered leggings, long hair held in a ponytail. Took Fenchurch a few seconds to place her. Rachel Jones. Mortimer's ex.

The uniform grabbed her and took her away from the car.

Fenchurch peered into the boot and saw the source of her distress.

Tony Wyatt. A bullet hole through his forehead.

Fenchurch walked over to Rachel. 'Who did this?'

'A man. I don't know who. That man—' She nodded at the car. '—came to my door and knocked me out and took me in the car and...'

'Do you know where he went?'

'He was talking about the boiler room.'

Same as at the O2.

'Thanks.' Fenchurch followed Burridge over through the yellow wall of stewards and into the bowels of the stadium.

As glamorous as they tried to make them seem on telly and in the build-up, the reality of a football stadium, even a state of the art one like this, meant you were only ever a flight of stairs or a security door away from a breeze-blocked corridor. And here they were.

Fenchurch's buggered knee meant he couldn't quite keep up with Burridge and his steward mate, but at least there were signs pointing to the boiler room. He turned the corner and followed the path to another door, then opened it.

A big lump of a man stepped through first. Slicked back hair, eye bags resting on golf balls. He looked Fenchurch up and down. 'You?'

Fenchurch took a second to recognise him. 'Jack Walsh?'

'Right. Got a bone to pick with you. Lost my job at Shadwell because of you.'

Fenchurch couldn't remember much about that old case. Football manager who shagged anything that moved. And a few things that didn't. 'Sure it wasn't because of who you were sleeping with?'

'I used to be lord of my own manor, now I'm youth coach here.'

'Isn't that a step up?'

'Is it hell, I've got to put up with—'

'Sir, I'm attending an official police matter. I don't want there to be any bad blood between us, so why don't you call me on Monday morning.' Fenchurch handed him a business card.

Walsh stared at it for a few seconds, and it seemed to pacify the big brute.

At least enough to let Fenchurch slip past and into the stairs down to the boiler room. He took them slowly, one a time. Hoping the timer wasn't running. His knee gave in and he almost tumbled forward, just managing to grab hold of the banister.

Christ.

He clutched the railing that bit tighter and took it that bit slower.

He heard Burridge down below. 'I'm arresting you—'

A gunshot, loud enough to be close.

Fenchurch had to hurry now. He jumped down the rest of the staircase and shouldered the door, breaking out into the boiler room.

Lezard was standing over Burridge, pointing his gun at him.

Fenchurch hadn't been spotted, so he held the door and eased it shut behind him.

'You faking it?' Lezard kicked Burridge.

Nothing.

Then again, harder.

Still nothing.

'Why is it always little old me, eh?' Lezard laughed to himself, then walked over to the boiler, which Fenchurch could feel the heat of from over by the door.

Lezard still hadn't seen Fenchurch.

Something was stuck to the side of the boiler. Looked like it'd been made on a kitchen table. Wires hanging everywhere. A clock radio in the middle.

The timer, connected to the detonator.

Christ.

Fenchurch got out his baton, then eased it out slowly and quietly.

Not slowly or quietly enough.

Lezard wheeled around, training the pistol on Fenchurch. 'Well, well. If it isn't old Skidmarks Fenchurch.'

'What?'

'That's what we used to call you. Thought you were the big shot, didn't you? On your way to the top. But your pants were full of skidmarks.'

Christ, he had lost it big time.

'You don't have to do this, Rob. It's okay.'

'Okay?' He laughed. 'Hardly. I'm going to blow this place up. You move, I shoot you. Understand?'

'Right.' Fenchurch raised his left hand in the air, keeping the baton behind his back. 'Why are you doing this?'

'Why not?'

'Steve, it's okay.'

'Steve?'

'Steve Vickers. Right?'

'Steve's dead.'

'Rob, why are you killing that old team?'

'I haven't been. You've been looking for James Mortimer, haven't you? Poor guy lost his marbles. Still, he can build a very good bomb.'

'You're assuming this is going to go off.'

'Oh, it will. Old Tony Wyatt's round at Rachel Jones's flat just now. Ready to kill her if this doesn't work.'

'We found Wyatt's body in the car.'

'Oh.' Lezard nodded over towards the door. 'Anyway. Once the timer's running, it'll be you in here. Copper going mad, losing his marbles over his wife's adultery. Lost the plot over the traumas he's experienced over the years. So sad, but the name Fenchurch will be ruined. Skidmarks Fenchurch.'

'What did I ever do to you?'

'Because *you* kicked me off the force. I was just doing my job. And you kicked me off.'

'I never did anything.'

'You did! I've seen the paperwork. DI Simon Fenchurch. You signed it.'

'You have any idea how many forms I fill out every day?'

'This is me you were doing it to. Me!'

'You lied under oath!'

'So now you remember?'

'No, but you can't lie. It undermines everything. We can't convict people if cops just lie.'

'Well, you deserve everything you get in here, Fenchurch.'

This wasn't over. Not by a long shot.

Fenchurch jerked his arm forward and tossed the baton through the air.

It arced away from Lezard, but his gaze followed its path. His aim shifted slightly.

Enough that the gun wasn't pointing at Fenchurch.

He launched himself forward, shoulder first into Lezard. Crashed him against the wall. He screamed out.

Something caught Fenchurch in the groin.

He went down.

Lezard stood over him, pointing the gun at him. 'Time to die.'

Something blurred through the air, knocking Lezard into the boiler.

Someone stood over Fenchurch, holding out a hand. 'You okay, Dad?'

He took a deep breath. 'I'm fine.'

'No you're not.' Lezard pressed the button and the timer started.

48

The numbers on the giant red digital display slipped away.

    9:57

9:56

Fenchurch grabbed Lezard and pushed him against the wall. 'How do you turn this off?'

Blotchy red skin cracked around Lezard's cheek. He laughed, with the mad eyes of a fanatic. 'Nothing. There's nothing you can do.'

Fenchurch tried pain first, twisting his arm around his back and slamming his face into the breeze block wall. 'How?' He grabbed his manbun. 'Do?' He tugged at it until Lezard screamed. 'I?' He let Lezard recoil. 'Stop it?'

'It's impossible now.' Despite the fresh blood, Lezard was still laughing. 'You'll die a famous death.'

Fenchurch yanked at his St Christopher, but he just tore it off.

Pain wasn't going to work.

He looked around the room.

Chloe stood over Burridge, finger to his neck. 'He's still alive.'

'I'm fine.' Burridge coughed. 'Totally fine.'

But Chloe was frowning like she knew he wasn't. 'Hey,

remember you were going to tell me what happened in your first month?'

Asking the kind of question that would keep people alive in films.

Fenchurch looked at the bomb, tried to trace the wires back to the detonator. Sweat trickled down from his forehead, blocking his vision. He wiped it away, but all he saw was a tumble of wires. No way to spot what did what.

Burridge coughed like he'd spat up a lung. 'Made a mess of taking a statement because my sergeant was pressuring me, so had to let this goon go. Daft sod did the exact same thing the next day. But I caught him this time. And I learnt a lesson from that. Don't rush things. Do it all properly.'

Which didn't exactly help Fenchurch. He was sweating like he'd run a 10k. 'Chloe, get him away to safety.'

'I'm not leaving, Dad. There's no time.'

Lezard laughed again. 'Oh, you have even *more* incentive to defuse this bomb.'

Chloe stomped over to them and grabbed Lezard by the wrist, then slapped on a handcuff and attached the other one to the bomb. 'We're keeping this arsehole right here with us. He's got front row seats for the explosion.'

A slight amount of doubt crept into Lezard's forehead, knitting into a frown. 'Just because I died first, it won't save you.'

'It's not about me.' Chloe crouched down. 'It's not even about my brother or my grandfather up there. Fifty-odd thousand people are here. Tons more in the surrounding area. We're saving them.'

'Forget it. I'm not helping you, I'm just going to watch that tick down.'

8:01

8:00

7:59

She looked over at Fenchurch. 'We're not getting anything out of him.'

He'd come to that conclusion during the pain session, but her attempt at reason and understanding just underlined it.

7:37.

He got out his radio. 'Control, Alpha-One-Four.'

'Control receiving.'

'Tell Owen the bomb is real. Repeat, the bomb is real and we have seven, repeat seven minutes. Over.'

'Shit.' Owen didn't say 'over'.

'Do I cut the red wire?'

The joke didn't land. 'Okay. Listen, I'm here with Mortimer. Can you get your phone and FaceTime me? Over.'

'No reception.' Fenchurch looked over at Chloe. 'Have you got any?'

'Don't even think about it. Everything was slower than Grandad eating.'

'Right.' Fenchurch put the radio back to his mouth. 'Negative. Over.'

'Shit.'

7:02.

'Chris, I've got seven minutes.'

'Okay, you're on with James Mortimer.'

Mortimer's breath was a harsh whisper. 'What can you see?'

Fenchurch looked at the box again. He had to wipe even more sweat away.

Lezard shifted his body so he was in his way, but Chloe cracked him on the back of the knee and he went down. She pinned him there.

'Right, I've got a box stuck to the boiler. Lots of wires. A clock, that's saying 5:50 now.'

'Okay, good. Can you follow the wires from the timer and tell me where they go?'

'There's like six cans attached to it.'

'Christ. It's like the one they had me working on. Okay, so each of those cans is big enough to blow up a tank. Six of them... Had that back in Iraq and—'

'I'm at 5:30 so if you could cut the reminiscences?'

'Sure, sure.' Mortimer coughed. 'Right, I've got a quick way of doing this and a very, very long way that's much safer.'

'How long are we talking?'

'Well, about thirty minutes longer than you've got, and you need a toolkit and five years training and experience, so let's just focus on the simple method.'

'Go on.'

'Go to the clock end.'

Fenchurch didn't touch it, but got as close as he could while still being able to focus his eyes on it. 'Got it.'

'There should be a master control wire. The clock will tick to zero and it triggers the detonation by an electronic signal. That signal goes into the splitter, which goes six ways to the cans. Each can will then receive the signal and detonate. Now, there should be failsafes in here, but when I saw this, they hadn't been engaged.'

Lezard was on the floor, looking up. Laughing.

'This prick's laughing.'

Mortimer gasped. 'Ignore him. Can you see the splitter?'

'There's a wire that goes into a little black box, like a cigarette packet. Blue light on it.'

'Excellent, that's it. Right. You need to check for an orange box, about the size of a matchbox.'

Fenchurch scanned the box. Nothing was that small. A cigarette packet, maybe. He tried to ignore the voice in his head screaming that his son and his father were upstairs. 'Can't see one.'

'Shit.'

'Is that bad?'

'No, it means the failsafe's engaged.'

'What does that mean?'

'Well, it explains why he was laughing. He's removed it. Christ, it was still on. Okay, so what it means is, if you remove the signal splitter, it'll send the signals to the cans and detonate.'

'So?'

'So that's it. Shit, we don't have time to evacuate the stadium.'

3:49

'There's no other way?'

'Simon, there is, but I'm halfway across London in an ambulance and my hands are cut to ribbons.'

'Listen to me, if there's any way I can dismantle this, you tell me. My little boy is upstairs. Fifty thousand people are here and they'll die. I'm not giving up without a fight. We don't have time, but that means we're free to try the last, desperate throw.'

'Okay. It's not going to be quick.'

'What do I do?'

'You need to snip each wire at the can ends.'

'With what?'

'Just tug them out. But you have to be very, very careful. If the reverse signal triggers, then that's it. Game over. This needs steady hands.'

Problem was, Fenchurch's were shaking.

THE FATHER

The Newcastle players were first out, getting into their huddle ahead of the match, but the bubble machine was kicking into gear, meaning it was only a matter of time now before the home side were out.

Ian Fenchurch looked along the row, but he couldn't see Chloe. He rubbed his grandson's head. 'Where's your sister got to with that cup of tea?'

'Grampa, Daddy said blue.' Ally pointed to the pitch. 'But ye-wow.'

Little guy was obsessed with colours, just like his old man. He remembered bringing Simon to his first match at Upton Park, Liverpool at home, and he was more interested in the hoardings behind the goal at the far end than the teams. How times changed.

Still, it was parky out and he could do with another lovely cuppa, though that rooibos stuff Tammy had been giving him would have to do.

'Where's Ko-wee, Grampa?'

After what they'd all been through, Ian always got that little tickle in his heart when Chloe was incommunicado. No idea how Simon or Abi coped with it. Or even if they did.

The little guy had been through his own travails, but that kind of separation was nothing compared to what happened to her.

'Sure she's just got stuck at the queue, Al.' Used to be that every time he used that name, he got a pang of pain at the little guy's namesake. Now, it was just every so often.

A man in a blazer ran onto the pitch then made his way to the Newcastle team. He spoke to that big lump, the captain who Chelsea had tried to buy. His name was on the tip of Ian's tongue. He spoke to his teammates, then they walked off.

The crowd noise got louder, drowning out the Stone Roses.

Something wasn't right.

Ian's old police instincts were kicking in.

The crowd were on their feet, like the Hammers had just scored, but there was no joy or release in their shouting. It wasn't just Ian Fenchurch who smelled a rat, instead they were fleeing the ship. A couple of men pushing past on their way to the exit.

Ian grabbed Al's hand and got him to his feet. He couldn't see Chloe, but he'd find her. He lifted Al up. 'Make way. Kid's gonna crap himself!' He carried Al along the way, much easier when they were all confused and standing up and avoiding a small child.

'Don't need, Grampa!'

'Yes you do! Oh it's a big one. Sorry, the wee lad crapped himself. Can you smell that? Need to get to the toilets. 'Scuse me, coming through, coming through. Little lad's been to the toilet.' He got to the stairs, then set Al down and led him up to the concourse.

Virtually empty, just a few stragglers watching the TVs and supping their drinks.

No sign of Chloe.

Ian needed to get the little lad out of here. Do some good. 'Come on, son, this way.'

A hand grabbed his shoulder.

He spun around ready to throw a punch.

Simon caught it. 'Careful, Dad. Knock someone's block off with that.'

Ian laughed, but it turned to frost when he saw the fear on his face. 'You okay, son?'

'Had better, Dad.'

'You look like you've crapped yourself.'

Ally cast an angry glance at him.

Chloe was next to him, eyes wide. 'Grandad, you should've *seen* what I just did.'

49

FENCHURCH

A few miles away, the match was finally kicking off, but the Fenchurch family weren't there. Three generations stood in the Leman Street station car park, pretty full for this time on a Friday.

Dad and Chloe stood there, hands in pockets.

Fenchurch held Al in his arms. Still just about small enough to do that. 'No, son, you need to go with your mother.'

'Daddy!' He was wriggling and kicking. 'Ah-wee stay with you?'

'I'm going to be busy, son.' It was the wrench that drove a wedge through his entire life. Separating his professional and personal worlds. And when they intersected, his instinct was to double down. 'I'll pick you up on Monday morning, then we'll go to Legoland again.'

Al stopped. 'For weal?'

'Really.' Fenchurch hoped it was open. If it wasn't, Harry Potter World or somewhere else would be. Anywhere over that way, just a big park. Sod it, he could drive up to the National Football Museum in Preston. If it was still there. 'We'll have a good time, just you and me.'

'Okay.'

'Good lad.' Fenchurch carried him over to Abi's car, then put him in the baby seat in the back. He leaned in, checked everything was triple locked, then kissed him on the forehead. 'Have a good night, yeah?'

'Did we win, Daddy?'

'The good guys won.'

'Yay!'

Another peck and Fenchurch shut the door.

Abi was frowning at him. 'Are you okay?'

'I just helped my daughter disarm a bomb that was powerful enough to blow up a football stadium, against a timer. I'm wired out of my head, Ab.'

'What was she—' She swallowed. 'Let's not get into this just now, yeah?'

'Sure.'

Chloe joined them, rubbing both of their arms. 'Mum, is it okay if I stay the weekend with you and Super Ally Fenchurch?'

'God yes.' Abi's mouth hung open. 'You don't need to ask.'

Chloe smiled. 'Be good to spend some time together.'

Fenchurch felt himself join in the grinning. 'I'll pick you up on Monday.'

'Dad, I'll get the tube or a Travis.'

'No way are you getting in one of them.' Fenchurch grimaced. 'No, I'll pick you up. Monday lunchtime.'

'You're going to be working all weekend on this case, aren't you?'

Fenchurch nodded. 'I wish I had the time off, but...'

'I get it, Dad.' She kissed his cheek, then got in the back with her brother.

Fenchurch smiled at Abi. 'I hope you have a good weekend, just the two of you.'

'Sure we will.' Abi bit her lip. 'About us, I need to think it all through.' She looked at him, eyes twitching and glowing. 'But I need the truth from you, Simon. Did you have anything to do with what happened to Brendan?'

'No.'

'Simon, I saw the video. Him getting shoved into a car. Did you do it?'

'No. And I swear on Al and Chloe's lives.'

'You better be telling me the truth.'

'I'm not the one who's been lying here.'

She shut her eyes. 'I deserved that.'

He reached out a hand for her to take. 'Let's talk this all through next week. Okay?'

A smile flickered across her lips, fleeting but it was there. 'Okay.' She got in the car and drove off.

Taking the family man with her.

Leaving the angry police officer.

FENCHURCH STOOD in the obs suite, watching Will Merton on the screen. His earlier co-operation had faded to a wall of silence.

Reed and Ashkani sat opposite, but each question just got a shrug.

'Bloody hell.' Fenchurch collapsed into his seat. 'He must know he's screwed.'

Owen nodded. 'At least we got hold of Mortimer. At least we stopped a bloody bomb going off.'

Fenchurch stared into space. He kept seeing Chloe's fingers touching the wires, tugging them out of the cans. One by one she'd done it, hers way steadier than his.

The only thing either one of them could've done.

Hard to think that if she hadn't, he'd be dead. His son and his father too.

Christ.

The door opened and a uniformed constable peered in. 'Sirs, that's Angus Percival here.'

Owen was already on his feet. 'Does he want time with his client?'

'Said he didn't.'

'Excellent.' Owen was rubbing his hands together. 'Come on, Simon, let's do him.'

'Sure about this?'

'Oh, yes. I can't let you out of my sight, remember?' Owen was first out into the corridor.

Fenchurch followed, but his head was thumping. So much stress over the years, and this on top of it all? Defusing a bomb? Christ.

He entered the room and Owen was already talking, sitting alongside Nelson.

Fenchurch had to stand and his knee was throbbing. Fantastic.

Owen leaned forward. 'Okay, so you decided to blow up a football stadium. Why?'

Lezard was sitting back, arms folded, looking at the clock above the door. 'I didn't.'

'Mr Vickers, you were—'

'The name is Lezard.'

'Steven Vickers. That's your name. Not Rob Lezard.'

He shrugged. 'Suit yourself. Thing is, I didn't do anything.'

'You shot two people. James Mortimer. Adam Burridge. And you tried to *bomb a football stadium*.'

Lezard snorted with laughter. 'Did nothing of the sort.'

Nelson frowned. 'What's up?'

'Well, it's just gone ten o'clock. I believe you've already faced a timer today, Simon. One you allege I set to blow up the London Stadium. I did set another one, though.'

Another bomb? What? Fenchurch tried to stay calm and level. 'What are you talking about?'

'Not a bomb, if that's what you're thinking. No, if I don't click on a link on my website, this little app I've got publishes a video to my YouTube channel. Very interesting stuff.'

Fenchurch felt like he had been blown up. He got out his phone, the one Owen had given him, and checked the page.

Sure enough, a video posted at ten o'clock on the dot.

The truth about DI Jon Nelson

Nelson looked like he was going to throttle him. 'What the hell is this?'

'Oh, there's a good chunk of stuff in there. Some leaked stuff about James Mortimer, but also about you, DI Jon Nelson. How you made a mess of a few investigations. How you dropped the bollock on the Mortimer case and framed him. Naughty boy. I mean, I've served as a cop and I've seen it happen. Sometimes investigators get confirmation bias, and they include stuff that supports their theory and bury the stuff that doesn't.'

'What is it?'

'I'd rather you watched it than I just told you, Jonathan. Remember that I was a cop back then. Same rank as you. I had access to the same stuff as you, you idiot. But you didn't listen.'

Nelson frowned. 'What are you—'

'I met you in the canteen at Scotland Yard. Remember? I told you everything that Dean Hatton was up to. How he'd been the one who planned to blow up the stadium. But you didn't listen. You had him if you looked, but you didn't and you sent me away and told me to keep silent. But you didn't listen. Just tried to frame Mortimer. Toady up to your bosses.'

'Hatton? It was you who—'

'Nope. He did it. He was your bomber. Not me. Trouble is, he set that bomb a few days ago, then accidentally set himself on fire. Does a lot of harm to you.'

Fenchurch didn't know what to think. 'You were the one who was bombing a stadium.'

'I'll use the James Mortimer defence. I was just trying to defuse it.'

Fenchurch found it hard to breathe. Yeah, he was going down for what he'd tried to do, but he seemed so confident.

'I've got that recording of Jon Nelson. From the car. Threatening Will Merton. DI Nelson is going down.' Lezard laughed. 'Just think, all those convictions that hinge on his testimony? They're going to throw them all out. Jon, the stuff in that video is proof of your corruption. You're going to lose your job, your life, your pension.'

Nelson towered over him, looking ready to smash his face in.

Fenchurch grabbed his arm and pulled him away. 'He ain't worth it.'

'Oh, Simon, I so am worth it.'

DAY 3

Monday
16th March, 2020

50

Th e door opened and Abi stood there, looking him up and down. 'She's gone to the shops to get some more football stickers for Al.' She walked into the kitchen and looked out of the window at the street. 'Back in a few minutes.'

Fenchurch looked out of the window too. 'You want me to wait down in the car?'

'You sure? I can get you a cup of tea? A coffee?'

'I need my bed. Lost my weekend to... Well. Helping a mate, but it's a lost cause.'

'Jon Nelson?'

Fenchurch looked away. 'He's in trouble, Ab. Deep trouble.'

'He'll lose his job?'

'Probably.'

'My God. He's a good cop, isn't he?'

'I thought so, but... It's not looking good for him.'

Abi pointed at the window, the same one Fenchurch had stood in front of eleven years before, doing the bloody dishes while some vermin kidnapped his daughter. Abi staying here had been a determined act, a way of taking ownership of it.

He'd had to get out of there, buy himself a bachelor pad where he could drown his sorrows.

Christ.

He wanted nothing more than to live back here.

He looked over at her. 'Listen, we should talk.'

'You want to clear the air now?'

'I do, but I'm just so bloody tired.' Fenchurch sighed. 'Listen. Bugger the counsellors, let's just get dinner and see how it goes.'

She smiled at him, widely now. 'I'd like that.'

'Tomorrow night?'

'Sounds good.' Fenchurch made for the door, but she stopped him.

'Simon, do you have any idea where Brendan is?'

'Holding? No. I've got my best guys on it. Kay's team. They'll find him if he wants to be found.'

FENCHURCH LEANED against his car and put his phone to his ear.

Chloe answered it straight away. 'Dad? You okay?'

'Yeah, just here to pick you up.'

'Oh. Right. Can you wait with Mum?'

'Yeah, I'll be in the car outside.'

'Oh. Right. Well, we're just at the checkout now. Be five minutes.'

'Don't sweat it.' He ended the call and put his phone away.

The sun was warm but the wind picked up the dirt and was flinging it at him, making him close his eyes. Made him feel like he was back here and his daughter was being taken.

Yeah, maybe he shouldn't live here. Maybe moving out to Leigh-on-Sea was what they should do. Get away from bloody London.

A car pulled into the street.

Fenchurch blinked hard and saw a high-end Mercedes rolling towards him.

The window slid down. 'Good afternoon, Fenchy.' Younis peered out.

What the hell?

Fenchurch tried to speak but couldn't.

'Oh, my love. Look at you. Lost for words, ain't you? You so aroused to see me?'

Fenchurch swallowed hard. 'How?' That was all he could manage.

'Got out already, didn't I? All thanks to DI Nelson's blunder. Judge gave me emergency bail ahead of my appeal. Case against me fell apart. Truly sorry about O'Keefe, though. I liked him. Bit greedy, though.'

'You paid him?'

'You think that was a ruse? He was as bent as a nine-bob note, him.' Younis grinned. 'Wanted more money, wanted it sooner, wouldn't listen to my advice on best practise on bribing a cop and getting away with it. But I did the best I could.'

Fenchurch was dumbstruck again.

'Oh, and glad things worked out with you finding Lezard; you can thank me later.'

'What? Why?'

'For Will Merton? He works for me, after all. Gave me all sorts on your mate Rob Lezard once I got him squealing. About how he gave him access to that video of Jon Nelson threatening him.'

Fenchurch felt like he'd been in the car crash. Of all the people... Jesus Christ. 'You were going to blow up the London Stadium?'

'Heavens, no. He was just stalking your missus. Did a cracking job until, well, he got caught up in a little car crash. Those Priuses ain't cheap, let me tell you. But seeing as it's you, Fenchy, I'll pass this little nugget on. See, one of my people was approached to participate in fixing Lezard's bomb, but there's no profit in innocent dead people. Besides, I'm West Ham myself. Put two and two together and I got worried that Lezard—or whatever he called himself—was going to blow you up. Fenchurch, as much as I love you and your body, you're worth more to me vertical and six feet tall, than horizontal and six feet under. No, Will spotting Lezard was just a bit of luck. I've had him following Abi for ages. Heard that Lezard had you as targets for some big exposé. Didn't want that coming out, did I?'

Younis had Fenchurch by the balls now. 'If you think I'm going to do anything for you, think again.'

'No, mate, I ain't gonna get you to do anything for me.'

'What are you up to?'

'Nothing. Just enjoying my freedom. And I must say I expected a bit more gratitude from you. Surely you don't think I'm *Holding* back on you, Fenchy?'

The window wound up and the car slid off, joining the traffic on Liverpool Road.

Fenchurch felt like he'd been punched in the stomach.

If Younis had Holding, nobody would hear from him again.

And he was a free man. Fenchurch knew his life was going to get a lot more complicated again.

AFTERWORD

Thank you for reading this book.

I don't think you can appreciate how much it means that I've been able to write it. When I did the previous book, DEAD MAN'S SHOES, I wasn't well and was suffering from heart arrhythmia. Luckily at the end of November, I had a procedure that restored it to normal and has stayed in "sinus rhythm" ever since. Touch wood. So being able to write this without my heart thundering my chest was a blessing.

I hope you enjoyed seeing inside Chloe's head. And I hope Fenchurch is changing in your eyes. Still tough as nails, but he's softening. I hope.

Anyway, huge thanks to James Mackay for the editing work at outline stage and after the first draft, it fixed a lot of howlers. Also thanks to John Rickards for his copy editing, which tightened a lot of the text up. And finally to Mare Bate for proofing it, nailing down the few stragglers and eliminating the errors I put back in during copy editing. If you notice any errors, all my fault, then please email ed@edjames.co.uk and I'll fix them.

Finally, I've put the ninth Fenchurch book, THE LAST THING TO DIE, on preorder, so I hope you enjoy it when it comes. It's a year away, so if enough of you preorder it, I'll do a tenth. Deal?

And if you could leave a review on Amazon? That'd be a huge help, cheers.

Thanks again,

Ed James

Scottish Borders, October 2021

OTHER BOOKS BY ED JAMES

SCOTT CULLEN MYSTERIES SERIES

Eight novels featuring a detective eager to climb the career ladder, covering Edinburgh and its surrounding counties, and further across Scotland.

CULLEN & BAIN SERIES

Six novellas spinning off from the main Cullen series covering the events of the global pandemic in 2020.

CRAIG HUNTER SERIES

A spin-off series from the Cullen series, with Hunter first featuring in the fifth book, starring an ex-squaddie cop struggling with PTSD, investigating crimes in Scotland and further afield.

1. MISSING
2. HUNTED
3. THE BLACK ISLE

DS VICKY DODDS SERIES

Gritty crime novels set in Dundee and Tayside, featuring a DS juggling being a cop and a single mother.

1. BLOOD & GUTS
2. TOOTH & CLAW
3. FLESH & BLOOD
4. SKIN & BONE

DI SIMON FENCHURCH SERIES

Set in East London, will Fenchurch ever find what happened to his daughter, missing for the last ten years?

1. THE HOPE THAT KILLS
2. WORTH KILLING FOR
3. WHAT DOESN'T KILL YOU
4. IN FOR THE KILL
5. KILL WITH KINDNESS
6. KILL THE MESSENGER
7. DEAD MAN'S SHOES
8. A HILL TO DIE ON
9. THE LAST THING TO DIE (December 2022)

Other Books

Other crime novels, with Senseless set in southern England, and the other three set in Seattle, Washington.

- SENSELESS
- TELL ME LIES
- GONE IN SECONDS

- BEFORE SHE WAKES

FENCHURCH WILL RETURN IN

THE LAST THING TO DIE

1 December 2022

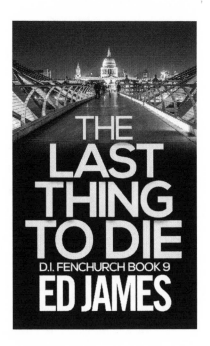

Hope is the last thing to die

DCI Simon Fenchurch has everything under control. His marriage, his family, even his job, where he's starting to lose the imposter syndrome that has plagued him.

But a mysterious death on the border with the City of London leads Fenchurch into a murder inquiry crossing three jurisdictions.

All signs point to one man.

Dimitri Younis, recently released from prison and running the East End with an iron fist, spreading his talons into London. And even more determined to appear to be squeaky clean.

As Fenchurch homes in on a witness with evidence that could put Younis away forever, the tables are soon turned.

Is Fenchurch going to be the last thing to die? Or will it be the hope that he can live a normal life?

Preorder now at https://geni.us/EJF09b

By signing up to my Readers Club, you'll access to **free, exclusive** content (*such as free novellas!*) and keep up-to-speed with all of my releases, either by visiting https://geni.us/EJFReadersClub or clicking this button: